To Mary Ann,
Best Regards
Peter

If It's Not One Thing, It's Another Murder

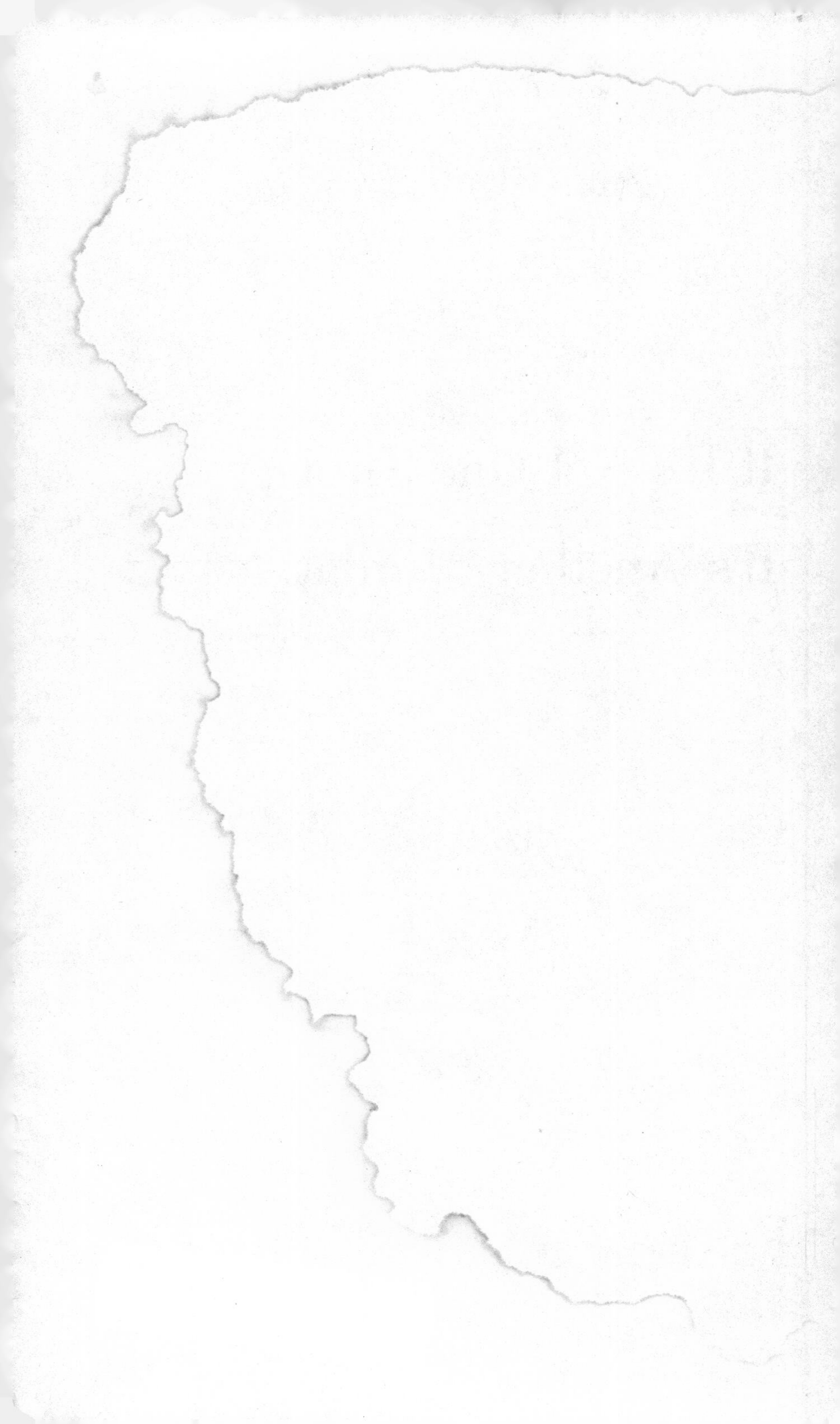

If It's Not One Thing, It's Another Murder

Peter Helmberger

ISBN : Softcover 1-4134-5669-3

This is a work of fiction. Names, characters, places and incidents either are the product of the author's imagination or are used fictitiously, and any resemblance to any actual persons, living or dead, events, or locales is entirely coincidental.

This book was printed in the United States of America.

To order additional copies of this book, contact:
Xlibris Corporation
1-888-795-4274
www.Xlibris.com
Orders@Xlibris.com
24949

Chapter 1

His name was Burley Smokes. His testes weighed 360 grams apiece, which together with the rest of him, brought his total weight to 1029.9 kilograms. He carried gut, bone, and hide with aplomb on four sturdy legs. His body commenced with a massive head and ended in a tight rump swept by an inconsequential tail in the now-and-again mode of a windshield wiper. Over the course of his service with the Upper-Midwest Breeders Cooperative, Burley Smokes had produced roughly 9,000 milliliters of semen. Thanks to artificial insemination and the advent of frozen semen, his progeny were numbered in the thousands and were spread over all the continents of the world save Antarctica, that most inhospitable place for the husbandry of cattle. He had sired two U.S. national prize-winning Holstein cows each producing at the height of their productive careers more than 35,000 pounds of milk per annum.

If there were one thing wrong with Burley Smokes, and there surely was, it was that he was mean. "You've gotta watch out for *that* son of a bitch," the semen collector at the Breeders Cooperative used to say, which explained in part why Mr. Dennis Mc Quade, the deceased former owner of Green Valley Farm, one of the world's foremost producers of purebred Holsteins cows, had been judged eccentric, or senile, or both by his acquaintances, for when the time came to retire Burley Smokes in favor of younger, more productive bulls, Mr. Mc Quade had stepped forward with his checkbook to save the old bull from the slaughtering plant.

Mr. Mc Quade had been entirely correct in believing that Burley Smokes, though uncelebrated, was truly one of America's great animals. His contribution to the nation's national product far exceeded that of such notables as Man o' War and Seattle Slew. Roy Rogers' horse Trigger? Not in the running. Seabiscuit? An overachiever. Willy the killer whale? He was, well, a killer. Lump together all the pandas in America's zoos and what would you have? Furry creatures that live in trees and do nothing much but munch. And the males drive zookeepers crazy, approaching the females with the hesitancy of Prince Hamlet (to mount, or not to mount), totally unlike Burley Smokes who once launched himself onto an obliging steer with such exuberance that he fell off and damned near killed the semen collector.

At present, Burley Smokes was confined to a small grassy pasture with a brook that babbled during the summer and froze hard as stone during the winter. The one tree in his pasture, a big white oak, provided shade when it was hot and sunny. In the wintertime he had a cozy room to himself in a barn for heifers and a few riding horses. He had everything a Holstein bull could possibly desire except a herd of cows to call his own, which might explain why, after a lifetime of five ejaculations per week into the artificial vagina held by the Breeders Cooperative's nervous semen collector, Burley Smokes had become meaner than ever. Heavy of brawn and light of brain, he had of course never contemplated risking his life to save cloven-hoofed brethren spread out all across the length and breadth of America. But now we're getting way ahead of our story.

One day, as he nibbled sparse April grass, Burley Smokes was annoyed by a crow that flapped raucously up into the sky. He lifted his head and saw movement in a copse of evergreens along the southwest border of his pasture. His suspicious yellow eyes discerned a man standing in shadow. The man wore army camouflage. He had black hair, a swarthy complexion, and a prominent nose that hooked downward above a rebellious moustache. In short, he was just the sort of person most likely to be ignored at an airport security checkpoint as guards scrutinized the wedgies of an old lady from Duluth. Burley Smokes didn't like what he saw. He rarely did. After a moment he lowered his head threateningly. A muffled thunder rumbled up from the bowels of his deep chest. With hooves the size of horseshoes, he clawed the earth, flinging into the air dirt, pebbles, and clods of turf that landed on his back, which seemed to further itch his irritation.

Annoyed by this display the man picked up an egg-sized stone and threw it as hard as he could. Burley Smokes watched the projectile, thinking it was some kind of fast-flying thing (we would call it a bird) that might land on his back and peck those small biting things (we would call them flies). Instead the projectile bounced off a rib and hurt like the devil. He shifted his weight and grunted. He sniffed the stone in disbelief. As far back as he could recall, he had never been mistreated by man, except for the time when they put a ring through his nose and, oh yes, when he was but a calf and was dehorned by an electric iron. The bastards. Could it be that such remembrances explained why Burley Smokes did something he had never done before? Which was to charge a man on the other side of a fence? The man fled in terror, but when he hazarded a glance over his shoulder, he saw the bull had pulled up short. He laughed at the stupid beast, at its being thwarted by mere strands of wire. He maneuvered to get a clear shot and threw another stone. This one was deflected by a steel post, however, and fell harmlessly to the ground.

"Come Id al-Adha," said the man to the bull, "we will tie you down and cut your throat and your blood will be pleasing in the eyes of Allah." Then he disappeared behind boughs of spruce and pine.

One week after his run-in with the thrower of stones, Burley Smokes encountered still another stranger, but Professor Myron Willgrubs was a different sort of character altogether. At the invitation of Green Valley Farm's current manager Troy Olson, he had come to observe the spring migration of exotic waterfowl that sat down by the hundreds in a marsh adjoining Green Valley

Farm. After observing the wildlife for over an hour, having shot a half-role of film through a telephoto lens, the professor now headed back to his car parked near the farm's grand old yellow brick house. The trail he followed, used mainly by snowmobilers, wound its pleasant way through a deciduous woods. He stopped to take pictures of wild plum trees brimming with swollen buds. Further along the path he came again to a small pasture for a solitary Holstein bull. He had noticed the bull before, on his hike to the marsh, but the bull had then been on the far side of the pasture. Now he stood no more than ten feet from the fence that ran along the path. Several sections of baled hay lay at his front feet. At first the professor thought the bull was chewing an ear of corn, for his head was held high as he worked his jaws laboriously. A closer examination revealed, however, that the bull was in some kind of trouble. He seemed unable to close his jaws. Even more alarming was the immense effusion of bloody slobber issuing from his mouth.

That poor beast has something caught in his mouth, the professor thought, and he wheeled into action. He laid his camera and binoculars on the ground. He took off a Harris tweed jacket with leather patches on the elbows. He found a place in the fence where the woven wire that formed its base sagged below the lowest of several strands of barbed wire. Carefully, he pushed down on the woven wire and maneuvered his pear-shaped body through the fence. He hurried to the impaired bull, held its head up slightly, and looked into the gaping maw. He saw something foreign. Without a moment's hesitation, he reached into the bull's mouth, grasped the offending object, and pulled it out. It was a short piece of dried wood, perhaps a fallen twig from a tree. Apparently the twig had hardened through time and had somehow gotten mixed in with the bailed hay. The stick had lodged vertically in the bull's mouth, and the harder the poor beast clamped his jaws, the more it bore into the top of his mouth till it had become firmly lodged. Professor Willgrubs looked at the stick in disbelief. He had, after all, been reared on a dairy farm, and as a professor of agricultural economics had often came in contact with farmers, county extension agents, and veterinarians. Never in his entire life had he heard of a head of cattle so afflicted. He wiped the offending stick against his pant leg and put it in his pocket to show Mr. Olson. He would warn Mr. Olson about the baled hay. Professor Willgrubs was always on the lookout for sage advice that could be given to his acquaintances. He watched the bull tidying up his nose, rolling his great tongue first up one nostril and then the other. The professor scratched the bull behind the nearest ear.

"Nice bully-bull," he said. "Mmm, you like that, huh?"

After a moment or two, the bull moved its head sideways, as if gently to butt the stranger aside.

"Oh, you want me to go away, huh?" the professor said. He then scratched the bull's face, concentrating on the area between mean yellow eyes that crossed in an effort better to see the offending fingers. "Nice bully-bull," the professor repeated. After a time the bull lowered its head and sniffed suspiciously at the hay, which was the clue to the professor to be on his way. He crawled back through the fence, put on his jacket, grabbed his gear, and walked on.

When he saw Troy Olson headed toward the house, he hurried forward to intercept him, eager to tell all. He was sidetracked when Mr. Olson said from a distance, "Well, hello, professor. Did you see many ducks?"

"Oh, my yes," the professor replied, "hundreds of them." He hurried forward and stepped up close to Mr. Olson, too close, adding "And I saw five whistling swans as well. I don't mind telling you that that was a real treat."

Aware of the professor's propensity for conversing nose to nose, Mr. Olson stepped backward to the more conventional distance of eighteen inches and said, "And did you get some photos?"

"I did indeed, sir," the professor replied, stepping nine inches forward. "I'm sure I shot a half-roll of film at least, but I have something to tell you about your bull. You see when I . . ."

He was interrupted just then when a woman in a apron opened the front door and yelled, "Mr. Olson, the veterinarian's on the phone."

"I'm coming," Mr. Olson yelled back. "We've got a heifer with the scours," he said to the professor before turning on his heel and striding quickly away.

"But, but," the professor said, reaching into his pants pocket for the dry twig.

On the front stoop Mr. Olson opened the front door but thought to shout a warning before going in. "About that bull," he called. "Stay clear of him. He's mean as hell. He even goes after my horses."

Magnified by thick glasses, Professor Willgrubs's pale blue eyes opened wide with horror and incredulity. "But, but," he said, but it was too late. Mr. Olson had disappeared inside.

"Dear me," he said quietly to himself, ruminating on the danger he had escaped, no doubt narrowly. "Oh, dear, dear me," he said, fingering the piece of wood.

Professor Willgrubs turned to look back at a pasture mostly concealed by service buildings, but the killer bull had apparently ambled off. The professor climbed into his car and sped for home, eager to relate his adventure to his wife Edna, his niece Miss Emily Peterson, former runner-up in the Alice in Dairyland beauty contest, and Miss Peterson's fiancée Patrick Delaney, the Plattefield Police Department's youngest detective. He would call Mr. Olson later in regard to his defective legume.

Coach Lawrence W. Coneybear, of square jaw and sinewy frame, sat alone in his office, enshrouded in a gloomy attitude. It was late Saturday afternoon and the Plattefield Yellow Jackets had just won an exhibition game with their arch rival in the Dairyland Eight Football Conference. The attendance had been remarkable for a spring game; the weather had been perfect. His team had moved with the power and precision of the Pentagon's smartest bomb, smashing to smithereens the opposing team's defenses. The hoopla surrounding the victory, which promised great things in the fall, had now died away. The footballers had showered, changed into their street clothes, and decamped in a noisy flurry of plans to party. A reporter from the *Plattefield Gazette* had asked the usual inane questions and the coach had drawn freely from his repertoire of inane answers. There would be a write-up in the sports pages of the Sunday's edition that would bore him totally. The band had packed up their instruments, too, and, save one, the cheerleaders had stowed their pompoms as well. Miss Sherree Lang would be stopping by momentarily, which made the coach sigh—there were so many women in his life demanding satisfaction. Jeez, he sometimes wondered, particularly when feeling sorry for himself, don't they realize I'm only human.

But there was still another reason for the coach's present funk, a reason more serious than service due a libidinous cheerleader. Lawrence W. Coneybear *was* a good coach. He was just too damned good, and therein lay a tale of his potential undoing. According to a reporter, an official from the University of Michigan had come to watch today's game and had been very impressed not only with the game itself, but with how the football program at Plattefield had been turned around. When Coach Coneybear took over the coaching of the Yellow Jackets three years ago, they were the weakest team in the conference. They were now the conference powerhouse. Coach Coneybear knew that someday (it was only a matter of time) one of the top college football teams in the country would consider making him an offer. Unlike the pissant Plattefield campus of the University of Wisconsin, a big-time university would almost certainly go through his resume with a fine-toothed comb. And when they did, they'd dislodge a nit fat as a pea. His career would grind to a halt, sink like a stone, go up in flames, go down the drain; the metaphors for a guy's waterloo being endless. And what would his wife say? Not to mention his superrich father-in-law.

Judas priest, he muttered under his breath, talk about shit hitting the fan. Elephant turds are gonna hit the fan.

He needed a picker-upper. He unlocked the lowest left-hand drawer of his desk, lifted out a flask of Scotch, and rummaged through vials, packets of pills, plastic bags of dried vegetation, and tubes of god-knows-what. Mmm, he thought, when you're down and blue, two pinks should do. He downed two pink pills with a swig of whisky. He waited a few minutes, but nothing much happened. Not wanting to come up short he fished around in the drawer, found a bottle, and took a couple more pills. The taste was surprisingly familiar. He looked more closely at the bottle. Good god! he thought. Viagra. He fished in the drawer for something else until he found a plastic bag of blue capsules. He popped a couple of blues and swallowed more whisky. Then he rolled his chair away from the desk, tipped it back, and rested his head against the wall. In a moment a wave of euphoria swept him out to sea. Wooo-eee, he thought. Thank you Dr. Jackson. (Dr. Harold Jackson from Sports Medicine freely dispensed creative drugs to both the football team and its coach.) Time's pleasant passing was interrupted by a gentle tapping at Coach Coneybear's office door.

"Come in," said the coach, without opening his big brown eyes. His visions were much too vivid to be muddied by a real world view. He heard the door open and close. There was the telltale rustle of pompoms.

"That you, Sherree," he said. The coach was continually amazed by the things Miss Lang could do with her pompoms.

"Who else?" Miss Lang replied.

His eye corners crinkled handsomely when he looked up and smiled. Miss Lang floated toward him in slow motion, a phantom of desire, blond-haired, blue-eyed, gorgeously bosomed and bottomed. He closed his eyes. There was the rousing rustle of pompoms. He felt her settling down on his lap. He felt her open mouth pressing against his. He tasted her tongue. Mm-mm, was she raised on a dairy farm? he wondered vaguely, nourished on peaches and cream?

"Did you lock the door?" he murmured.

"Don't I always."

"Ooo, ooo," he cooed. "Move a bit. You're compressing my organ."

An hour later Coach Coneybear walked through the front door of his upscale split-level home into a beehive of activity. He stood mouth agape for a moment or two, not entirely sure he was in the right house. For one thing there was a great scurrying about. A bevy of cheerleaders seemed to be dusting, vacuuming, arranging flowers, and fetching trays of nibblers from the basement refrigerator. This should not have surprised the coach. His wife Jane Coneybear often invited the cheerleaders to her parties, not only to spark middle-aged male guests, but to acquire free help in preparing for the party and cleaning up afterwards. The smart and sassy coeds were onto Mrs. Coneybear's scheme, but what could they do? They all knew that the director of women's sports who was responsible for selecting and coaching the cheerleaders, a big striking athletic woman with closely cropped hair and a bit of a moustache, was on peculiarly good terms with the coach's wife, which they correctly surmised explained why Coach Coneybear wandered far afield in his quest for affaires d'amour.

"Where in the hell have you been?" Jane Coneybear yelled at her husband. "The party is supposed to start in fifteen minutes. Get the bar set up. Hurry up, goddamnit. Just don't stand there."

The coach swayed forward toward the kitchen to fetch citrus, ice, and maraschino cherries from the fridge. He had the strangest feeling that his feet weren't actually touching the floor, that he was walking on air. The fuzzy white refrigerator, bifurcated by a groove of dark handles, slipped into and out of focus and was strangely arousing. He felt an uprising inside his briefs, but his efforts to brush the thing down only made matters worse. Damned those pills, he thought. Wooo-eee. He breathed deeply and watched a foxy cheerleader slicing a salami, which seemed to help.

Later in the evening he caught his wife refurbishing a tray of cheddar cheese when there was no one else in the kitchen. He sidled up behind her, put his arms around her, and pressed his privates against her bottom.

"How about a quickie?" he muttered. "I'm hotter than hell."

"Are you nuts?" she replied. "Go away."

Jane Coneybear could easily have pressed a cheerleader into passing a tray of cheese, but the time had come for her to check up on her guests. What were they talking about? she wanted to know. Were any of the men getting too drunk to drive? Were any of her guests dullards who should not be invited again? Offering tidbits was a perfect way to spy. She could dally here and dally there and join in lively conversations only when it suited her. She could flee from people who were boring. She could avoid entirely wallflowers who stood about stupidly, not knowing how to get involved in conversation. Those who contribute little to my party don't get cheese, she thought, and I'm not of a mind to discuss the weather, for chrissake, or plans for new street construction, or the current business of the school board, or any other crap like that.

With her tray refurbished, she headed for her guests. In the dinning room, near an etagere filled with Lladro kitsch, she joined Councilwoman Betty Bluestone, Detective Phillip Moran, and three right-wing businessmen. They seemed to be competing over who could become the most incensed by Wisconsin's not having the death penalty. Jane Coneybear moved the tray around without joining in the conversation. Fat fingers fumbled over crackers and cheese.

"So what if once and a while an innocent guy does get the ax," Mrs. Bluestone was saying. "After all innocent people occasionally go to jail and no one says we should dispense with prisons. I mean no judicial system is perfect."

"You can't scramble eggs without breaking some of 'em," Detective Moran put in, spewing cracker crumbs. "That's what I always say."

"Yeah, but how are we gonna git around them liberals in Madison?" asked the owner of a Kentucky Fried Chicken franchise.

"Yeah, and those blacks in Milwaukee," added the owner of Fastflow Industrial Blowers.

"Money and organization," Mrs. Bluestone replied. "We need a grassroots campaign."

"Hey, Moran," said the owner of Pickles Perfect, "what does your chief think about the death penalty?"

"Well, he's against it of course," said Fastflow.

"If you ask me, the old fool's suffering from salinity," Moran said.

Jane Coneybear fled toward the great room. In an arched entrance, she took a moment to admire the room and its furnishings. An area rug with a southwestern motif underlay a sofa, love seat, padded armchairs, and tables with softly glowing lamps. Several recessed flood lights glowed softly from a cathedral ceiling decked by what the builder had called boxcar siding. Flames fueled by natural gas licked artificial logs in a fieldstone fireplace flanked by pyramidal glass windows. And there were her things, her precious things: paintings by New York moderns, Chihuly glass, a genuine Roman head, and artifacts from ancient cultures. Jane Coneybear loved her things and spent a lot of her time and a lot of her dad's money acquiring them.

As she looked out over the boisterous throng, she decided her guests were a bunch of hicks. She was suddenly bored and angry. Her principal guests had gone. Chancellor John Olivier and his wife Professor Penelope Olivier had stopped by to congratulate the coach and have a quick drink. They had to rush off to dine with some dignitary visiting the campus, they said. On his first try for public office, Mr. Olivier had nearly beaten a popular state attorney general in the primary for the Democratic candidate for governor. It was agreed by everyone in the know that he was a rising star in state politics. The chancellor had swept around the room, beaming, shaking hands, and impressing everyone with his knowledge, forthrightness, and friendliness. Jane Coneybear had watched the chancellor working the room and laughed aloud. The man must have balls the size of a chimp's, she thought. But now the Oliviers had gone and of those who remained none would seem to have any real appreciation for her objets d'art.

The Coneybears' party ended on the same sorry note their parties nearly always ended. After the remains of the buffet supper had been cleared away and most of the guests had departed, Larry Coneybear sat down at the upright piano in the family room and began to play and sing an oldy-mouldy. The coach could play and sing just about everything. He was quickly joined by several guests who were inebriated to varying degrees and clueless about when to go home. They tried to sing along without quite recalling the right words. Now, as Jane Coneybear listened to a lamentable rendition of a *Bicycle Built for Two*, climbing a half-flight of stairs to the great room to turn off the fireplace before going to bed, she remembered the first time she saw the man she'd later marry.

The occasion had been a frat house party and she had been impressed by the handsome lug seated at a badly chipped black grand piano. The piano was out of tune, but that didn't matter to the player. He played and sang his heart out as pretty coeds fussed over him and made requests. Jane Coneybear now felt a pang of regret for her husband. It wasn't his fault, really, that he had married a woman who could never love him, even though she had at one time convinced herself that she did. She used to listen to his singing with pleasure, but that was years ago. Now she thought she'd puke her guts out if she heard *Hello Dolly* one more time.

Meanwhile, back in the coach's office a man from Physical Plant rested his push broom against the closed door. He walked to the desk, sat in the coach's chair, and began rifling through the drawers in search of the key to the one drawer the coach kept locked. His nosiness had been piqued by the girl he saw leaving the coach's office. She looked the worse for wear. Her hair was mussed and her short skirt was slightly askew. Flaccid pompoms, once so bouncy and perky, now dragged on the floor as she schlepped toward a back door. Slut, he had muttered under his breath as pornographic images flitted across the lobed landscape of his mind. He had to get into that locked drawer. Only there was no key; not one that he could find anyway. He would have to think of something else, but his suspicion had now reached a fever pitch. He had to find out. He bent apart a paper clip and poked a wire inside the lock, but it seemed that no amount of poking and twisting could coax the lock into betraying its trust. He scratched his beard. His dark eyes narrowed as he thought, what to do, what to do. And then he remembered a tool he once bought to help a friend replace the shingles on his roof, a tough piece of steel designed for prying. The drawer would yield its secrets. One week from tonight. He rubbed his hands in anticipation. This might just be the source of money we'll need for our operation, he thought.

Chapter 2

Professor Myron Willgrubs found Detective Patrick Delaney an invaluable friend, not only because he would one day become a member of the family, but because he more than anyone evinced a genuine interest in whatever it was the professor wanted to describe, explicate, or expound upon. Detective Delaney had been invited to join the Willgrubs for dinner on the very day of the professor's encounter with Burley Smokes. The detective would no doubt be fascinated by the professor's brush with death.

Thus, when the doorbell rang at six-thirty that evening, the professor hurried to the front door. As expected, the broad-shouldered detective was waiting on the front stoop with a merry grin on his cherubic face. It was generally agreed that no one could possibly look less like a policeman than Detective Patrick Delaney. The professor's eye was as quickly drawn to the paperback in the detective's right hand as it was then averted. His embarrassment at having noticed the book was sensed by the detective, who held the book forward as if in all innocence (innocent in a pig's eye!) and said, "I brought a book along to read while Emily does her homework."

"Yes, of course," the professor replied, affecting a matter-of-fact attitude. But was he not a man? Had he not once been young and violently in love? He was onto the detective the very first time he arrived for dinner with the ready explanation for the book he had in hand. And the professor knew the basic essentials of what to expect after supper. Emily would likely offer to help Edna clean up, but Edna would say something like, "Oh, no, my dear. You have too much school work to do." And, with telltale red splotches in his cheeks, a sign both of embarrassment and what was to come, Delaney would say something like, "I brought a book to read while you study, Emily. Would that be OK?" And she would say something like, "Yes, of course, honey," and she would look demurely at nothing in particular. And in a while the lovers would climb the stairs to Emily's room, and one or the other would gently close the door. Later, several hours later, the detective would let himself out the front door, locking it behind him and walking out into the cool morning air with what Professor Willgrubs assumed (Had he not once been young and violently in love?) was the certain knowledge that life is good for the man who weds and beds, though not necessarily in that order, the woman he will love till the end of his days.

Edna Willgrubs would likely frown as her niece and the detective mounted the stairs, for she had suspicions about what went on up in Emily's room. Although the young lovers were engaged, Mrs. Willgrubs did not approve of intimate relations before marriage. She didn't approve entirely of intimate relations after marriage, come to that, and the professor could easily have complained, were he of a mind to do, which he was not, being the very soul of discretion in matters of intimacy, that his life had been one of rather short rations.

The detective and the professor were soon comfortably seated in the living room, the first drinking heartily from a bottle of beer, the second sipping sherry from a Waterford glass. While the women clattered about the kitchen putting the final touches to supper, the professor regaled the detective with the details of his encounter with a killer-bull at Green Valley Farm. He was not disappointed by the detective's attentiveness. The story even spilled over into the dining room as the foursome laid waste to a bowl of salad and a great pot of beef stew and dumplings. Mrs. Willgrubs had heard the story before of course, but she now thought to ask whether the woman who had summoned Mr. Olson to the telephone was his wife. The professor couldn't say. Detective Delaney asked if Holstein bulls tended generally to be dangerous animals and the professor assured him that was indeed the case. Delaney's thoughts began at last to stray from the incident at Green Valley Farm when Mrs. Willgrubs chided her husband a third time for being so reckless. As before, however, she quickly softened her criticism, if indeed it was a criticism, by emphasizing the professor's wide reputation for his empathy for all god's creatures. This prompted Miss Peterson to remark on the story of *Androcles and the Lion*, and she wondered aloud whether the nasty old bull might someday repay the professor for his kindness. It was agreed that this was extremely unlikely. After a time, when it was clear the professor's adventure had been mined to the last nugget, with nary an interest on the part of anyone to sift further through the tailings, Miss Peterson changed the subject.

"About the hit-and-run accident today," she said to Delaney, "were you involved in the investigation?"

With his mouth full of dumpling and beef, Delaney was unable to reply, which allowed the professor to inquire,

"What hit-and-run accident?"

"It was on the radio just before I came down to help Auntie with dinner," said Miss Peterson.

"It happened over on Greenbriar Road," Delaney said.

"Oh, my," Mrs. Willgrubs said, "I hope the person wasn't badly hurt."

"I'm afraid he was killed," Delaney replied, and he then told what happened.

Which was this: At 6:35 in the morning, the Plattefield Police Department received a 911 call reporting a hit-and-run accident on Greenbriar Road. The dispatch operator immediately alerted the only detective on duty, Detective Patrick Delaney. An inveterate early riser, despite the late hours he sometimes kept with his fiancée, Delaney gulped what was left of his second cup of coffee, grabbed his handgun, and took off. Daylight was just breaking through a cold, gray sky when he turned onto Greenbriar Road ten minutes later.

He was hailed by a woman in baggy jogging clothes a quarter-mile further on. He stopped his unmarked car, reached for a flashlight, and jumped out.

"He's over here," the woman called.

As he hurried over she said, "I'm the one who called. Are you an officer?"

"I'm a detective," Delaney replied. "I hope you haven't tried to move him."

"No, no. I just put my jacket over him to try to keep him warm. I'm a nurse, you see, and I've been checking his pulse. He's still alive, but barely."

Delaney flashed a light on the body crumpled on the side of the road. He lifted the jacket to see. "Oh, boy," he exclaimed.

"Yes, he's in bad way."

"Did you see the accident happen?"

"No. I was jogging when I found him. Oh, I do hope the paramedics will get here soon."

Delaney returned the woman's jacket to the man's chest, straightened up, and looked about. He guessed Greenbriar Road was rarely used. The shoulders of the road were narrow and gave way to woods on either side. There were no curbs, sidewalks, or streetlights: a perfect place for accidents, he thought. The victim had probably been walking or jogging on the right side of the road, and it would have been easy for a driver to stray onto the shoulder. Even in the poor light Delaney could see tire tracks in the loose gravel. There was the glint of broken glass amongst mowed weeds and grass. He stared for a moment at an object some distance off before realizing it was likely the victim's headset radio.

In a few minutes the siren of an ambulance began its crescendo, shimmying the crisp morning air.

"That'll be the ambulance now," Delaney said. Then he remembered to introduce himself and show his badge.

"We'll need your statement later," he said.

"Yes, of course," the woman said. "My name's Caroline Maidin." She offered her hand.

In a few minutes the ambulance screamed to a stop. Red strobe lights flashed over the victim and the ground where he lay. Two paramedics bounded over to him. They examined the man and seconded the nurse's prognosis; he was alive. He was quickly strapped onto a gurney, hoisted into the back of the ambulance, and whisked away even as other police vehicles began converging on the scene. Tom Willison, a senior detective and Delaney's mentor, chatted briefly with Delaney before taking charge of the investigation. Soon there was the crackle of two-way radios and the irreverent chatter of men at work. A photographer took stills of the tire tracks and the place where the man had lain. An officer from the lab team pulled on plastic gloves and got down on his knees to put scraps of blood into tiny plastic bags. There would be a forensic examination of tire tracks, skid marks, chips of paint, and broken glass. One of the officers was dispatched to the Plattefield Memorial Hospital to check on the victim's identification and condition and to summon any family the man might have.

"It's cold," Delaney said to Mrs. Maidin, "and we'll want to keep your jacket for a time, just in case it picked up evidence. Would you mind waiting in the car? If it's OK, I'll drive you down to the station and we'll take your statement there. Then I'll take you home."

On the way to the station a short while later, Mrs. Maidin said, "I should phone the hospital to tell them I'll be late. I work at the hospital."

"Yeah, sure," Delaney said. "Here, use my phone."

She told someone named Carla what happened and said she wasn't sure when she could come in.

Over coffees in the interrogation room, Delaney ran through a list of stock questions and wrote down Mrs. Maidin's replies. He went by the book in his interrogation. His holster and handgun were stashed in the cubicle he thought of as his office. He had taken off his jacket and rolled up his sleeves. His manner was low-key, thoughtful, nonthreatening. He watched her carefully, trying to size her up without being conspicuous.

That Caroline Maidin jogged was understandable; she was overweight. He guessed she was about five-foot-seven. She had blond hair, a chubby face, and a nervous smile. At one time, Delaney surmised, she had had trouble with acne. If asked to guess, he would have said that she was a responsible, no-nonsense kind of young woman, but that she was probably unhappy, and not just this morning. There was that about her eyes, a hint of sadness. Dressed in gray sweatpants and sweatshirt, she had apparently been listening to the headset radio that now rested on the table by her coffee cup.

Her name, she explained, was spelled with an I-N, not E-N, and she gave her address and telephone number. She was married, but had no children. Her husband Joe Maidin was a student at the university majoring in biology. To lose weight, she said, she had taken up jogging and often jogged down Greenbriar Road before going to work. She had seen no other person or vehicle on the stretch of Greenbriar Road where the accident had occurred. She had never seen the downed man before. All and all, she could offer little information of value. She sipped her coffee and nervously fingered her headset radio. Near the end of the interview Delaney asked if she was OK and she said she was. He thanked her for her cooperation and drove her home to a large colonial in a ritzy new development. On the way back to the station he wondered how the Maidins could afford such a grand new house, certainly not on Mrs. Maidin's salary as a nurse. Then he remembered that Mrs. Maidin had called the hospital, but not her husband, which he thought odd. He put himself in her husband's shoes and decided that had he been the husband, with no children to attend, he would have gone back with his wife to the scene of the accident. He would have waited with her until the police arrived. Maybe the husband wasn't at home.

Shortly after getting back to the station, he and Detective Willison drove to the Plattefield Memorial Hospital to see how the victim was faring and to question his wife. The victim Harold Salvati was still in the operating room when they arrived. They joined Mrs. Connie Salvati in a small lobby just down the hall.

She was a short plump woman, middle-aged and smartly dressed. Her hair was suspiciously blond and piled high with curls. She wore lots of makeup, and Delaney wondered whether she had done her face before or after the summons from the hospital. She seemed on the verge of breaking down.

Detective Willison made introductions and apologized for intruding during her time of distress. After a perfunctory display of badges, he offered his sympathy and asked if she felt strong enough to answer a few questions. She said she did.

It turned out the Salvatis had only recently moved to Plattefield from Philadelphia where they had been in the real estate business. Mrs. Salvati said she and her husband had no children and had not yet found jobs with any of the local realtors. She said her husband had taken up jogging in the morning only four days ago, but couldn't say whether he jogged regularly on Greenbriar Road. The interview was interrupted when Doctor William Jensen appeared. He shook hands with the detectives and chatted with them briefly before asking Mrs. Salvati to come with him. The detectives watched as the doctor guided Mrs. Salvati down the hallway and into a room on the right. Before closing the door behind him, he looked back at the detectives and shook his head sadly.

A reporter from the Plattefield Gazette joined the detectives a little later and took notes on what they had to say. The interview was interrupted by a muffled scream from the room down the hall. After several minutes passed, a sympathetic nurse led the grieving widow back to the lobby and sat with her on a sofa. A second nurse appeared with a glass of water.

Mrs. Salvati accepted the glass, stared at it for a long moment, and then threw it across the room. An arc of water spilled in flight. The glass struck a framed poster of a painting of a suggestive purple iris. Glass shattered and fell to the floor; water leaked from the naughty iris and ran down the wall.

"Those bastards," she screamed. "Those goddamned marshals. They were supposed to protect him. They promised he'd be safe in this . . . this goddamned red neck of the woods."

The onlookers were stunned. Mrs. Salvati's red mouth made a little O, as if she hadn't intended to spill the beans.

"Are you referring to U. S. marshals?" Delaney blurted out in astonishment.

"Who else, dumbo!" she replied. "My husband was in the witness protection program, if you want to know. And look what they've done to him—ran him down like a dog." She burst into tears and would not be consoled.

Detective Willison took charge at this point and shooed everyone out of the lobby and out of the adjoining corridors. He told Delaney to keep his eye on the public entrance to the lobby and to be on the alert. From an incoherent story punctuated by tears and outbursts of anger and threats, the two detectives learned that Harold Salvati, formerly Michael Patriarca, was from New York City, not Philadelphia, that he had provided crucial evidence in the prosecution of New York mobsters and had been only recently enrolled in the witness protection program. The billfold in her husband's jacket gave his new identity, address, and telephone number. The other sources of identification were equally bogus. She explained that she and her husband had moved into their new home on Saturday, April 13. She wasn't sure but believed her husband started jogging on the following Wednesday and was usually out for, oh, maybe 45 minutes. She had no idea where he jogged. Willison assured Mrs. Salvati that the local police would provide protection until the federal authorities could be summoned, and she said with bitter sarcasm that she felt *so* reassured.

The Gazette reporter was waiting for Mrs. Salvati when she exited the hospital escorted by the two detectives. In spite of gentle coaxing on the part of Detective Willison to say nothing to the reporter, Mrs. Salvati stopped to give a brief interview, explaining that she was going to sue the federal government for millions of dollars and insisting that she, too, was probably on the Mob's hit list, but that she didn't care anymore, because she had lost the only man she had ever loved. Understandably, in her hysterical lamentations, she failed to give any hint of how it came to be that her husband had had incriminating evidence in the first place. Nor did she indicate the jail sentence he had avoided by turning state's evidence. And she certainly said nothing about her husband's $500,000 life insurance policy naming her beneficiary.

"Well, that about wraps it up," Delaney said in conclusion.

Burley Smokes was not longer an object of interest at the Willgrubs dinner table.

"Well, how extraordinary!" Professor Willgrubs exclaimed. "Surely the mob is responsible. Don't you agree, Patrick?"

"Everyone seems to think so," he replied.

Miss Peterson recognized her fiancée's hedge. He's not convinced, she thought. She looked at him affectionately. When he caught her eye and smiled, she wondered how she could have ever supposed that green eyes, a rounded freckled face, and a thicket of sandy hair much too curly to be subdued by brush or comb, were other than the stuff god would use to conjure a handsome man. That his ears were too big and stuck out a little, well, that simply added character.

Miss Peterson was suspicious of Hollywood looks. She had discovered in her senior year at Eau Claire High that her steady, a star athlete considered a perfect specimen by everyone who knew him, was making out on the side, so to speak, with a freshman tart. She decided then and there never again to be bowled over by a man's good looks. It was Delaney's boyish appearance that had attracted her in the first place: that plus the way he looked at her and how she felt when he said her name, a hunk with a quiet voice saying, "Emily," as if in a prayer.

"Oh dear, what a terrible blot this will be on the U. S. Marshals," the professor said. "Do your men have any leads on the culprit?"

"Not many, but the paint chips and glass from a broken headlight will give a good indication of the vehicle involved. Finding the vehicle is nearly always the key to hit-and-run cases."

"Who found the victim?" the professor asked. "Anyone we know?"

"Her name is Caroline Maidin," the detective replied.

"Mmm," the professor murmured. "The name doesn't ring a bell."

Up in Emily's room, Delaney sat in a worn but comfortable overstuffed chair. A floor lamp illuminated the open pages of *Huckleberry Finn*, which he was rereading as part of a self-improvement program. He was always on one self-improvement program or another, sometimes on several at once. But now his mind was restive. It kept flitting from a raft floating down a wide river to a car speeding down a narrow road.

He lay his head back against the chair and closed his eyes to think the tragedy through for the umpteenth time. It could have been an accident, he thought. Someone speeding down the road half-asleep. With his lights on? Maybe reaching for a thermos, cell phone, map, whatever. Wasn't that how Steven King got clobbered? Some darned fool not paying attention. If the driver's local, it shouldn't be too hard to find him. The vehicle will give him away. Someone will notice. But of course, everyone thinks organized crime is behind it, and they're probably right. The driver would not be a local then. But, but, but: there were so many buts. The victim's wife said this was only the fourth time he had gone out for an early jog. Is that enough to project likely behavior? Would a professional killer have known what to expect? And I've never heard of a case where someone in the witness protection program was killed. No one at the station had either, except in those instances where the security precautions were ignored by a foolish witness. Hmm. By a foolish witness, or in this case by a foolish wife. Maybe this guy's wife dropped a postcard to her mom. "Dear Mom, here we are in Plattefield, Wisconsin. (See over.) Looks like a nice place, but there's only one mall. Can you believe it?" Well, that angle of the investigation will no doubt be explored by the FBI, Delaney concluded. Ditto the New York end of it. There might not be much for us to do here in Plattefield, come to think of it.

And then Delaney lifted his head, blinked, and rubbed his nose. Could it be the killer got the wrong person? Was Mrs. Maidin the intended victim? Nah, he decided. That's too far out. But if true, she could still be in danger. Hmm. Maybe I'd better snoop around a bit, he decided.

Detective Delaney was unaware that Emily Peterson had been watching him. She went to him, removed the book from his hands, and settled down into his lap. "What's the matter, copper?" she said, smiling and putting an arm around his neck. "Can't get your mind off your work?"

"It's that hit-and-run," he said. "There's some darned funny things about this case."

Miss Peterson began unbuttoning her blouse, murmuring, "I'll bet I can make you forget the case."

"I'll bet you can too, Emily," he replied. He lifted a strand of blond hair from her face and held it to his nose. He ran his fingers lightly over her face, her eyelids, cheeks, and lips.

"What are you doing?" she said, blinking at him.

"You know what they say," he murmured, "about taking the time to smell the roses. I'm smelling the roses." In Detective Delaney's unbiased opinion, Emily Peterson was a dead ringer for a young Grace Kelly.

Miss Peterson didn't ask about those "darned funny things about the case." She even regretted having asked about the case in the first place, although she knew the crime would sooner or later have become the topic of conversation at the Willgrubs dinner table. Mrs. Willgrubs would have insisted upon it. What the world was coming to was her favorite subject. But Miss Peterson had for some time been thinking about being a cop's wife and had come to an important conclusion. When her husband came home from work (and there was no reason why she shouldn't start here and now before they were married; they had, ahem, started other things), she would help him forget about crooks, crimes, and misdemeanors. She would be there for him and he for her. And, in time, there would be kids to rear and household chores to attend. That's how it should be, she had decided, and now, with Delaney's big hands cupping her face gently as a flower and pressing his open mouth against her lips, her plan seemed to be working like the devil. She suddenly felt a flush of warmth.

Side by side sat Professor and Mrs. Willgrubs in the room below, reading books and half-listening to the evening concert on public radio. Edna Willgrubs was a fleshy woman, big-boned and taller than her husband by nearly two inches. She and her husband thus cut a quaint couple as they bought groceries, attended Sunday services at Calvary Baptist Church, and frequented learned symposia at the Plattefield campus of the University of Wisconsin. Though given to fretting and nattering, Mrs. Willgrubs was not to be taken lightly once her dander was up. At about ten-thirty the professor heard a suspicious cadence of noises from upstairs. He quickly moved to turn up the volume of the radio, but he was too late. His wife had heard the sounds, too.

Her mighty bosom swelled with indignation. She lifted her eyes to the ceiling and said, "Well! I mean really! I'm of a mind to march upstairs and pound on the door."

"No, no, my sweet," the professor said. "Let us retire for the evening and give the young people a little privacy."

"Harrumph," declared his wife. "It seems to me we've given them too much privacy already. Oh, very well. I don't know what the world's coming to."

The Willgrubs washed their faces, brushed their teeth, and changed into their night clothes. Propped against pillows with the two bedside lamps burning brightly, they again took up their reading. The professor tried to concentrate on a book centering on the mysterious malaise that had struck the Japanese economy. After a time he put his book down, stared at the ceiling, and wondered if Japan's difficulty might be traced to the new competition from other Asian countries that were simply imitating what Japan had done earlier. He read a little further before again examining the ceiling, this time thinking about Green Valley Farm instead of incompetent Japanese bankers. Oh, dear, he thought, this has been some day. He remembered the sandpaper quality of the bull's tongue against the side of his hand. Then he remembered something else.

"Did we get anything in the mail today?" he asked.

"Mostly junk and bills," his wife replied. "Oh, come to think of it, there was a letter for you. I left it on the desk. I'll go get it," she added without moving.

"No, no, my dear. I'm sure it can wait until tomorrow."

The professor opened his book again, but it was hopeless.

"Who was the letter from?" he asked.

"I believe it was from the International Association of Agricultural Economists."

"Well, maybe I *will* fetch the letter," he said in another moment. He folded back the beige duvet and its matching sheet with pink roses and embroidered top hem, put on leather bedroom slippers with red and green plaid flannel lining, and padded out to the kitchen desk where Mrs. Willgrubs always sorted through the mail. He returned with the letter and in bed began to read.

"What was the letter about, dear?" his wife asked after he had finished reading and was once again absorbed in contemplating the ceiling.

"Oh, nothing really," he replied. "It's about the international meeting of agricultural economists in Dublin. Remember I told you about it some time ago. Seems a discussant of one of the papers has passed on and they're interested in whether I might be willing to fill in. I've never gone to the international meetings. Too expensive."

"But, of course you have, dear," his wife replied. "You attended the international meetings in San Francisco. I remember because I went with you to see the city. I couldn't understand what all the fuss was about, though. All those men holding hands and parading down the sidewalks just as nice as you please. You have to wonder what the world is coming too. And I can still remember the awful smell at Fisherman's Wharf. Harrumph. They have nothing that can compare with the Mall of America in the Twin Cities."

"You're quite right, my dear. I mean about the meeting in San Francisco. I forgot. But that was a long time ago, wasn't it?"

"When exactly is this meeting to be held?" asked Mrs. Willgrubs. "The one in Dublin."

"From August twelfth through the fifteenth," was her husband's reply.

Mrs. Willgrubs's eyes opened wide. The professor must be plum tuckered, she thought. Doesn't he remember that Emily and Patrick will be in Ireland at that very time? On their honeymoon! And haven't I often said I'd like to visit Ireland someday?

"Maybe we should go," she said. "We can afford it. Yes, definitely we should go."

"Yes, perhaps," the professor replied, catching her expression out of the corner of his eye. To himself, he muttered, Dear me. Oh, dear me. I wonder what Patrick's going to say about this?

By 1:00 in the morning the Willgrubs house had fallen silent, save for the random creak of timbers and the occasional hum of electric motors. In the position of spoons, the lovers upstairs had drifted away on blissful dreams. Downstairs, the professor lay on his back with his hand touching one of his wife's great hips. When the Willgrubs were abed, whether asleep or awake, one or the other of the professor's hands always moved about until it lay gently against the love of his life. Mrs. Willgrubs knew this and was gratified by the attachment of such a learned man.

Such scenes of nocturnal bliss as those at the Willgrubs's contrasted sharply with that at 502 Mayberry Street. Caroline Maidin stood barefoot in the hallway just outside the master bedroom of her swank new home, nervous and confused. She could hear her husband pacing the living room, back and forth, back and forth, back and forth. The underflooring had been improperly nailed to the joists and she could hear now and again the creaking of wood, which she found strangely vexing. What in god's name is he fretting about? Is this because he didn't want me to call 911? That as a Muslim he's afraid of the police and didn't want to get involved? I can understand that. She wanted to go to him, to put her arms around him and make him know that everything would be all right, but she was afraid of how he might react. She waited a few minutes more, shivered, and returned to bed. And tomorrow, she thought, trying to sleep. Oh, god, tomorrow. It'll be such a long day and I'm so tired.

Had she known how close the hooded specter had passed her by, how close had been the whisper of his scythe swinging through the cold morning air, she would have run screaming into the night.

Chapter 3

You'd think the day a write-up in Sports Illustrated said Coach Lawrence Coneybear was one of the best young coaches in the country would have been a great day for the coach, but no: it was the worst day of his life, well, not counting the day a 200 pound tackle made a pretzel of his right leg. The day got off to a terrible start. On arriving at work, he learned that someone had broken into his desk and discovered his trove of drugs. Had some of his little friends been lifted? He checked, but couldn't decide: there were so many. Then he discovered that a batch of newspaper clippings recounting his high school football career was gone, which stopped him cold. He had been a fool to save them. Anyone reading those clippings, particularly about the knee injury he sustained during his last football game, would know that his gridiron glories at Ethan Dinglebarry College in California, as occasionally noted in the press, were totally bogus. He certainly had *not* been the starting quarterback during his senior year at Dinglebarry. People who stopped by the coach's office beaming with pride and wanting to pump his hand came away puzzled. Assistant coaches hoping to hitch a ride with a rising star were baffled. The coach seemed so distracted, as if the Sports Illustrated article meant nothing to him. Didn't he realize he was fast becoming a national celebrity?

The coach's day got much worse later on. After the support staff had mostly gone home, a janitor strode into his office and closed the door. Yeah, a fucking janitor, he thought afterward. Jeez.

"We need to talk," said Basim Hachem, "and I'm gonna get right to the point. I got a plastic bag of drugs taken from your drawer. They got your fingerprints on them, don't they? What's more, I know you've been lying about your background in college sports. So here's the deal. You help me. I help you. Eh? That's what it comes down to. I got my eye on a good used car, and I need a loan. I need $10,000. One week from today you're gonna make me a $10,000 loan, otherwise I'm gonna call the newspapers. That's all I have to say."

"What's this?" the coach replied, moving to the edge of his seat. "You're after *what*?"

"You heard me. I want $10,000, else I'm calling the newspapers."

"You bastard!" cried Coach Coneybear, rising to his feet. "I'll teach you to break into my drawers. How would you like it if I busted your fucking skull?"

"Hold on, hold on. Think what you're doing." (A switchblade flashed in Hachem's hand.) "Be reasonable," he said, stepping back and brandishing his weapon.

"Reasonable? What about you, you bastard. You fucking snoop. How in the devil am I going to raise that kind of money? How the devil am I going to explain this to my wife? She watches every goddamned nickel I spend. I'm not giving you a dime. You bring me down and I'll turn you over to the FBI and they'll ship your ass to the land of camel fuckers."

"You'll get the money," said Mr. Hachem. "One anonymous telephone call. That's all it would take and your career would be over. Think of the disgrace, the shame. Remember, one week from today—same time, same place."

Mr. Hachem left the office and closed the door behind him.

Coach Coneybear sat at his desk in a sorry stew of incredulity, bellicosity, and self-pity. He had contemplated disaster many times, but never one quite like this. I'm not going to give that bastard a dime, he concluded. (He got up and paced the floor.) He's bluffing. Yeah, yeah. (He sat down.) I'll call his bluff. Not a dime. (He stood up and shadow boxed around the room. He sat down.) Where in the hell would I get $10,000? I'll just ignore the bastard. Maybe he'll go away.

The enormity of the coach's problem slowly put a dent in his suspension of rational thought. Options were eventually analyzed; benefits and costs were reckoned and compared; long-run considerations were given their due. And in the end, he knew he was screwed. Damn, he thought.

He reached for the flask of booze in the damaged drawer and fished around among the assortment of his remaining pills. He helped himself freely before wheeling his chair away from the desk so he could lean back and rest his troubled head against the wall. He closed his eyes. After several minutes he didn't feel so bad. Dum-de-dum-de-dum, he hummed a little tune to himself. There must be fifty ways to kill an A-rab, he thought.

Just stab 'im in the back, Jack. Shoot 'im in the head, Ned. Drown 'im in the tub, Bub. His sing-along with Paul Simon was interrupted by a loud knock on the door.

"Come in," he hollered.

Stubby Olson stepped in. "Hi, Coach," he said. "I've got the printout of the statistics on the game. Should I just put 'em on your desk."

"Okey-dokey," said the coach, without lifting his head.

Just hit 'im with a bat, Matt. Hang 'im from a tree, Lee

"Huh?" said Olson, arrested in the doorway by the sound of music.

"Nothing," the coach replied with a silly grin.

That night Coach Coneybear stayed up late thinking how he'd kill Basim Hachem, in spite of his knowing right off that he didn't have the balls for that sort of thing. Not when it came right down to it. It was merely a pipe dream induced by alcohol and drugs.

In the morning, he headed to the credit union for a $10,000 loan. He worried about collateral. He worried what his wife would say when she found out about it. You gotta think up some kind of story, he told himself. You could say you had to lend some money to a friend who's got a sick mom who needs an operation or something. Yeah, yeah. You've gotta think of something like that.

As he walked along, unconsciously eying pretty young coeds who had shed their winter wraps, an idea came to him out of the blue. He remembered a buddy from the past, an old college roommate and fellow pothead Maxim Kutsenko, a student from Russia. What made Maxim Kutsenko an object of interest was a claim he once made that his uncle was in the KGB, and it was this plus something else. Just the previous week the coach had read in the dentist's office a magazine article claiming that on the breakup of the Soviet Union many KGB agents had joined the Russian Mafia. Now he wondered whether good old Max's uncle had turned in his red-star-studded epaulets for the more genteel shoulder pads of a dark Armani suit, one well tailored to conceal a soft leather holster.

Coach Coneybear slowed his pace. Might Maxim Kutsenko's uncle be just the man to deal with the bothersome Basim Hachem? God, he thought. Just think of the names of these guys. This is all so . . . so un-American. Hmm. Maybe you should put off paying the money; stall the bastard. You could plead for time. Yeah, yeah. Plead for time. Maybe you could arrange for a change in the terms of payment, maybe paying not too large a sum every month. You could say that that way your wife might never find out about it. You could have your paycheck deposited in a new bank account, your very own. Yeah, and you could make payments to that bastard on a monthly basis. You could stall him. You wouldn't have to call his bluff completely. Make a counteroffer. Maybe gain some time to arrange a little surprise for the prick. You've got to get in touch with Max pronto.

Coach Lawrence Coneybear turned on his heel and strode back toward his office. Put the poison in a pill, Phil, he sang to himself. There was hope. Life was looking up.

The car that struck down and killed Mr. Harold Salvati (a.k.a. Michael Patriarca of New York) on Saturday, April 20, was discovered on Monday, April 22. As often happens in hit-and-run cases, the car was spotted by an irate homeowner, in this particular case by Mrs. Darling Turnquist. Mrs. Turnquist had become irritated by a unfamiliar car parked in front of her house over the weekend. As it happens, she was prodigiously proud of her spring garden, a riot of windflowers, early daffodils, and glories of the snow. When she realized that a rust bucket was obstructing the view of her garden by passing motorists, she began asking around. A neighbor lady wondered aloud whether the offending car might be the very one the police were looking for. The two ladies exchanged alarmed glances and hurried to the street to take a closer look. To their horror they discovered the car had a dented right front fender and a broken headlight. They rushed inside and locked the door. Mrs. Turnquist called the police while her husband, alerted to the danger, ran to the bedroom for the handgun under the T-shirts in the top drawer of his highboy. Then he paused in bewilderment. Where in the devil had he cached the bullets?

A rusty green Taurus with a dented fender and a broken headlamp was subsequently towed to the fenced-in holding area just to the side of the police station. There, on weary springs, it rested unevenly. Though final determination would require forensic tests, everyone assumed the offending vehicle had been found. The car had Illinois license plates, wouldn't you know, and had been reported stolen in Chicago. As word of the discovery of the car together with its origin spread through and beyond the Plattefield community, the people of Dairyland were reminded once again of the misfortune of sharing a border with the likes of Illinois.

Hurrying to be on time for a meeting with the Chief of Police Eugene Smedegard, Detective Tom Willison, and someone from the FBI, Patrick Delaney pulled open the backdoor to the station just as Detective Phillip Moran came busting through. Delaney mumbled something about being sorry, presumably for being in the way, but Moran, Plattefield's most senior detective, sneered, shouldered the young detective out of the way, and didn't even slow down. A troop of SWAT guys, outfitted in Kevlar helmets, night-vision goggles, body armor, and camouflage fatigues, and armed with an assortment of pistols, shotguns, and submachine guns, marched smartly out of the station single file with shoulders thrown back and guts pulled in, though it may be noted in regard to the latter that the effect was less than proportional to the effort. No matter: the SWAT guys looked ready to kick ass, to take on the entire Al Qaeda network, if needs must be, with any remaining remnants of the Taliban thrown in for good measure. Bring 'em on, Moran had once said stupidly. Delaney held the door and grinned as the troop passed by. It was well known that he shared the chief's opinion, which Detective Moran liked to tell fellow officers was typical of Delaney's ass-kissing, that the organization of a SWAT team was Plattefield's most absurd response to the 9/11 catastrophe.

As Moran's men piled into olive green Humvees, one said to Detective Moran, "Hey, I liked that shoulder check you gave Delaney. Ha, ha, ha."

"Yeah," replied Moran, "I got him good." Then, thinking ahead to the day when he would be the new Chief of Police, he mumbled more to himself than anyone else, "That boy's gotten too big for his bridges, by god. Well, we'll see where he stands when I cut him off at the knees."

With his men loaded, Moran jumped into the lead Humvee and said to the driver, "Let's go." With that the SWAT team roared out of the parking lot in a cloud of spent fuel and testosterone and headed for an abandoned house on the outskirts of town. There they would simulate an attack on a hypothetical cell of terrorists. Delaney watched the departing Humvees, momentarily forgetting his appointment and thinking that some day the SWAT team might do some real damage. When he remembered what he was about, he hurried to the chief's office.

Chief Smedegard sat in a high-backed, padded swivel chair. He was elderly and in bad health. Thin wispy white hair atop his head contrasted sharply with a ruddy complexion and a large purple nose. Flesh sagged pitifully from a rack of large bones that had once framed a powerful man. Nearly everyone wanted him to retire, but he had been hanging on year after year, fearful that if he *did* retire, the mayor, whoever he or she might be, would make Detective Phillip Moran the new chief. This he could not countenance. He would rather die with his boots on, he told his long-suffering wife.

The chief's office was furnished with walnut-veneered furniture and a beige Berber carpet. Book shelves had ample space for a bit of pottery and mementos from a long illustrious career. Dusty US and Wisconsin flags hung from poles standing in a corner. An oblong table had been pushed up against the desk in a T-configuration, which allowed the chief to hold small conferences in his office without surrendering his I'm-the-chief chair.

"Delaney," the chief said, "I'd like you to meet Bud Kohler from the FBI. Bud, this is Patrick Delaney."

There were how-do-you-do's and a hand shake. Delaney joined Kohler and Willison at the table and poured a glass of water from an insulated pitcher, all the while thinking Kohler was *so* FBI, all spit and polish with firmness of grip and openness of eye.

The friendly chitchat that followed left off when Agent Kohler said they should get down to business, which was what he did by assuming the chairmanship of the meeting. He began by recounting some history of Michael Patriarca and the role Patriarca had played in bringing to justice a murderous mid-level boss in the Gambino family. The history was both sketchy and unnecessary. The Plattefield police had been in contact with the New York City police. Voluminous faxes now on file at the station had been reviewed at some length. But the three Plattefield officers let the FBI agent ramble on. Mr. Kohler's revelation that Michael Patriarca and his wife Connie had both received nips and tucks from a plastic surgeon was the only tidbit not already in the faxes from New York.

Of greater interest was Agent Kohler's report that Connie Patriarca was the named beneficiary of a $500,000 life insurance policy taken out by her husband. She had also told her sister that she and her husband were being settled somewhere in Wisconsin. Had she said where in Wisconsin? Had she passed along her new last name? Had she revealed her new telephone number? She adamantly denied breaking the seal of secrecy in any of these ways, and her attorney had turned thumbs down on any but the most tender of interrogations.

Willison remarked that a driver of a stolen car would have been reluctant to call 911, which he thought increased the possibility that the driver might simply have been some local punk. Kohler eschewed any such likelihood, saying that the FBI was over 90 percent sure the driver was a mob hit-man. Delaney wondered aloud why a professional hit-man would have taken the trouble of stealing a car and running Patriarca down. Why not simply rent a car at Chicago or Milwaukee, drive to Plattefield, and gun the man down? he asked. Kohler speculated that the mob might have wanted the murder to look like an accident. Delaney had planned to say the driver might have run down the wrong person, that the intended victim might have been Caroline Maidin, but he changed his mind. Kohler had become defensive, as if the locals had no business questioning the wisdom of the FBI. The chief, moreover, weighed in with the view that the killer was most surely in the employ of organized crime. The session ended with the understanding that the Chicago police would investigate the theft of the car and try to discover who the thief had been: that the New York police would investigate suspected hit-men: and that the Plattefield police would undertake a local investigation, just in the off-chance (Kohler's characterization) the hit-and-run had nothing to do with the witness protection program. The FBI would play a coordinative and integrative role, Agent Kohler explained.

Delaney and Willison rehashed the meeting in Willison's cubicle. Delaney said Caroline Maidin might have been the intended victim. Willison was skeptical, but Delaney persisted, noting that Michael Patriarca wasn't much larger than Mrs. Maidin, that both were dressed alike and had headset radios. Patriarca could not have been jogging on Greenbriar Road very long, Delaney argued, whereas Maidin jogged there often. Willison finally agreed that it might not be such a bad idea for Delaney to have a little chat with Mrs. Maidin, just to see if there might be someone with a motive for running her down. This was all the encouragement Delaney needed.

Caroline Maiden was surprised but pleased when she answered the doorbell and found Detective Delaney on the front stoop. She was embarrassed, as if unaccustomed to company and unsure what to say.

"I called the hospital," Delaney said, "and was told you were off today. So I thought I'd swing by just to follow up on the hit-and-run. Do you have a few minutes?"

"Of course," she replied, stepping aside to let him in.

"Would you like some coffee?" she said.

"Yeah, sure. Thanks."

Without being invited, Delaney followed her into the kitchen, wondering if her husband was at home. While she measured coffee into a filter, he looked around and said, "Boy, is this a nice house."

"Oh, thank you," she replied. "I love it, though I'm afraid we have more room than we need."

"Did you buy the house as is, or did you have it built?"

"We had it built."

"I'm in the market for a house myself, but I could afford nothing like this. Not on a cop's pay. I've been wondering about building, but it seems a little scary."

"It's a challenge. I'm not sure we did the right thing."

Caroline Maidin then talked about the time that goes into designing your own house, all the decisions you have to make, and how she and Joe were unskilled in the business and had made mistakes. She complained about the builder and the subcontractors and the beer-swigging carpenters. Delaney sat at the kitchen table as he waited for the coffee to brew. He listened, watched, and asked questions both out of curiosity and to keep her going. As she talked she loosened up; she seemed to enjoy his company. Delaney decided she was a lonely woman who didn't make friends easily and was perhaps trapped in an unhappy marriage. He knew women like that.

After complaining about a ceiling fan that didn't work, Mrs. Maidin changed the subject.

"You said you were interested in getting a house, are you married?"

"No, but I'm engaged."

Mrs. Maidin knew Detective Delaney's marital status perfectly. A few years back he had become famous for cracking a case of a serial killer and was nearly killed trying to make an arrest. His picture and story had been on TV and in the papers. Though not on Mrs. Maidin's ward, he had spent several days at the Plattefield Memorial Hospital. Some of the nurses at the hospital knew things about Detective Delaney that would have made him blush. They had been following closely his engagement to the lovely Emily Peterson. Detective Delaney's sometimes bumpy romance with Miss Peterson had become an item in Plattefield society.

With the prospect of gossiping with her fellow nurses, Mrs. Maidin was prepared to fish shamelessly for the latest news about the couple. She was unaware that Delaney, too, was playing a game: that he was prepared to lead her on and to ask at propitious moments questions that on the surface had little relevance to the hit-and-run accident on Greenbriar Road.

"Congratulations, Patrick. When are you going to tie the knot?" (Mrs. Maidin had become a little flirty.)

"In August. August 3rd. That's why I'm thinking about getting a house, something small to start with."

"You must be very busy with marriage plans and all. Are you planning a big wedding?"

"Oh, yeah. Big. Big. It's not my idea, but Emily—Emily Peterson is my fiancée. Well, she wants a big wedding. Her aunt would have Pope John officiate if she had *her* druthers."

Mrs. Maidin laughed at the joke and said, "Have you decided where you're going on your honeymoon?"

"Sort of. We're thinking of going to Ireland. I've never been abroad. Neither has my fiancée."

"Oh, do go to Ireland!" Mrs. Maidin cried. "I love Ireland. Have you picked out the places you want to see?"

"No, not yet. That's the problem. We don't know for sure where we should go, what to see. We only started thinking about Ireland recently."

"Well, I've been to Ireland many times. You see my mom was Irish and we used to go there every summer after my father died. I have a recommendation if you want one free of charge."

"I'm all ears," Delaney replied. He and Mrs. Maidin laughed at his figure of speech, for Delaney's ears stuck out a bit. It wasn't something that would go unnoticed.

"Well, OK. My mom and I often stayed at the Derrycross Hotel in Sneem. Sneem's in Southwest Ireland, my favorite part of the country. The scenery is breathtaking and the hotel is just the best. Wonderful rooms and service, and you can avoid the touristy stuff at places like Killarney and Blarney. That's where I met my husband, in Sneem."

"No kidding. Is Joe from around here? Is that why you've settled here?"

"Heavens no. He's from Egypt. You see his family is famous in Cairo. A family with a long tradition of surgeons and physicians. Quite well-to-do. They often vacation in Ireland and stay at the Derrycross Hotel. And that's where we met, Joe and I. I must have some brochures about the house somewhere, probably in an unpacked box. I'll try to find them and send them to you if you'd like."

"Great," Delaney replied.

Mrs. Maidin then waxed lyrical in her description of Ireland: the scenery, historic places, and the people. The questions Delaney asked should have been a clue to Mrs. Maidin that he was not as ignorant of Ireland's attractions as he had led her to believe.

"Is your husband a citizen?" Delaney suddenly asked. "You know how crazy the world has gotten since 9/11."

"Yes," she replied. "He became a citizen last year."

"Is he very religious? I've often wondered how American women cope with men who are devout Muslims."

"Joe isn't too religious. That's never been a problem for me."

"Do you have many relatives? People you're close to?"

"Oh, I guess I have a few second cousins in California. I hardly know them."

"Caroline, I don't want to take too much of your time, but I do have a few questions about the hit-and-run. I know you . . ."

"Isn't it incredible that the victim was in the witness protection program? Are you making any progress on the case. I mean things you can talk about?"

"We haven't made much progress at all. But I wanted to ask you something. When you jog, do you always take Greenbriar Road?"

"Well, I used to jog there a lot, nearly every morning. I don't go there anymore, though. Why do you ask? Didn't I explain this before?"

"Well, I'm still interested in whether you remember seeing anything suspicious during your workouts. It's less likely you did if you always run the same course." (It was a lame excuse for his question, but Delaney could think of nothing better.) "I noticed you jog with a headset radio. I've been wondering about getting one. Do you like listening to the radio when you jog?"

"It's OK. I've not used it very long."

"I like to listen to birds when I jog, especially in the spring. You know, the sounds of nature and all that. I'm not sure I'd like a radio clamped on my head. Are they very expensive?"

"I really can't say. It was a present from Joe."

"Was it a birthday or something?" he asked.

"No, I think he just wanted to make jogging less onerous. I try hard."

It would also make it harder for you to hear a car coming up behind you, Delaney thought, but he only said, "Well, I suppose I should get going so you can enjoy your day off."

"You mean get all my housework done."

"Doesn't your husband pull his load?" (Delaney grinned handsomely and affected a manner as if to share confidences.)

"You forget where he's from. Would you like more coffee?"

"No thanks."

Delaney rose and he and Caroline walked to the front door. Delaney opened the door and then stopped. "One more thing," he said. "I need to ask you a rather far-out question. Do you know of anyone who might intend you any harm?"

Caroline Maidin held Delaney's eye for a long moment. Her expression changed. The levity disappeared.

"That's what this was all about, wasn't it? You were letting me run on."

"Sometimes a cop has to explore alternatives that seem remote, even ridiculous . . . . Do you, Mrs. Maidin? Know of anyone who might intend you harm?"

"Patrick, I know of no one who would want to *kill* me."

"One other thing. Where did the money come from for this house? From your husband?"

"No, from me. You see, my mom died a few months ago. She was quite wealthy."

I see, thought Delaney. He got citizenship and money. I wonder what she got. "Where did your mom live?" he asked.

"Here, in Plattefield. She lived here in her later years. She had Alzheimer's."

"I see. Sorry. What was her name?"

"Margaret Schroeder."

"The name is not familiar. Well, I hope I haven't alarmed you, Mrs. Maidin. Please take my card and call me if you can think of anything more. And oh, about Ireland, I really am interested in—what was the hotel? Derrycross Hotel? If you find those brochures I *would* like to have them. You see, Mrs. Maidin, I enjoyed talking to you and I'm concerned about you. I wish you well. Good-day."

Even before Delaney had backed out of the driveway, Caroline Maidin remembered where she had put the brochure on the Derrycross Hotel. She tried to remember the detective's exact words. What had he said? That he cared for her? What a nice guy. She forgave his milking her for information. He was only doing his job. She would send the brochure to him. She'd get it in the mail today before she forgot about it.

As Delaney drove away, he had little idea that his nice-cop speech would in the end pay a handsome dividend: that the Derrycross Hotel would prove to be the key to everything.

Chapter 4

On the very afternoon he was to fork over $10,000, Coach Coneybear sprang his plan to run out the clock on Basim Hachem. Buy now, pay later. It was all *so* American. The coach would buy Hachem's silence and pay on the installment plan. He would give Hachem $1,000 per month for ten months on the proviso that would be the end of it. There will be no more payments after that, the coach insisted, and, with a sneer, Hachem agreed. Coach Coneybear wondered if Hachem was so stupid as to believe that he (the coach) believed that the ten grand would in fact be the end of it. Dumb ass, he thought. On the very next day he flew to Portland, Oregon, ostensibly to do a bit of recruiting, actually to arrange for murder in the first degree.

He landed at mid-afternoon, rented a car, and drove to the Markov Rhody Motel, the newest addition to the Markov chain of motels on the West Coast. At seven o'clock he picked up Maxim Kutsenko at his home. They drove to a bar to quench their thirst and thence to the Red Steer Palace where they drank some more and ate charcoal broiled steaks. Coach Coneybear picked up the tab. After that they drove to the Markov for a night cap. The coach got a bucket of ice and opened a bottle of Jim Beam. After more booze and small talk, he finally got around to the matter of murder.

He explained his situation vis-à-vis Basim Hachem and mentioned Kutsenko's uncle in the KGB. "You see, Max," he said, "I read this magazine article the other day that said that after the breakup of the Soviet Union, a lot of guys in the KGB went over to the Russian Mafia. So, what's happened to your uncle? Didn't you once say he was hoping to come to America? Can you get in touch with him? I need someone to solve my problem. I'm not a rich man, but I could scare up, say, $20,000. Anyway, there it is. I'm looking for some one who can rid me of a blackmailer, and I'm willing to pay."

"You want this guy killed?" Kutsenko said, hunched forward. "Look, I'm not going to get involved in anything like that. I've got a wife and two boys to think of."

"Well, I didn't say I wanted this guy bumped off . . . exactly. I mean we have to be careful what we say here. All I'm saying is I want the problem solved one way or the other. I don't care how. If you don't want to get involved, I'll contact your uncle myself. All you have to do is tell me how to get in touch with him?"

"Sorry pal, my uncle has retired from the business. He'd never want to get involved in something like this."

"OK, listen. Just listen a minute. A while ago we were talking about college football and you said you and your buddies have been making some bets with your local bookie. You said how pissed your wife got when you lost a bundle at Las Vegas betting on the Sugar Bowl game. OK, a couple of Saturdays ago, a guy from Michigan came to our spring exhibition game and was damned impressed. They're looking at me, Max. Think of it. Suppose I become the head football coach for a team like Michigan. You want tips on the games? You want inside dope? You help me out here and we could work something out. And there are other possibilities. Think about it."

"God, I'd really like to help you, Larry. And yeah, I can see where you'd be in a helluva good position to guess outcomes. But what the hell can I do?"

The words were no sooner out of Kutsenko's mouth than he began rethinking the payoff, not the tips on likely game outcomes, but on the other possibilities his friend mentioned. He thought about shaving points, throwing games. Visions of rigged Sugar Bowls danced in his head. The song of a cash register tinkled in his inner ear. Ka-ching, ka-ching, ka-ching was the happy refrain. Hmm, perhaps there *was* something he could do.

"OK," he said after a pause. "How about this? My uncle is living in the US, but I'm not saying where. I've been meaning to visit him anyway. It's been a long time. So, I'll go see him, tell him what you said, what you need. Then it's up to him. If he has a name or two, well, I could pass them along to you. OK? That's all I can do."

"Hey, man, you're a real pal."

"Well, you helped me out once. You know, that silly rape thing. She was just trying to get even with me, of course. You know, for dumping her."

"Yeah, but that was a long time ago. I'm not asking for payback or anything. It's just that I'm a dead man if I don't get some help. Oh, one more thing. God, I hate to push, but I'd really appreciate your acting fast, real fast."

"Yeah, we'll see. One thing, though, we'd better break off any further contacts for the time being. You know, until after all these matters are taken care of—one way or the other. It's too bad I told my wife about your coming here. Well, it's too late to do anything about that now. If you were ever asked why you flew to Portland, could you give an explanation?"

"I told my secretary I was off to do a bit of recruiting, but that might not stand up under close scrutiny. Who did I recruit?"

"Well, you'd better think of something."

Petrouchka's offered the best Russian cuisine in Los Angeles. Because the restaurant was new, however, neither the food critics nor the nouveau riche were aware of its sumptuous fare. Located at the intersection of Happy Valley Road and Fairy Rose Street, about a half-mile off the Santa Monica Freeway, its exterior consisted of a red brick façade capped by a no-nonsense marquee painted black with "Petrouchka's" appearing in large red letters. Its Spartan exterior gave the lie to the over-the-top opulence of its interior, where a white marble-floored vestibule opened onto a dining room as luxurious as a Faberge egg. The floor was covered with a thick blue carpet. The motif for walls and ceiling came from the Paris Opera Ballet's rendition of the *Petrouchka* Ballet as staged by Nicholas Beriosov. The domed ceiling rendered a night sky with a quarter moon, falling stars, and fierce black cats swooping about on broomsticks. Dancers in colorful costumes decorated the walls in scenes of a Shrovetide Fair. The ballerina, Moor, and Petrouchka were forever locked in their tragic pas de trois. Cavorting about them were drunken Cossacks, circus performers, peasant girls, and corrupt policemen. An ominous black bear on a chain stood to the side with his master waiting to take his place at center stage.

The patrons of Petrouchka's sat in padded chairs with flaming red leather backs and seats. Sound proofing materials assured patrons of the chance for quiet repartee, with the background hum of conversation, laughter, and clattering dishes providing no more than the ambiance of people at pleasure. Side rooms were available for large parties. A powerful fan cleared the cigar room of smoke, thus contributing its bit to Los Angeles's polluted air.

The menu at Petrouchka's included homemade flavored vodkas and smoked salmon, sturgeon, peroshki, and caviar served with chopped egg, onion, and blini. With sauces, wines, and blood-clotting creams, entrees of lamb, chicken, beef, and fish were prepared in the best tradition of Russian cookery. Prices guaranteed the exclusion of the unwashed.

Now, as it happens, the owner of Petrouchka's was Victor Malakhov, former major in the KGB and the very uncle of whom Maxim Kutsenko had spoken to his friend Coach Larry Coneybear. Mr. Malakhov had acquired enormous wealth through the purchase and later sale of shares in a Russian oil company, a company that had acquired a large oil field at a fraction of its true value. The banker who had lent him the money in return for protection (from Malakhov's own thugs, as you might have guessed) was now among the ten richest Russian oligarchs. The FBI had investigated Mr. Malakhov at length and concluded that his business strategies had much in common with those of John D. Rockefeller and were therefore quite in keeping with the finest traditions of American capitalism. He was therefore not indicted for criminal offenses. In addition, the information he had provided on former officers of the KGB together with spies in various US intelligence agencies provided the quid pro quo for US citizenship. Victor Malakhov thus had it made, as the saying goes.

His LA home was large and comfortable. The windows at the back of the house looked out on a lovely garden with a water feature. Those at the front afforded a distant but nonetheless pleasant view of the Pacific ocean. Mr. Malakhov was a contended man. His wife loved California: the climate, flowers, endless beaches, and stores and shops overflowing with a cornucopia of goodies. Mr. Malakhov's ancient mother was happy as a mama bear with a salmon. She sat in the family room and watched TV day and night. Her English was not the best, however, and from time to time she cried out in Russian, even when she was the only person in the room, "What did he say? What did he say?" For supplemental income, an elderly émigré often sat with Grandma Malakhov, translating sitcom English into fractured Russian, which sometimes led to spirited disagreements. Now and again, the émigré flounced out of the family room in a royal snit.

If there was one disappointment in Victor Malakhov's life, one tiny cloud in an otherwise sun-blanched sky, it was his son Mani. Whereas Victor was squat and square, Mani was slender and svelte. A long neck connected stooped shoulders to a delicate jaw. His fair hair was groomed at Saks Boutique Hair Salon on Hollywood Drive for $225 per cut. There, its natural wave was ironed to flatness. Straightened hair was severely parted. The cut was not particularly long except for a lock that was supposed to hang down over his right ear but fell forward in front of his right eye instead, as if in compensation. Because of a slight speech impediment (all his "r's" were turned into "w's"), he sounded as if he were affecting a British accent, which his friends found endearing, but which his father found sissified.

As a young man Victor Malakhov had been a boxer and was known as Killer Vic. His son Mani, on the other hand, wanted to be a ballet dancer, though he had all but given up on a dream he felt would never come true. Instead he worked in the kitchen of his father's restaurant. He washed lettuce, shredded red cabbage, diced beets, and helped with the cleanup after closing. He labored under his father's tutelage to learn the business from the ground up. One day he would inherit a world-famous restaurant, his father assured him. He was advised as well to stop hanging out with those faggy beach boys with dark tans and sun-bleached hair who carried surfboards around all the time and paraded about half-naked showing off ripped muscles that were as much the product of anabolic steroids, in Victor's opinion, as the lifting of weights. Contrary to his father's dark suspicion, Mani liked girls and they liked him back. It's just that he loved to sing and dance, go to the movies, wear smart clothes, get facials, and shop for grooming products. He had an eye for movement, music, color, patterns. His love was show biz, not food biz, and he bridled at his father's tutelage day in and day out. Not only would he never dance ballet, he would never earn his papa's love and respect. Sometimes he cried himself to sleep, for a sensitive young man was this poor Mani Malakhov.

One day the Malakhovs were paid an unexpected visit by Maxim Kutsenko, a visit that would forever change Mani Malakhov's life. The Malakhovs were thrilled to see Kutsenko. They had few friends, and nearly all of their relatives, with whom they were not on speaking terms anyway, lived in Moscow. Maxim was treated like a long lost son. He was feted to the best food he had ever eaten in his life. Ditto the vodka that poured like, well, wine. It was emphasized time and time again that he must visit LA more often: that he must bring his entire family and plan to spend weeks and weeks in LA. In fact he was told that living in Portland was ridiculous when he could just as well live in LA. The winters in Portland are so bad, he was told: all that rain. He was treated so graciously that he hated to bring up the real reason for his visit. But, on the evening before his scheduled departure, that is what he did.

"Uncle, I need to talk to you about something that's rather delicate," he said to Victor Malakhov. "Is there someplace we could talk in strict privacy?"

The issue was thus broached. Maxim watched and waited while his uncle took his good sweet time lighting a cigar. It occurred to him that Victor Malakhov projected a sinister, rather reptilian air. He had black hair, a spotted swarthy complexion, and a big potato nose skewed to the left. His eyelids lay heavy over dark eyes. His shoulders hunched up around his thick head-neck continuum. His movements were slow and deliberate, as if the sun's warmth hadn't yet penetrated his innards. Maxim sensed rather than knew that if ever his uncle decided to strike, it would be with the deadliness of a Gila monster.

"Let us go to yard in back," Mr. Malakhov said after wreathing his head in cumuli of smoke.

They visited a garden. The scent of roses hanging in the air was soon snuffed by the smoke of cigar. A jet of water tinkled as it splashed down in a circular pool. Gold fish finned warily under lily leaves. Mr. Malakhov guided his nephew to a secluded bench backed up to a planting of small bamboo. He was unaware that just behind the bamboo, in a yoga position on a stepping stone, sat his son Mani listening to Ravi Shankar playing Gershwin melodies on the sitar. Mani had seen his father and cousin headed his way, and for reasons he himself could not explain (perhaps it was fate) had turned off his radio and lifted the earphones from his head. He then sat still as the intrepid heron that sometimes touched down in the Malakhov's water feature and pretended to be a stick.

"Well, I don't know where to begin exactly," Maxim began uncertainly. "You see there's this guy who did me a big favor when I was an undergraduate at Ethan Dinglebarry College. I mean, I really owe this guy. Well, now he's the football coach at the University of Wisconsin, not at Madison. That's Big Ten territory. He's coaching at the Plattefield campus. It's a small campus, you see. Anyway, he needs help. He's being blackmailed."

"This coach of football," Mr. Malakhov said, "He did something bad. Yes?"

Maxim explained how an Arab named Basim Hachem had rifled the coach's desk and discovered the coach's secrets.

"Once long ago," Maxim confessed, "I told Larry, Larry Coneybear—that's the coach's name—that I had an uncle in the KGB. Larry now seems to think the KGB has become the Russian Mafia. So he figures you might be able to help him. He doesn't know a thing about you. I've never even told him your name. Anyway, he's got this crazy idea that for, say, twenty grand or so, you might help him out. I said no way: that you were never mixed up with the criminal element. But he's desperate. He thought you might just know of someone." (For a long moment there was only the sound of tinkling water.) "God, I hope I haven't hurt your feelings, uncle. I feel like a real asshole even mentioning this, but you see Larry is desperate and I *am* heavily in his debt. I mean, I could be in jail right now if it wasn't for Larry. I said I would be seeing you anyway and that I would ask. There, I've paid off my debt. I'll tell him anything you want me to and we'll forget it."

"It is possible some of my fellow officers did take up crime element," Mr. Malakhov said, fingering his cigar. "When the Union of Soviet Socialist Republics collapsed was tough living for some of us. When I come to America all my connections get cut. I never do thing that be against law. You see, I cannot assist your friend."

"That's what I figured. That's what I told him. I'll just mention one thing more. Larry is one of the finest young coaches in the country. There was an article in a recent issue of Sports Illustrated that discussed the rising new crop of coaches that would one day hit the big time. Larry Coneybear received a glowing report. He's going to become a coach of a really first-rate team one of these days. I mean a team like Michigan or Florida State. OK, so he's going to be in a really good position to swing close games one way or the other, providing he's given the proper motivation. You see what I mean. I mean just imagine the money that could be made if you knew Michigan was going to lose a game in the Rose Bowl. We're talking many thousands of dollars here."

"Ah, you be his friend not so good. You blackmail him to throw game. Eh?"

"No, no. I'm not saying *I'd* blackmail him, but someone could. The thing is, he's desperate and he rather hinted that he might some day be willing to, well, do favors. Anyway, what else can I do? I mean what he's willing to do to get rid of Basim Hachem, well, that's his business."

"Hmm," hummed Mr. Malakhov. "The betting angle is of quite interest. I admit to that. But still, I think this thing I stay away from. I give it thought, yes. Can't promise anything. Shall we go back in?"

Just in case he was spotted by his father or his cousin as they headed for the house, Mani Malakhov put his earphones back on and turned on the radio. He wouldn't have wanted to be accused of eavesdropping. Later, as he slipped around to the front of the house, his heart beat wildly, for he knew what he would do. The plan was dangerous, but the payoff would be a goodly chunk of change, just the sort of thing he'd need to get his BFA in Dance Performance at the University of California: Irvine. And there were long-run possibilities, too. What did he know of betting on sports? Nada. And football was his abhorrence; it was so . . . so unnecessarily rough. But he could learn sports. And it wouldn't hurt to have a coach in a position to fix games. Mani Malakhov would at last become a real man, a tough guy like his papa. Maybe then his papa would show him some respect. All he had to do was bump off a crooked Arab. Well, he could do that. True, Mani Malakhov had never before considered killing anything bigger than a bug, but he knew or at least figured his dad had killed lots of people. How hard could it be to do in a really bad person? he asked himself. A blackmailer. Ugh. You point a gun and, bang, like in the movies. He didn't want to think in detail about actually doing it, about actually pulling the trigger, not just yet. When the time came he'd do it. He could kill just like his papa used to do. Right? Poor Mani Malakhov didn't know who he was, but he would find out soon enough that he was no more cut out to be a crook than a cook.

The investigation of the hit-and-run accident on Greenbriar Road had hit a roadblock. In spite of a great expenditure of time and resources, the FBI could find no link between the Gambino family in New York and the death of Michael Patriarca. True, the car involved had been found, but that was weeks ago and nothing came of it. The car, stolen in Chicago, had fingerprints aplenty, but they belonged to the previous owners and their three sticky-fingered kids. The parents had never been arrested, never been to New York, and never known any New York mobsters. It was the lack of progress as much as anything that caused Detective Delaney to decide one day to go over the Patriarca file line by line. He had hardly gotten started when he noticed something odd. The 911 call from Caroline Maidin had come from 836-5559, which was not her home number. He logged on the internet and discovered that 836-5559 was the number for John and Heather Bellman who lived next door to the Maidins. Now this is an oddity, he thought. He would talk to her in person, not over the phone.

He drove to the Maidin residence, but there was no one there. Then he drove to the Plattefield Memorial Hospital and made arrangements with Caroline Maidin's supervisor to speak with her. They met in a small room normally used by doctors in the examination of patients. While he waited for Mrs. Maidin, he read the health tips posted on a bulletin board and vowed to cut back on bacon and eggs and grilled brats.

"Hello Patrick," she said after closing the door behind her. She offered her hand, but her expression was guarded. She sat at a small desk that supported a computer monitor. Delaney sat in one of the two chairs presumably intended for patients.

"Is there something I can help you with?" she asked.

"Mrs. Maidin, when you called 911 to report the hit-and-run, you used your neighbor's phone instead of your own. Why was that?"

After a nervous hesitation, Mrs. Maidin replied: "I tried calling from my place, but the phone was out of order."

Some people are not good at lying, and in Delaney's opinion, Caroline Maidin was one of them. He decided to push the issue.

"What was wrong with your phone?"

"I don't know. It just wouldn't work."

"Well, did you get a dial tone?"

"I don't remember, but I dialed 911 and nothing happened."

"Did you try again?"

"I can't remember. I was in a panic."

"You must have more than one phone in the house. Did you try another phone?"

"No, I just assumed our other phones were dead, too."

"So you went to the Bellmans and called from their phone. Is that right?"

"Yes."

"How did you explain your request to use their phone?"

"I told her my phone wasn't working and I had to call 911."

"You talked, then, with Mrs. Bellman, not Mr. Bellman. Was Mr. Bellman present at any time you were using the phone?"

"No."

"Did you call the phone company to report that your phone was out of order?"

"No, you see when I got home I found the phone was working after all. I think I must have dialed the wrong number in the first place."

"Did you tell your husband about it? About the hit-and-run?"

"Yes, of course."

"When did you tell him? Before you tried to call?"

"I told him about it before I called. I rushed in and told him before I called. Before I tried to call. And then I rushed out of the house. You know, to go to the Bellmans."

"Did you tell him the phone didn't work?"

"Yes, and then I rushed out of the house."

"Did he try to use the phone after you left?"

"I don't know. I suppose he might have."

"Did you talk about it after I took you home? Didn't you ask him about it? After you returned from the station?"

"Yes, and we agreed that I must have misdialed."

"So he *did* try the phone and when he did, it worked. Is that right?"

"I guess it must have."

Delaney stared at her in disbelief and anger, for he was sure she was lying. She held his gaze until her eyes brimmed with tears.

"Are you sure, Caroline, there is nothing more you want to tell me?"

"I'm sure."

Delaney's next stop was the cramped reading room of the Probate Court of Jefferson County. There he learned that Mrs. Anne Schroeder had left her entire estate to her daughter Caroline. From the listing of stocks, bonds, and real property, he guessed the estate must have been substantial, probably in the millions of dollars. But the real surprise, a surprise that made the detective sit back and rub his nose, was that Mrs. Anne Schroeder had been the owner of Green Valley Farm, which now belonged to Caroline Maidin. He frowned as he recalled Professor Willgrubs's encounter with a mean Holstein bull at that very place. Coincidences were such a bother, always demanding explanations. Though his knowledge of Wisconsin's laws on inheritance was far from fresh, he suspected that Joe Maidin would end up with diddly if he and Caroline were divorced. Not so if Caroline died in an accident, however, depending on her will, if she has one, that is.

That afternoon Detective Delaney walked into Detective Willison's cubicle, plopped his butt down on a chair, and said, "You got a minute?"

Willison pushed a half-completed activity report toward the back of his desk and said, "What's up, Pat?"

"I've been thinking about our hit-and-run," Delaney said. "I think the FBI might be off on the wrong track, which might explain why they're coming up with zilch. And we've not come across anything that would suggest a local car thief, either."

"Ah, so you're back to thinking Caroline Maidin was the intended victim. But I thought you said you talked to her and didn't pick up on anything."

"I've made a list," Delaney said, holding up a sheet of yellow paper for emphasis. (Willison was familiar with Delaney's fondness for doodling and making notes on tablets of yellow paper.) "Maidin had been jogging on Greenbriar Road for some time. We don't know where Patriarca jogged, but he might not have established a routine. There wasn't much time. The two of them were about the same size and wore similar clothes. Both wore headset radios. Caroline told me that her husband bought her the radio, but not for any particular occasion, like a birthday or something. A radio would block out the sound of an approaching car."

"You think Caroline's hubby could be behind it?"

"Maybe. Maybe. There's more. Caroline says her husband's from Egypt. Her mom died of Alzheimer's awhile back and I checked her will in probate court. Her mom left her a bundle. I'm not sure how much of that would go her husband in the event of a divorce, but he'd likely get it all in the event of death. So, did handsome Joe marry plain Caroline for citizenship and money? A couple other things: On the way to the station, Mrs. Maidin called to say she'd be late for work, but she never called her husband. I think that's odd. Also, why didn't the husband go back to the scene of the accident with his wife. You see they have no children. He didn't have to stay home with the kids. Again, I think that's odd, that he didn't go with his wife."

"But here's the oddest thing of all, Tom. Mrs. Maidin didn't use her home phone to call 911. She used her next-door neighbor's phone. When I asked her about it, she said she went next door because her own phone wasn't working. She said she must have misdialed because it was working later on. I think she's lying."

"Well, she might have been embarrassed at having misdialed. It seems plausible to me. Anyway, why else would she have run next door?"

"You tell me. Assume she's lying, that she didn't misdeal.

Can you think of any reason why she would have gone next door to use the phone?"

"Mmm. Well, let me think . . . . OK, her husband didn't want her to call 911."

"Yeah, and if he had planned to have her killed that morning and she came rushing into the house saying someone was run down on Greenbriar Road, would he have been receptive to her calling 911? In a panic, he might have argued that it was best not getting involved, that it would be better if someone else found the victim. If he had attempted murder, the last thing in the world he would want is to draw the attention of the police."

"But the victim wasn't dead. Any decent person would be eager to call, hang the consequences. A nurse would know that time was of the essence."

"Exactly."

"I think you've put together enough evidence to go after subpoenas. Let's go talk to the chief. Hang the FBI."

The Student Records Office was housed in Jackson Hall. Mrs. Faith Cummings was in charge. Detective Delaney introduced himself, showed his ID, and said he wanted to examine the file of a student named Joe Maidin. He presented a subpoena. Elderly and suspicious, Mrs. Cummings looked askance at the subpoena lying on her desk. She wiggled her mouse, fingered her keyboard, and said, a little too gleefully, that there *was* no student at Plattefield by the name of Joe Maidin.

"This is strange," Delaney said. "I've talked with his wife Caroline Maidin. She says he's a graduate student in biology. She says he's from Egypt. Are there *any* Maidins going to school here?"

"Yes."

"How many?"

"One."

"Ah, perhaps Mr. Maidin changed his name. If the Maidin you've found is from Egypt, then he's very likely the man I'm interested in."

"Well, we do have a Yussef Maidin," she said sheepishly. "I could check his file. If he's from Egypt and if he's married to a woman named Caroline, well, then I suppose Yussef and Joe are the same student."

Hello! thought Delaney contemptuously. "Please," he said.

Joe Maidin and Yussef Maidin were of course one in the same, and at a small table not far from Mrs. Cummings's desk, Delaney set to work on a thick file.

Joe Maidin left home to begin his education in the United States in 1995, according to the record. The admissions officer at the university certified that Maidin's application for admission was complete and that his credentials were in perfect order. He had graduated in the upper ten percent of his class at Highbridge College, a highly rated private preparatory school originally built by the British for the well-to-do. His English was excellent. Mr. Maidin had not participated in sports at Highbridge, according to one of the letters of recommendation, which seems to have been the only blot on his record. Maidin's teachers gave glowing accounts of his scholarly abilities. There was no question but what his family had the resources to send their boy to college in the United States. At Plattefield he had earned a BS degree and was now working toward his MS. His grades were outstanding, but he participated in no extracurricular activities. In particular, it appeared that he had never been a member of the only Islamic group on campus, not that there would have been anything wrong with that.

Delaney's next stop was the Plattefield Memorial Hospital where he talked to the head of personnel and examined Caroline Maidin's work folder. He learned that she was a well-respected nurse and had graduated with honors from the School of Nursing at the University of Wisconsin-Madison. Her maiden name was Caroline Schroeder, but this he already knew. The personnel director said that her mother had died at William and Judy's Hospicecare in early 2002 after a long illness.

One morning shortly after his visit to the hospital, Delaney parked his car some distance from the Maidin residence and watched. When Mrs. Maidin left for work, he drove to her house, parked in the driveway, and rang the doorbell.

"Hello," Delaney said. He gave his name and showed his ID.

"Are you Joe Maidin?" he asked.

"Yes," Maidin replied. "What do you want?"

He was a slender man of medium height with a dark complexion and refined features. Delaney thought women would likely find him attractive. He was barefoot and wore a baggy T-shirt and jeans.

"I just have a few questions," Delaney replied. He paused for a moment and said, when it was clear that he was not going to be invited in, "Mr. Maidin, your wife reported a hit-and-run accident on the morning of April 20th. She used the neighbor's phone. How would you explain that?"

"You've already talked to her about that, so why are you bothering me?"

"To find out if you agree with her explanation? What I want to know is: did you try to stop her from making that call?"

Mr. Maidin and Detective Delaney studied each other. Nothing was given away on either side.

"If you don't stop harassing us," Maidin said, "I'm going to call our attorney." Then he closed the door.

Chapter 5

Overlooking that his father might one day himself arrange the demise of Coach Lawrence Coneybear's nemesis, Mani Malakhov set out to do it on his own. He would shoot Basim Hachem and collect the money. That was the idea. His friend Tuck Meadow owned a handgun and was careless where he put it. It was always lying around somewhere. The modest house on Vine Street that he shared with his girlfriend Sharon was often overrun by people looking to party or hang out. His handgun was passed around, commented on, and treated like a toy. Mani's plan called for surreptitiously borrowing the gun and learning how to use it. Perhaps he would drive out in the country and shoot at tin cans. The gun would of course be returned on the completion of his work, so it wasn't as if he were stealing from a friend.

Important among the unknowns in Mani's benefit-cost analysis were those measured in dollars. How much would this Coach Coneybear be willing to pay? he wondered. Hadn't Max mentioned $20,000? Which didn't seem like very much for popping a guy. Was that after taxes? When the time comes, should I demand cash, he asked himself, or would a check do? Cash, probably, was his reply. A check might bounce, but a stiff is stiff forever.

In addition to fine tuning the payoff, he had to think up an excuse for getting away from home and traveling to someplace in the Midwest where he could rent a car and drive to Plattefield. It was by mere coincidence that one of his friends had decided to return to Minneapolis, his hometown, and enroll at the University of Minnesota in the fall. Couldn't Mani pretend that he, too, was interested in attending the University of Minnesota? They could drive to Minnesota together.

At lunch with his family one day Mani explained what his friend was planning to do and said that he, too, was interested in getting a degree at Minnesota. He acknowledged that he had already written for an application. He asked if he could take a few days off from work to go to Minneapolis to check out the campus.

"And what would you study?" Victor asked his son, wary as usual in regard to his son's histrionic proclivities.

"Minnesota's Department of Food Science is famous worldwide," Mani replied. "I thought I might major in food science." Because of his speech impediment, "department," "world," and "major" came out "depawtmnet," "wowld," and "majow."

Fwuitcake science would be more like it, his father thought uncharitably.

"Oh, how nice," cooed his mother Alina Malakhov, "but this place is where? This Minneapolis."

"Goodness gracious," declared Grandma Malakhov, speaking in Russian. "It's up north, dearie, along the Canadian border. It's like Siberia in the old country. They have a good hockey team, too. I saw them on TV. You should try out for the hockey team," she said to Mani.

"I don't know how to skate, Grandmamma," Mani confessed in Russian, "although at one time I was rather keenly interested in figure skating."

His father shot him a withering glance from under his black, bushy eyebrows.

It was soon decided that, yes, Mani would be allowed to take a week or two off from chopping vegetables to check out the University of Minnesota and that, yes, as regards the bill, his parents would, in the words of his father, "Pick up the foot." (Tab, Mani corrected him.) Mani's friends used the occasion of his departure for Minneapolis as an excuse to throw a party at Tuck Meadow's house. They were all agog that Mani would even think of giving up LA and the surf in favor of Minneapolis and the snow. Mani was sorry about lifting Tuck's handgun, but the entertainment soon took the edge off his guilt. One of the guests, a former Gopher, sang a lusty rendition of the University of Minnesota's fight song. There were karaoke, original songs, and several funny skits. Mani and his girl did a jitterbug routine to Glenn Miller's *In the Mood* that elicited whistles, bravos, and bravas. The party went on most of the night. Mani's girl became teary as daylight crept in through an open window, but Mani, ever the gallant, kissed her and held her close and promised he would call every day.

Uncertain what to expect after his visit with Maxim Kutsenko, Coach Coneybear got a $15,000 line of credit from the credit union. He'd use the money either to protect his reputation for ten months, or make a down payment to a KGB hit man if one ever came along. Hachem had demanded ten grand, but an extra five might come in handy along the way.

Two weeks went by after his visit with Maxim Kutsenko before anything came of it. One day after work, as he was examining the defaced bumper sticker on his Grand Cherokee Laredo, which now read, "God less America," glad at least that Old Glory still waived triumphantly out the rear window in the form of a decal, he was approached by a young man. The man was well-tanned. Bright blue eyes strained to see through a bleached forelock of hair.

"Coach Coneybear?" the man said in a base voice. Because of the man's speech impediment, "Coneybear" came out "Coneybeaw."

"Yes," the coach replied.

"I understand you've been having a problem with Basim Hachem. I'm here to solve that problem for you. We need to talk."

Coach Coneybear was shocked to the marrow. He had been praying for a hit man without quite believing one would ever show up. Now that one had, he wondered incredulously, This guy's *it*? Jeez, he looks like a gay model from New York City.

"Are you KGB?" he asked stupidly. A momentary pause allowed reflection. No one who looks like this could possibly be KGB, the coach decided, while Mani Malakhov wondered how best to answer an unexpected question.

"In a business like mine, Mr. Coneybear," Mani replied, "its best not to answer too many questions. But we shouldn't be standing out in the open like this." (He glanced right and left for a possible eavesdropper.) "We should meet someplace in private," he added in his normal tenor voice, forgetting his intention to talk machoese.

"OK," the coach agreed. "My wife's gone to visit her family in Milwaukee. So why don't you swing by my house later on—you know, when it's good and dark. Ten o'clock. Now listen, don't park in front of the house. Park a block or so away. Do you know where I live?"

"Yes."

"Good. And don't ring the front doorbell either. Just take the sidewalk to the left of the driveway. That'll lead you out back to our patio. We'll talk."

"See you then," Mani replied. He walked away.

Coach Coneybear drove home, turned onto a spacious driveway, and disappeared inside his two-car-plus-one-boat garage. The garage door slammed down with a bang. Inside he hurried to a half-bath for a nervous leak. He rinsed his fingers and studied himself in the mirror. He ran a hand through dark wavy hair, which made it stand on end. "Wooo-eee," he said to his image, "now what the hell are you going to do? Are you really going to do this?" Several drinks later he was still undecided. In the kitchen, he couldn't decide whether to eat leftovers or a bowl of corn flakes, so he had another drink instead. Doobie-doobie-do, he hummed, thinking about his ten o'clock rendezvous. He burst suddenly into song.

Stranglers in the night, exchanging glances. Stranglers in the night, what were the chances. Bugger, bugger me. La-la-la-la, la-la.

At ten o'clock sharp he stepped bravely out a French door onto the patio.

A deep voice said from the dark, "Good evening, Coach Coneybear."

"Jeez!" the coach replied. "I didn't see you sittin' there. You scared the crap out of me. Hey, you wanna drink?"

"Sure," replied Mani Malakhov, still in a base register.

As they went inside, the coach said, "Scotch all right?"

"Sure."

Mani looked about as he sashayed into the house, impressed by what he saw. The people who decorated this place had style, he decided. He stopped momentarily to look at a denim vest secured against an off-white mat. It was beautifully framed. There was printing at the bottom. "Vest worn by Cat Stevens at his 1971 Concert in Liverpool," it said. Awesome! thought Mani. Would I ever like to get my hands on that.

Fortified by drinks the two men sat on overstuffed chairs in a dimly illuminated great room. The drapes had been drawn. Only one lamp burned.

"I simply love your décor," Mani said in his normal voice. "It's so eclectic," he added, lisping and spitting a little.

"Huh?" the coach responded, puzzled by the inconstant voice and surprised that a hit man should have an interest in interior design. "Oh, yeah, my wife's doing," he said. "You want a few of these?" He held out a hand filled with light green pills.

"Sure, what are they?"

"I don't know. I got 'em from the team doctor. Good stuff though."

Mani washed down two pills with a swig of Scotch and said, "OK, Coach, let's talk business. You got a problem with a Basim Hachem. I'm here to solve it for you no questions asked. But it won't be cheap."

"How much?"

"Fifty grand." (Low voice again.)

"Oh, Christ, I can't raise that kind of money. On my salary? You must be nuts."

"Fifty thou is peanuts for this kind of job. You have to look at it from my point of view. This is business. You think I don't take risks?"

"You've done this before?"

"Lots of times." (Mani looked at his nails as if contemplating the need for a manicure.)

"I'm not disputing the fifty grand. It's just I don't know how I'm going to get my hands on that kind of money."

"Hey, I'm looking around your house, and you know what I see? Money. Big time money. You're loaded, so don't give me any shit."

"It's my wife's dough," the coach said. "Her dad is filthy rich. Used to own a ton of stock in Johnson Controls or some damn company in Milwaukee. If she ever found out what I've done, you think she'd stand by her man? What a joke. Stand *on* her man would be more like it," he added bitterly, thinking that stomping on his balls would be more like it still.

"OK, I understand you've been thinking about $20,000. That's not enough, but it's enough to get the job done. You know, as a down payment. But you'll have to pay me the rest, say, oh, over a three-year period. Ten thou a year for three more years. That's the deal." (Normal voice now.)

"Yeah, so what you gonna do with this guy? Kill him?"

"I said I'd solve the problem. And I will, too, to your complete satisfaction. Money back guaranteed. Boy, these pills are terrif."

"Listen, I don't know who the hell you are, where you live, or nothin'. I give you money and you take off. Then I'm standing in shit deeper than ever."

"Hey, hold on a minute here. We gotta trust each other. If I was out to get you, well, I could just play the blackmail game along with Hachem. You'd have two blood suckers hanging on your butt. If you don't trust me, well, I'll just go home and we'll forget about the whole thing."

Mani stood up to leave, but sat down quickly when he lost feeling in both legs.

"OK, OK. But how are we gonna proceed?" the coach said. "I don't have $20,000 under the mattress that I can just hand over here and now."

"Well, what kind of a down payment can you make by tomorrow night?"

"Ten thousand, but I'm not paying it all up front. Damned if I will."

"When is your wife coming back?"

"Oh, I don't know. Three days at least."

"OK, I'll be here tomorrow night at ten. Five thousand dollars now, with the remaining five the night after I've done my work. Then you pay me $10,000 per year for four more years."

"Hey, that's $55,000."

"Interest. Is this a deal?"

"It's a deal. Lets shake on it."

"I'll just leave the way I came," Mani said. "I noticed you've got a lot of expensive looking stuff in your house," he added, heading for the patio, but stopping to appreciated the framed vest. "Is some of this art worth something?"

"That frickin' vest you're looking at belonged to Cat Stevens. Cost close to $10,000. My wife's crazy about that kind of stuff. She's a rock and roll nut."

"Yeah, well, you ever think about lifting some of her stuff and selling it?"

"Burgle my own house you mean?"

"Sure, to finance our deal. You've got insurance, don't you?"

"Never thought of that."

"Give it some thought. I know some people in LA who'd pay a pretty penny for that vest." Oops, thought Mani. I shouldn't have mentioned LA.

I'll bet he's from LA, thought the coach. I wonder if that's where Max's uncle lives.

Basim Hachem pulled himself out of bed to answer the doorbell. For a long moment he eyed the stranger standing on the front stoop. In the first instance, he thought, Ah, a new Muslim brother has come to Plattefield; he wondered if something big was afoot. Such thoughts were scuttled almost immediately, however, when he noticed his new brother's button nose and blue eyes. The black hair was a obviously a wig; the beard was fake. What the devil? he asked himself.

For his part, Mani Malakhov, fortified by three shots of vodka on an empty gut, stood paralyzed by fear and indecision. Just as Hachem was beginning to think this was a prank of some kind, the stranger took a gun from his pocket and aimed it at his (Hachem's) head. There was this incredible pop. Mani watched as Hachem, falling backward, seemed to be making a grab for the gun. His head hit the floor with a thunk. Mani passed out. When he came to he found himself sprawled across Hachem's legs. Rather than checking to make absolutely sure Hachem was dead, which had been part of the plan, he fled in terror. He jumped in his rented car and sped recklessly back to his motel.

The stars that twinkled in Hachem's head when he hit the floor exploded and then fell into a black hole. When he came to, he scrambled to his feet. He felt of his head, his chest, his butt. He looked for blood on his fingers, but there was none. Except for the egg on the back of his skull, he couldn't find a thing wrong. The crazy infidel with the gun must have been using blanks, he decided. He peeked out the window, scratched his beard, and walked about the living room of his dinky, down-at-the-heels house in total amazement. Then he noticed neat holes through a lamp shade. A further search quickly revealed a hole in the wall as well. The bastard shot a bullet all right, but somehow missed, he muttered to himself. Allah be praised.

Coach Coneybear shuffled papers on his desk that required attention, or at a minimum, his signature. His secretary had prepared some letters of recommendation and a couple of travel requests. Her printout of the minutes of the last faculty meeting needed checking for accuracy. It was all so boring. Some of his friends would soon swing by on their way to lunch. Perhaps the paperwork could wait until after lunch.

He was roused from his lethargy when an enraged Basim Hachem burst into his office, slamming the door behind him. Hachem put his hands on the coach's desk and leaned forward.

His eyes blazed. For a few moments, his mouth worked in search of articulate speech. And then,

"You sent an assassin to kill me, but he failed. At point blank range, he fired a pistol at me and missed. Now I've got you good, you bastard, not only for lying about your football career, but for attempted murder as well. So what do you say to that?"

"You're crazy. I never hired anyone to kill you."

"You think I can't prove it, huh? A neighbor heard the shot and saw your friend pulling away from in front of my house. She took down his license number. I told her not to worry, that it was just a friend pulling a prank. But look at this. It's the bullet I dug out of the wall."

"Dumb son of a bitch," the coach mumbled, thinking about his incompetent hit man. Professional killer, my ass, he thought.

"This morning I rented a safety deposit box at one of the local banks. I have in it all the evidence regarding your drugs, lying, and attempted murder. I've arranged a little surprise for you in the event of my death. All the stuff that's in the bank gets turned over to the police. Do you believe in god, Mr. Coneybear?"

"I believe in god and country," the coach said defiantly.

"Well, then you had better pray that nothing bad happens to me. I don't get sick. I don't get run over. I don't get shot by a hired killer."

"Yeah, yeah, yeah. So what do you want?"

"Our previous agreement—about the $1,000 per month—all gone. Gone up in smoke, gun smoke. I know you're getting paid over $90,000 per year. I read it in the paper. I don't care if you have to move into a cave and live off tea and moldy bread. Ditch your wife if she gets in the way. Starting next month I want $4,000 per month from you and I'm not taking a dime less. And you know what else? This is going to go on as long as I want it to. When you get a raise, I get a raise. As of today, you are my infidel slave, and there's not a damned thing you can do about it."

Mr. Hachem turned to leave but stopped before opening the door. "One week from today," he said, "you'll hand over the first payment: $4,000."

Coach Coneybear sat still for several moments after Hachem had gone. Then he rose quietly from his desk and gently closed and locked the door. He turned off the lights and slumped at his desk. He held his head in his hands. Tears filled his eyes. His life was over. Long ago and far away, when he was a college senior in California, he put down a falsehood on his vita. It got him what he wanted: that first coaching job at Durham High in Minnesota. All he had ever wanted was to coach football. Was that asking too much? he now wondered in a wave of self-pity. Now you must die. End of story. Tough shit. It all seemed *so* ridiculous, *so* ridiculous. He waited for a sad song to come to him, but none did. Had music deserted him, too? But he would be no one's slave, certainly not Basim Hachem's slave. But how would he do it? He remembered his wife's pearl-handle gun in the stand by her bed. And then he remembered something else, too: that frickin' KGB asshole. By god, the coach thought, he isn't going to get away with this. I'll shoot the asshole in the head. Then he'll know how it's done.

Coach Coneybear's rendezvous with Mani Malakhov came earlier than expected. After nightfall, but well before ten, the doorbell rang. Oh, my god, he thought. If this is Sherree Lang and her tickly pompoms, I'll send her away.

The caller was the KGB hit man, not Miss Lang. Mani didn't wait to be invited in. He simply brushed past the coach, rushed to the great room, and collapsed on a sofa. There he hid a tear-streaked face behind his hands and rocked back and forth most piteously.

Coach Coneybear looked down on his coconspirator in utter contempt. "I suppose you've come for the rest of your money, you swine" he snarled. He hadn't decided what all he would do to KGB, Jr.; maybe he'd just kick the shit out of him. He was unnerved by what happened next.

"No, no," cried Mani. "Oh, no. I've done a terrible, terrible thing. I don't want your money. Here take back the $5,000. I don't want it anymore."

He took from his coat pocket a bunch of one-hundred dollar

bills and dumped them on the coffee table next to one of Jane Coneybear's ancient sculptures. Some of the money slid off the coffee table onto the carpet. Judas Priest, the coach thought.

"What the fuck kind of KGB are you anyway?" he thundered.

"I'm not KGB. My father was KGB. He was a major. I'm just a, a lost soul."

"I'm sick of this bullshit. Who in the hell are you?"

"No, no. No names, please. It's best if we never see each other or talk to each other ever again. I've only come to return the money and to tell you I'm getting away from here as fast as I can. You see, I killed him. I killed Hachem. I shot the poor man right in the head. Oh, it was terrible, terrible."

"You little shit! You stupid fucking little shit! You didn't kill anybody. Hachem came to see me this morning. He said someone tried to shoot him at point blank range and missed. Jesus H Christ, this is all so, so un-American. I can't believe it."

"That can't be true. I shot him and he fell over."

"Well, all right, have it your way. I could have sworn Basim Hachem came into my office this morning, but maybe it was his twin brother. He told me what happened and said you missed. Now he says I've got to pay him $4,000 per month, because now he says he's got proof I tried to have him killed."

"Proof? What proof? I was wearing a disguise."

"He said he talked with a neighbor lady who heard the shot and saw you drive away. She wrote down your license plate number and was going to call the police, but Hachem said he told her it was all a joke: that a friend of his was pulling a trick. And he has the bullet, for chrissake. He's got proof. You've ruined my life."

"But wait. Hold on a minute, Coach. Before I got to Hachem's house, I removed the license plates from my car and put them in the trunk—you know, just in case someone saw me taking off. No one could have seen my license plates."

"Huh, are you lying to me?"

"No, no. Scout's honor. I promise, Mr. Coneybear. He doesn't know my license number. He couldn't possibly know my license number."

"Ya, but what about the bullet. He's got it. He showed it to me."

"As proof goes, that doesn't mean anything. I'll throw the gun away. I'll throw it in a river or a puddle or something. Mmm. I wonder why he lied to you, though. About the license plates. Hey, I got an idea. Suppose he knows you tried to have him killed, but suppose he doesn't have any proof. A bullet without the gun means nothing. Maybe he's lying about the neighbor. Yeah, that's it. He doesn't have any proof. He's bluffing."

"Yeah, well. Maybe you're on to something. You want a drink?"

"Sure."

"OK, I'll pour. You talk. Tell me everything. Start from the time you left the motel. Oh, here, have a greenie."

"OK."

After greenies, drinks, and the dissection of a failed mission, Mani said, "Suppose you tell Hachem he doesn't have proof and you aren't going to meet his demands. It'll be up to him to show that he does have proof. Tell him to put up or shut up. No proof, no payoff. You've got to call his bluff."

"Hey, you're pretty smart, you know that? We've got to come up with an offense. You want another drink?"

"Sure. Now, let's go over everything. Let's figure this thing out. Oh, my god, I just had another idea. You read in the papers all the time about Al Qaeda cells: you know, those crazy Muslims wanting to blow up Disneyland and stuff. Well, these guys need money to operate. I'll bet Hachem is a terrorist. By god if he's a terrorist, the last thing in the world he would ever do is go to the police. Yeah, and he surely wouldn't want you to go to the police, either. My god, if he's Al Qaeda, you could be in danger!"

"Jeez," the coach said, holding out another large glass of ice and Scotch. "Hold on a sec, I'll get some more greenies."

"No more pills, Coach. Not until after we have this thing figured out. We've gotta figure this thing out."

"Yeah, but how do we know if he's Al Qaeda or not?"

"We've got to find out."

"Yeah, yeah, but how?"

"Well, we've gotta follow him around, don'tcha see. See if he's taking flying lessons."

"Yeah, yeah, by god. He's taking flying lessons sure as shit. You know, you're a clever little bugger. What's your name?"

"Mani, Mani Malakhov."

"Glad to meet you, Mani," the coach replied.

They shook hands. Thus did Larry Coneybear, coach supreme, and Mani Malakhov, song and dance man wannabe, begin a beautiful friendship.

Later that day, far away in LA, an ominous development unfolded in the cigar room of Petruchka's. Victor Malakhov was visiting with a middle-aged man he had never met before. The man's name was Gregori Samonovitch. They spoke in Russian. On the surface the conversation, though cool, was calm and polite; underneath, hot sulphurous gases rose up from fractures in the crust of hell. Although Victor hadn't known Gregori before this evening, he had known rather too well his father Nicholas Samonovitch, the former KGB operative turned gangster turned politician who had been gunned down in Moscow a few years back. Victor had been unaware that Nicholas Samonovitch's widow, daughter, and son, recently admitted to the United States, had settled in LA. He had been unpleasantly surprised one day when Gregori called on the telephone and asked for a meeting.

Victor suggested the cigar room at Petruchka's, which was where they now sat, drinking vodka and smoking cigars after closing time. Gregori Samonovitch was a dark ugly brute of a man with a really bad reputation. He was huge, a Goliath. He complimented Victor Malakhov on his fine restaurant, remarking that it must have cost a great deal of money. Victor thanked him, ignored the topic of money, and asked after Gregori's mother instead. Gregori said that his mother was in good health, but still despondent over the loss of her husband. He painted a grim picture of his family's financial situation. The family, he said, lived in a cheap two-bedroom apartment. His mother spoke little

English, and his own English was bad, making it difficult for him to find work. His young sister, he noted, was in high school. The implication of all this was apparent; he needed a job, money, or both.

Victor hinted several times that the hour was late, that perhaps their tête-à-tête should continue at some indefinite future date. But Gregori was in no hurry. Eventually he changed the subject to other Russian émigrés, how some had come to a bad end in their efforts to duplicate in America the burgeoning organized crime groups in Russia. Although Victor wanted to discuss in this connection the well-publicized failures of Russians at arson, extortion, Medicaid fraud, and trafficking in prostitution, Gregori was more interested in the theft of jewels. For reasons of his own, this was ground Victor cared not to tread.

Finally, Gregori remarked on the disappointment of his acquaintances at their failure to monopolize trade in diamonds smuggled out of Africa, diamonds used to pay for weapons used in civil wars, particularly in Angola and Sierra Leone. As Gregori spoke of this, of the trade in blood diamonds, he watched Victor carefully. He saw nothing. It would have taken a poker player far more skilled than Gregori Samonovitch to have noticed and appreciated the significance of Victor Malakhov's momentary stare, an extra second between the lazy blinking of black, flat eyes. But in that trifling stare, Victor had taken his measure of Gregori Samonovitch.

Later, after his unwelcome visitor had departed, Mr. Malakhov moved silently about his restaurant as he waited for the cleanup crew to complete its scrubbing of the kitchen to gleaming perfection. As he looked about, ostensibly to check that all was in order, he reflected on his conversation with Gregori Sonofabitch, his name for hell's agent.

Mr. Samonovitch had played his trump card, for it was Victor Malakhov who had provided the CIA with an invaluable tip on the Russian mob's intentions regarding trade in African diamonds. Had Nicholas Samonovitch gotten wind of the tip-off? Had he told his notorious son Gregori? It was doubtful that Gregori had proof, for Victor Malakhov had acted with utmost caution. It would be difficult now for Victor to quiz Gregori about what he knew without giving the game away. On the other hand, Victor feared that some remnants of the Russian mob in America might get the wrong idea about him and why he had been so royally treated by the U. S. authorities.

The cleanup crew completed its work. Mr. Malakhov bade them goodnight and said he'd lock up. Then he went to the bar to sip more ice cold Moskovskaya and think. He would make a decision before he locked the back door and headed for home. Should he buy Gregori's silence by steering him to a contract to kill? Or should he simply arrange to have Gregori shot together with his mother and sister as a warning to other presumptuous émigrés? Tough decision. Putting Gregori in touch with Max's friend would be doing the coach no favor. He would come to know the everlasting embrace of a grizzly bear. On the other hand, killing Gregori would be risky. The cops might find out who arranged it. The Russian Mafia might take umbrage at the slaughter of Nicholas Sonofabitch and his family. Decisions, decisions. Victor Malakhov yawned, patted the pistol packed in his shoulder holster (yes, it was still there), and headed for the back door.

Chapter 6

On a Saturday morning Detective Delaney drove to the Willgrubs's and learned the professor and his lady were away buying groceries, which meant he and Emily Peterson had the house to themselves. Emily led him to the living room where they snuggled on a rose plush sofa with antimacassars on the arms and back cushions. The room was packed with furniture, bric-a-brac, coffee-table art books, African violets, and lamps with fringed lampshades. A grandfather clock stood guard and officiously tracked the time, reminding Miss Peterson to murmur as Delaney's kisses became ardent that the Willgrubs would be home at any minute, just in case he had the idea of slipping upstairs, which in lusty fact he did. The conversation turned to Ireland, and once again Delaney complained about the Willgrubs coming along on their honeymoon.

"It's not going to be *that* bad," Emily said.

She changed her position, sat on her foot, and with her hands moved Delaney's face closer to hers. She gently slid a hand back and forth over his forehead.

"I'll bet I know what you're doing," he said.

"Oh, what?"

"You're ironing a frown."

"You're such a smarty pants. There. It's all gone. Now, think about this. We'll spend our wedding night at the Edgewater in Madison where we won't have to worry about making too much noise—you know, about upsetting my aunt and uncle downstairs. We'll make as much noise as we please. We'll fall off the bed, tip over the chairs, pull down the drapes, scream. We'll make a shambles of the place, if you like. Oops, do I detect a dirty grin? I'll have to do something about that."

With her fingers she tried to smooth downward the corners of her lover's mouth.

"Then, in the morning," she continued, "we'll drive to the airport, meet my uncle and aunt, and then we'll all fly away to Dublin. It's not as if they'll be sitting on our laps. And besides, shooting halfway around the world in a jet-propelled sardine can isn't my idea of a romantic journey anyway. Then, when we . . ."

"Don't you want to go to Ireland for our honeymoon?"

"Oh, I do, I do. I'm dying to go to Ireland. But the flight itself will probably be a bore. Now, about the hotel, last night . . ."

"We could fly first class."

"Oh, phooey. That would cost too much. Anyway, I'm trying to tell you I found the homepage for the Derrycross Hotel on the internet last night. Oh, baby, it looks too divine. I sent a little note to Caroline Maidin thanking her for the brochure she sent you. Anyway, we'll have four days there before my uncle and aunt join us, and when they do they'll be staying at the hotel and we'll have our own Derrycross cottage. The home page says the cottages are new, and you have to walk through the garden to get to the hotel dining room. And the professor says that during the day we can go our separate ways, providing he summons the courage to rent a car and drive down the wrong side of the road."

"And if he doesn't?"

"We must assume that he will. OK, so we'll meet for dinner from time to time, you know, to compare notes and discuss our adventures. That might be kind of fun. I know it won't be as romantic as if they weren't there, but perhaps there is someway I could make it up to you. How about this? You could plum your sexual fantasies and tell me what you'd most like me to do."

Emily raised her left eyebrow. Blue eye beams met green eye beams head-on and fused. Dust motes caught in the collision smoked, burned, and fell dead.

"Are you sure we don't have time to go upstairs?" Delaney

asked in a husky voice. "I don't think it would take me very long."

"But I like it long," she replied. Again that eyebrow.

Delaney grinned at this double entendre, but said, "Oh, fart," when the garage door went up with a barrage of grates and groans. Emily laughed, commanded Delaney to help with the groceries and ran from the room. Delaney had to wait a bit before he could comfortably walk out to the garage.

Once the groceries were brought in and put away, Professor Willgrubs invited the detective to see the gardens in the backyard. They meandered among island beds in full bloom. From time to time, the professor bent over to pull a weed, at one point complaining that with all the recent rains the weeds were trying to take over. Weeds are so opportunistic, he averred. From time to time Delaney voiced his delight and asked for the name of this or that cultivar. On completion of the tour, they sat on chairs on the patio under the shade of a honey locust. Emily brought out a couple of beers and returned to the house. Delaney remembered to mention a strange coincidence.

"Did you know," he said to the professor, "that Caroline Maidin and her husband own Green Valley Farm?"

The professor replied that he did not.

"Mrs. Maidin inherited the farm from her mother. Her mother's name was Anne Schroeder. She had a lot of money. Did you happen to know of her?"

Again the professor replied that he did not.

"It's odd, isn't it, that on the very day of your visit to the farm, the farm's owner reported a hit-and-run accident?"

"Odd, yes, but there could be no connection."

At this point the professor gave a little lecture on the propensity of people to imagine causation whenever they encounter simple correlation. The lecture didn't seem relevant to the coincidence Delaney had described, and he had, besides, heard the lecture several times before. Still, he indulged the professor, knowing how much the professor loved holding forth on scientific methodology.

Presently, the professor changed the subject. "I've been meaning to inquire about the hit-and-run. Has there been any recent progress on the case?"

"Very little, I'm afraid," Delaney replied. He didn't want to get into his recent investigation of Joe Maidin, which hadn't turned up a scrap of hard evidence.

"Your mentioning Anne Schroeder reminds me of something now that I stop to think of it," said the professor. "I seem to remember that a few years back the owner of Green Valley Farm was killed in an accident of some sort. Yes, there was an item in the paper. This might explain how Anne Schroeder came to own the farm."

"What kind of accident?"

"Oh, I don't remember, except that it was grisly. Yes, it was very grisly."

The men drank beer in silence, listening to the birds, hearing an occasional car pass by on the street out front, and in general letting life pass gently by. Summertime in an old but respectable neighborhood with not much going on. And the beer was cold and delicious. This is my idea of being cool, Delaney thought, but then he wondered whether he had grown old for his age. Shouldn't he be out playing golf or soft ball with his fellow officers, or maybe fishing on a nearby lake? Mmm. Maybe being really cool is not being cool at all. In a moment or two, his mind took a turn. He began thinking about Anne Schroeder. Was the professor right in thinking she had inherited the farm? Because of an accident?

"Patrick, you must tell me the truth," the professor said, rousing the detective from his meditation on crimes made to look like accidents. "Are you sure Edna and I will not intrude on your honeymoon? Our friends and neighbors say we should go to Ireland some other time."

Detective Delaney then repeated much of what Emily had said to him, thus assuring the professor that he and his wife would be most welcome, that a guy's having an uncle and aunt along on his honeymoon was just the thing, and that they would all have a wonderful time. The professor smiled happily. It occurred to him that in all the ways that really matter, Patrick Delaney had become the son he had always wanted, but never had.

The following Monday, Detective Delaney drove to Hunters Point to talk with George Summerfield, Sheriff of Crawfish County. Sheriff Summerfield had been surprised by Delaney's call, asking if they could meet to discuss the death of Dennis Mc Quade. The sheriff knew of Detective Delaney and wanted to meet him. He was also curious to know why the Plattefield Police had an interest in the death of Mr. Mc Quade.

After hellos, Sheriff Summerfield asked about it, and Delaney described what happened on Green Briar Road and set forth his suspicion that Caroline Maidin might have been the intended victim. He confessed that he was probably barking up the wrong tree: that she was probably not the intended victim of a hit-and-run. He said the FBI was sure organized crime was behind the death of Michael Patriarca, which Sheriff Summerfield already knew from what he had read in the papers.

"But what has this to do with Mc Quade?" the sheriff asked.

"Only this. Caroline Maidin owns Green Valley Farm. If she had been the intended victim of a hit-and-run, and had the attempt succeeded, then two owners of Green Valley Farm would have died ostensibly from accidents. It's the pattern that's puzzling. There's just the slim possibility that something's going on here. That's all. I'm just trying to touch all the bases."

The sheriff wondered why Delaney had bothered to come if he was so uncertain about his hunch. Maybe he's not as uncertain as he pretends, he thought.

"Well, let me tell you about Dennis Mc Quade," the sheriff said, "and then we can talk more after you've gone through the file. I know: I'll treat you to a piece of pie over at the Norski Diner when you're through."

"Sounds good to me, Sheriff," Delaney replied.

"OK, this is the way we have it figured. Three years ago, about the middle of December, Dennis Mc Quade apparently decided to take a walk about the farm. It had been cold, and

Green Valley Marsh, which borders the farm, was frozen over. Apparently, he walked out on the ice, tripped or slipped and fell forward and was impaled on a sharp stub of a willow tree branch that was sticking up through the ice. You see, the water level in the marsh has been high in recent years and some of the trees ringing the marsh have died. This includes a stand of willow trees. These dead trees had fallen in the water over the years and the branches were mostly but not completely submerged. We found many very pointed branch tips sticking up through the ice. A few were rotted, but some had hardened. Mc Quade had the misfortune of falling on one that was both hard and sharp. His heavy jacket had been opened, perhaps because he was heated up from the exercise of walking. At any rate, the end of the branch sticking through the ice was like a dagger. It ripped through his clothes and went clean through his body. The injury was massive. Apparently, he couldn't lift himself off the branch. He simply laid there and died. By the following day we had six inches of snow. The body wasn't discovered until after—well, the coroner puts it at five days, which jibes with how long he was missing. His farm manager Troy Olson was the guy who first reported that Mc Quade was missing. So that's about it. Helluva way to go."

The case was discussed a little further before Delaney asked to see the file. When he finished going through it, taking notes as he did, the sheriff delivered on his promise; he and Delaney walked a few blocks to the Norski Diner. They sat in a booth next to a large window looking out on lazy traffic on a hot summer's day. The waitress's name was Bernice. She brought two glasses of ice water and recommended the lemon meringue pie. Between swallowing hot coffee and bites of pie, the officers reviewed the bizarre details of the death of Dennis Mc Quade.

Over coffee refills, Delaney asked whether the sheriff thought there was any chance Mc Quade had been murdered. "Is it remotely possible, do you think?" he said. "It would have required at least two men."

"Probably more than two, and they would have had to know when Troy Olson and his wife were away. You see the Olsons lived less than a quarter mile away back then, before they moved into the big house at the farm, and Troy spent a lot of time doing chores there. He was doing most of the farm work; his wife pretty much kept the house. Mc Quade's wife died many years ago and he never remarried. We know that Troy and his wife were in town that day. They even had lunch with Mrs. Olson's sister. They were gone most of the day. There's just no way they could have had anything to do with murder."

"Yes, the killers either knew the Olsons' shopping habits, or they were watching the farm."

"But that would be hard to do. You know, without being seen by a neighbor or somebody. We asked around. No one saw anything that looked suspicious. Of course, I expect there might be inconspicuous places where you could park, if you were willing to walk."

"Maybe they scouted the place and knew where a car could be concealed."

"And how would they have known about the willow branches?"

"Perhaps the farm had been under surveillance for some time, during the wintertime in particular. Yeah, well, there are problems. I can see that, but let's assume the killers scouted the farm and the people who worked there. They wait till the Olsons drive away and then show up. They might catch Mc Quade outside, or they might go right inside the house. They confront Mc Quade with guns. Maybe they tell him to put on his jacket if he's inside. Then they bound him, maybe with strips of plastic, and they don't tie him up too tight. They don't want suspicious bruises to show up in an autopsy. Hmm. Maybe they bind him to a stretcher. Yeah, two guys could handle that. All the time they would keep a lookout for visitors. They carry Mc Quade out to the marsh tied down on a stretcher. They tip him over belly side down, lift him five or so feet in the air, and slam him down hard. Then they remove the bindings and the stretcher and take off."

"Well, I never thought through it quite like that," the sheriff confessed. "What you say is plausible. Of course, if it hadn't snowed, we might have found tracks. Could they have counted on snow?"

"Was there much snow on the ground at the time? At the time Mc Quade went missing?"

"You've got a point there. There was hardly any snow on the ground when the accident occurred. It would have been hard to detect tracks on the ice."

"It might have been hard to find tracks over frozen ground, too, and they might have counted on a considerable passage of time before the victim was discovered. Hmm. Maybe they were just lucky that it snowed when it did. The killers would have needed a lot of inside information. And you're sure the Olsons shopped only once a week?"

"Well, they usually shopped on Friday, but of course they did go to town on other days, too. And they have relatives about who they visit. But here's the central problem as I see it. Where's the motive? Who would want to kill Mc Quade? The farm went to his sister and she had a lot of money of her own. Her husband used to own the Hunters Point Cannery before he died. The plant was sold to Green Giant."

"Yes, but his sister had Alzheimer's. And Caroline and Joe Maidin might have known that the farm would come to them. If the sister died before Mc Quade died, might Mc Quade have made a will leaving the farm to others? Did you ever question Caroline and Joe about it, about whether they had alibis?"

"No, do you think we should have?"

"I guess not. After all, Caroline and her husband were due to get a lot of money when Caroline's mother died whether or not she owned Green Valley Farm. No, I think you got it right. It seems likely that it was an accident. The thing that sticks in my mind, though, is that if Caroline Maidin *had* been murdered in a hit-and-run, then it would be the case that Joe Maidin had come into a lot of money plus the ownership of Green Valley Farm merely through marriage and accidents. Darn quick way to get rich. Well, I think I'd better head for home. Could you tell me how to get to Green Valley Farm? I'd like to drive by the place on the way going back."

"Yeah. I'll draw you a map."

Detectives Willison and Delaney met to discuss whether Caroline Maidin had been the intended target of the hit-and-run on Greenbriar Road and whether her husband might have been behind it. The investigation up to this point had been little more than a tentative probe. There had been no wiretaps or surveillance of Joe Maidin's movements. There had been no questioning of his professors and friends. How far should the investigation be pushed? How invasive should it be? Did the evidence Delaney had uncovered amount to anything? The death of Mr. Mc Quade certainly seemed to be an accident, either that or a homicide skillfully crafted for an uncertain motive.

All of Delaney's suspicions, already in an advance stage of wilt, were put on hold indefinitely by a major FBI discovery. An undercover agent in New York learned that Peter Stubbs, known on the street as Pit Bull Peter, a suspected hit man for the Gambino crime syndicate, had flown from New York to Chicago on April 10. He next showed up at the Morocco Club back in New York on May 6. He was with his woman friend, and they were spending lots of money. He had been picked up for questioning, but his attorney wasn't letting him talk. It was apparent that he could easily have stolen a car in Chicago, or used a car stolen by someone else, driven to Plattefield, and killed Michael Patriarca. His plan might have been to make the murder look like an accident. An accomplice could have driven him back to Chicago.

A major investigation was begun to track Pit Bull Peter's movements between April 10 and May 6. The police departments of Chicago, Milwaukee, and Plattefield were enlisted in the investigation. Although assigned to the search for anyone who might have seen Pit Bull Peter in the bars, restaurants, and motels of Plattefield, Detective Delaney's heart wasn't in it. His heart was in getting the details right for his marriage to Miss Emily Peterson. He was discovering that getting married is a lot of work.

Late one night in Mani Malakhov's motel room, two days after Basim Hachem had dodged a bullet, Coach Coneybear and Mani plotted strategy. Plied with booze and party packs of Ecstasy, cannabis, and amphetamines, compliments of sports medicine, they put the finishing touches to their scheme to prove Basim Hachem was a terrorist. They would catch him, by god, if it was the last thing they ever did, and it might take time, so the sooner they got started the better.

On the following afternoon Coach Coneybear told his secretary that he had a headache (true) and that he was going home (not true). Instead he drove to Minneapolis with Mani Malakhov following behind in a rented car, which was dropped off at the Twin Cities airport. It was a long drive back to Plattefield and both men were exhausted. To keep awake Coach Coneybear began singing in a fine tenor voice. Mani joined in with harmony and scat. They laughed and had swell time keeping themselves awake. Then, after a period of silence, the coach sang a song in a falsetto voice that would have made the Bee Gees sit up and take notice.

Hey, bumper car baby, yo be big and strong,
But when you bump me baby, you do it all wrong.
Don't keep pushin' me hard up against the curb,
And then leave me stranded like an old dog turd.
Oh, bumper car baby, now don't get all pissed,
Just because I think you should see a therapist.

Mani joined in, beating gently on the dashboard with the palms of his hands and singing, "yo be, yo be, yo be" in a syncopated rhythm. After a few more verses, they stopped and laughed and Mani insisted they do the number again.

After finishing a second time, Mani said, "Hey, that must be new. I haven't heard that before. Who's doin' it?"

"Oh, that's just a little something I made up," the coach said.

"That is such a *huge* lie."

"No, no. It's a hobby of mine, making up stuff like that."

"Well, you're in the wrong business, Coach. You could get that song published. It would be a smash."

"You think so? Well, I thought it wasn't bad. Hey, I nearly forgot, I gotta get gas."

He swerved off Interstate 94 onto an exit, cutting off a van in the right lane. When the driver of the van honked his horn, the coach said, "What's the matter with *that* guy?" Mani opened his eyes and unclenched his fists, but said nothing.

The next day the coach gave Mani the keys to a white 1990 Buick. The car belonged to an assistant coach who hoped one day to tag along with Coach Coneybear when he leapt the fence to a greener pasture, and Michigan grass is about as green as grass gets. As it happens, the assistant had purchased a new car, but had decided to hang onto the old one. When the coach said for the second time over lunch that he had a friend who needed a car for a few weeks, his young colleague obligingly offered to help. Thus did Mani acquire the wheels to get the goods (the bads, actually) on Basim Hachem.

The next morning he parked on the street where Hachem lived. He watched and waited and was terribly bored. At ten minutes to two, he followed Hachem to work. Hachem parked in a university parking lot and walked into Johnson Hall carrying a lunch bucket. Unsure quite what to do next, Mani drove to Skywide Cinema and took in two movies. He drove back to the university and saw that Hachem's car was still in the lot, so he grabbed a quick bite to eat. He picked up Hachem's trail again at eleven o'clock that night, when Hachem got off work. Nothing much happened. Hachem went home, turned on the lights, and opened the windows to let in the cool night air. Mani tiptoed across the yard and risked a few peeks inside, but what he saw was very ordinary. In his underwear, Hachem ate a sandwich, had a bottle of beer, and watched TV in the living room. The lights went out at 12:30. Well, that was a total bore, Mani thought on his way home.

The following days varied little from the first, and when Coach Coneybear and Mani got together they wondered what the devil

Hachem did all day closeted in his house. Friday turned out to be one of Hachem's days off. He took his car to a garage and from there walked to Plattefield's only mall. He wandered about inside and bought an ice cream cone. He waited two hours while his car was in the garage. On his way home, he bought some groceries. That night he visited a tavern called the Fox's Inn. He sat at the bar, chummed with a few guys he seemed to know, and went home to bed.

Mani checked bases with Coach Coneybear and it was agreed that following Hachem around until he tipped his hand somehow or other might take a long time, which posed a problem. Mani couldn't stay away from home forever, and he was running out of cash. Eventually he would need call home and tell his parents some story or other to explain his long absence. And though the coach didn't mind giving money to Mani, he balked at handing over any to Hachem.

Such were the considerations that led the two conspirators to analyze the pros and cons of breaking into Hachem's house. The coach said for sure there'd be incriminating evidence in Hachem's computer; Mani said he was damned good with computers. The coach said for sure there'd be lots of manuals on jet airliners lying around; Mani said, bomb recipes, too. It was a foregone conclusion that sooner or later, Hachem would drive to Madison to take flying lessons, but how long would they have to wait to catch him in the act? A little break-in might speed things along very nicely.

Chapter 7

The day Patrick Delaney married Emily Peterson began inauspiciously, hit a sour note during the celebratory mass at St. John's Catholic Church, and ended in disaster at the Pine Hill Country Club. The first bad news came early. Father Schraufnagel, a longtime friend of the Delaney family, the priest who had baptized baby Patrick and had been hearing his confessions since his First Communion and was to perform the wedding ceremony, was called away to his mother's sick bed at the last moment. It fell to old Father Tripalin to do the honors. Father Tripalin was not only old: he was crotchety, borderline racist, consummately right-wing, and practically blind. It was this latter infirmity, which he denied having and tried to cover up by wearing glasses as little as possible, that facilitated a sacrilege during the church ceremony.

The sacrilege occurred at the most sacred part of the Mass, the consecration, when Father Tripalin invoked ancient incantations to convert bread and wine into the body and blood of Jesus Christ. He could see in fuzzy outline the pie-plate-sized host on the altar before him, but he could not see the shadow of markings on its downward side. And it was this side, the downward side, that was shown to the congregation when he grasped the host and raised it high above his head for all to see and adore. What the congregation saw clearly was a smiley face drawn on the host with a red magic marker. Father Tripalin had expected reverent silence. What he got instead were gasps and murmurs of outrage augmented in short order by the muted voices of those rendering assistance to a lady who fainted. The bride's shock soon gave way to concealed mirth. The groom's shock gave way to anger followed by curiosity. Which of his five older brothers had perpetrated this outrage? What could he do to get even? Mystified by the unusual sounds emanating from the faithful, Father Tripalin had no recourse but to stumble on, which is what he did.

The conversation at the dinner dance that evening touched only occasionally on Emily Peterson's being the most elegant creature ever to have been married in St. John's, or on how handsome and strong the groom had been in his black tux with a red rose, or on how utterly precious had been the flower girl and her young gallant following along behind the train of the bride's white dress. Because Emily's parents were no longer living, Mrs. Edna Willgrubs, with not a peep of dissent from the professor, had insisted on their taking the bride's parents' place by picking up the tab for the wedding. She (and the professor) had spared no expense, but the abundance of yellow roses, beautiful dresses, and lovely music meant nothing to the partygoers at the country club that evening. The only thing they wanted to talk about was the smiley face.

At first, there was widespread outrage. There were allegations, charges, denials, and counter charges. Father Tripalin, who had come to say grace (and to eat a hearty dinner, too), opined that the penalty for such a sacrilege, if only the culprit could be apprehended, would surely be excommunication. As the evening wore on, however, and as the two bartenders worked the free bar as if there would be no tomorrow, which for those who ate the chicken and pasta salad would almost be the case, the idea began making the rounds that maybe God could take a joke. After all, wasn't He supposed to be almighty? One of Patrick's older brothers, already a prospective candidate for excommunication, which would only have made him shrug his shoulders, even went so far in a conversation with a knot of dubious aunts, uncles, and cousins to speculate freely whether the faithful might discover on passing through heaven's porthole that god was rather put off by the endless bowing and scraping of religious zealots: that those who honestly doubted His existence and enjoyed the good life (good booze, good sex, football, and much laughter) might be the ones most closely grouped around His golden throne. A red-nosed uncle, apparently brought around to this view, said that God would surely prefer to hang with Johnny Carson than with Billy Graham. And someone else said, unless He's a total nut. And someone else brought up Billy Graham's anti-Semitic exchange with President Nixon, and the conversation then veered off in a whole new direction.

None of the partygoers had an inkling, of course, for what lay lurking in the chicken and pasta salad, one of several delectable dishes served at the buffet supper. A chef's assistant with an open wound on his hand had been careless in putting together a mayonnaise-based salad, which then stood around at room temperature before serving. The bacterium Staphylococcus aureus started with a dreamy waltz through the mayonnaise and ended in a lively polka. The bride didn't eat the salad; too many calories. The groom didn't eat much because by the time he got to the chicken salad, his plate was already filled to near overflowing. Still, by stacking a bun and a baked potato on a slice of ham, he was able to make room for a smallish helping.

At a quarter to one, with spirits running high and chaos building to its crescendo, the guests looked about and agreed that the bride and groom might have slipped away unnoticed, which in fact they had done. They drove first to the Willgrubs's home, where they changed into street clothes and loaded their packed suitcases. Then they drove to the Edgewater Hotel in Madison. It was a perfect summer's evening. A brisk wind from the northeast had blown away the heat and humidity of the day. The newlyweds began the drive in high spirits. Mr. Smiley Face was all but forgotten. There was so much to look forward to: to a night of romance in a swanky hotel, to Ireland where they would spend nearly two glorious weeks, and to the adventure of marriage and all that came with it: the beautiful babies they would have. Their lives would be good, they were sure. And the night would be perfect, too. Still . . .

By the time the car was parked in the hotel's underground garage and the suitcases had been delivered to their room, Delaney was getting sick. He put it down to the excesses of the day. He prayed it wasn't stomach flu. He swallowed, but said nothing about it. He willed himself to be well. Once the porter had accepted his tip and quietly left the room, Delaney turned off the lights and opened the drapes. He and his bride stood side by side and looked out over Lake Mendota. The wind had risen. Fluffy clouds skittered across the moonlit sky, hurrying shadows over black water frothy with white caps and foam. Lights twinkled in a grand arc along a faraway shore.

Stirred by an intense sense of being alive, Emily murmured, "Oh, Patrick, this is so beautiful, so wild and beautiful. When I am old woman," (she put an arm around his waist and held him closely), "and I have a grown daughter, and if she asks me when was the happiest moment of my life, I'll remember this moment. I'll say to her it was a moment on my wedding night when I stood next to your father and we looked out across wind-driven water in the moonlight. Oh, Patrick, I think I'm going to cry!"

"Emily?"

"Yes?"

"I'm not feeling so good."

It wasn't until morning, when Patrick Delaney's father called the hotel and spoke with Emily, that she and her new husband learned that, no, it had not been the champagne that caused Delaney to upchuck through most of the night, nor had it been the drive from Plattefield to Madison on a full stomach after a day of considerable stress, nor had it been a simple case of stomach flu. It had been a staph infection that had during the night struck twenty partygoers at least. Father Tripalin was in the hospital. When Emily asked about her uncle and aunt, she was told that Professor and Mrs. Willgrubs had passed through the line after the salad was all gone. The Willgrubs were at that very moment, she was told, headed for the Dane County Airport in Madison. (Had Emily heard her father-in-law striving to stave off a chuckle?) Poor Detective Delaney. What could he do, except say he was feeling better and would soon be right as rain. They, too, headed for the airport. Emily drove. They would fly first to Detroit and thence to New York City. The flight to Dublin would be a night flight.

The first leg of the flight was not the best. Emily could see her husband was still sick, and she knew the professor was terrified of flying. She had encouraged her uncle and aunt to go by boat, but the professor's fear of what he called the cruise-ship-illness syndrome was even greater than that of flying. She could not broach, of course, the alternative of their staying safely at home.

Detective Delaney's difficulties were not over. At Detroit, he noticed two young women (teenagers, he would have guessed) in the waiting area for the flight to New York City. They had with them their babies (one-year olds, he would have guessed) strapped in well-padded, brand new strollers along with all the other accouterments of their situation. Soft cuddly cases with Velcro fasteners seemed to hold all manner of things a baby could possibly need: disposal diapers, bottles of juice and milk, pacifiers, rattles, handy wipes, jars of baby food, and small bottles of what turned out to be medicine. What aroused the detective's ire was the fussing of the young mothers over their babies. It seemed to him that the two women were almost in a competition to see which one was the better mother. They were loud, bubbly, and excessively happy. There was incessant activity to see if baby was wet or dry, too cold or too hot, wanted milk or canned fruit, wanted this or that rattle, preferred jiggling in the stroller to resting quietly. It finally came to him in a fit of pique, as his head pounded and his bowels threatened disaster, that the two young mothers were not so much tending babies as playing dolly. And where were the fathers, he wanted to know? Good god, I'm going to die, he thought, averting his eyes to the other passengers in waiting and trying to think of something pleasant to say to Emily and Aunt Edna, or something that would buck up the professor's courage, but, in the end, too miserable to say anything at all.

The seating configuration of the DC 10 that would whisk them to New York was two-five-two. Patrick had taken pains to make sure that he and Emily sat on the side of the plane rather in the center, so they could hold hands and talk in some semblance of privacy. Moving down an aisle, Emily said she preferred the window. Patrick gladly agreed with this arrangement and looked around for the closest toilet. To be seated just behind them, he noticed with annoyance, were the two young mothers still making a fuss over their damnable babies and holding everyone up. They finally settled in their seats, filling them to overflowing with butts, babies, and blankets and their cuddly cotton cases. When the passengers appeared to be nearly all aboard and in their seats, with carryons stowed and buckles fastened, a flight attendant came down the aisle, stopped, and made a quiet announcement. It was against airline regulations, she said, for the two mothers with babies to be sitting next to each other. Why this was so she did not explain. She asked whether someone with an aisle seat would be willing to change places with the mother just behind Delaney. No one seemed eager to do so. The flight attendant asked again, this time with some urgency in her voice and her eye fixed firmly on the detective.

How could she know, he thought desperately, that I'm a sick man, that I might die, that I'm on my honeymoon? But was he not an officer of the law? Given to self-sacrifice where others were in need, or in danger? He turned to Emily and explained what he had to do, noting that it would be a short flight. She smiled at him sadly, caressed his sweaty unshaven cheek, and let him go. The seat swap took place and Delaney found himself next to one of the teenage mothers who said her name was Tamara and that her son's name was Tyrone. Her baby blankets and carryons invaded Delaney's space, but Delaney decided he would not be irritated: he would not. Tyrone starred at Delaney with bright-eyes and a happy face and burst into uninhibited laughing when Delaney made a face and goo-gooed. When his paroxysm of joy subsided he again stared at Delaney with the happy expectation of further entertainment. A bit of drool escaped the right side of his pink little mouth. Delaney's spirits lifted in spite of himself.

The great jet taxied for what seemed forever, waited in line, and then whooshed up into the sky in a show of unimaginable power. The fasten your seatbelt was no sooner turned off than Tamara said she had to take Tyrone to the toilet because of his wet diaper. With Tamara and Tyrone in the toilet, Delaney put his head back, closed his eyes, and tried to sleep. Just ahead of him, seated next to Emily, the other young mother seemed to be having problems. Soon her little guy was screaming his lungs out. Contrary to Delaney's assurances to his new wife, the flight was not short. It was very long indeed.

When the lead flight attendant announced that they would be landing in twenty minutes and asked the passengers to make the necessary preparations, Tamara said,

"Oh, dear. It must be time for Tyrone's medicine."

Wait! Wait! Delaney screamed silently. In twenty minutes we'll be on the ground. Wouldn't it be better to wait? He thought this, but said nothing. Big mistake.

A great deal of rummaging around was required to find both the bottle of suspicious-looking red medicine and a little plastic spoon. Once armed, Tamara gave Tyrone his dose of medicine. He swallowed, frowned, and licked his lips. Mother cooed and said good little boy. She moved baby to her right shoulder, the shoulder that she had been bumping against Delaney pretty much throughout the trip. The plane began a sharp descent. It shuddered alarmingly when the pilot lowered the landing gear and diddled with the flaps. That's when Tyrone threw up on Delaney's shoulder. Dreadfully apologetic, Tamara swung into action. She moved the baby to her lap and used a blanket to clean up. After making a mess of Tyrone's little corduroy jump suit, she turned her attention to Delaney's shirt. The plane banged against the tarmac, and it was only Delaney's deft movement that kept baby Tyrone from falling on the floor. Thus ended the flight from Detroit to New York City.

During the long arduous night flight to Dublin, with 225 passengers crammed butt to butt and shoulder to shoulder, a Boeing 747-200 howled like a banshee through a star-studded sky at 558 miles per hour, 37 thousand feet above the sea. On one side of Patrick Delaney, seated next to a window, Emily rested her head against his clean shoulder and fell sweetly asleep. On the other, a man from New York wondered why it was just his rotten luck to be sitting next to a guy who smelled from puke.

Coach Larry Coneybear's secretary Irma Six was a corpulent black woman who didn't take crap from nobody. Were it not for her competence and take-charge attitude, the coach's official affairs would have been like his private affairs, i.e., a mess. Mrs. Six relieved her boss of busywork and protected him from people, particularly students, who would waste his precious time. She drafted his letters, made up excuses when he was late for important committee meetings, and helped him decide which meetings to skip altogether. Budgetary matters were strictly her domain. In short, she made sure the only thing the coach had to do was pick the right athletes and teach them how to play football.

One day, as she tidied her desk before leaving for home, a huge man entered the office. With muscles, shoulders, and gut straining against the seams of a cheap dark suit, he approached her desk and grinned a sweaty grin that would have soured a mother's milk. He said he would have talk with Mr. Lawrence Coneybear. His accent was heavy, but from where had he come? Lower Slobovia? Mrs. Six hadn't a clue.

"Name please," she said.

"Paul Smith," the man replied.

"And what is it that you wish to speak to the coach about?"

"It is for woman not proper."

"Well, I'm afraid Coach Coneybear is a very busy man," Mrs. Six snottily replied, thus inviting a negotiation. You tell me what you want, she might as well have said, and I might let you see the coach. She knew even as she spoke that the coach was likely playing free cell on his computer. She was a zealous gatekeeper, however, and didn't appreciate big ugly strangers invading her domain and throwing their weight around.

Gregori Samonovitch's smile faded to contempt as he pictured the woman behind the desk wrapped mummy-like in dirty rags and stabbing fiercely at permafrost with a pickax. "Your football quarterback, Rod Schonenberg," he replied in a hush, hush mode. "In washroom at Badger Tavern he make pass at me. Showed me his—you know what he show me. Made suggestion. I say nothing to any person, but I have talks with coach about this."

Now, here was something Mrs. Six had no intention of taking in hand. "I'll just check with the coach to see if it's all right," she said. She hurried into the coach's office and said there was someone he just had to see. The coach said show him in, which is what she did. Then she grabbed her purse from a desk drawer and took off for home. Rod Schonenberg has always seemed like such a nice boy to me, she muttered under her breath as she walked down the hall. Who would have thought it? Standing in the gents with his you-know-what hanging out. I wonder what the coach is going to do.

Mr. Samonovitch closed the door behind him. He said he was Paul Smith, shook the coach's hand, and sat down. He looked around the office slowly and then pulled his chair a little closer to the desk. "Mr. Coneybear," he began, "Basim Hachem is blackmailing you I am informed. You want disposition of him. I am to do this for you. It will cause you to pay $75,000. You pay half of money before job and half after job. This is agreeable: yes?"

Coach Coneybear was dumbfounded. What the hell's going on here? he asked himself, mouth agape. Have they put up posters around Red Square for chrissake? "Wanted: one KGB hit man. See Coach Lawrence Coneybear." He didn't know what to say. This was all simply too much for him. He just wanted his troubles to go away. He wanted to be left alone. He wanted this goon perched on a straight-backed chair like a hippo on a lily pad to simply disappear, preferably in puff of smoke.

"Well?" said Samonovitch.

"Go away," said the coach.

"Huh? Half-way across country I come and you say go away? Not so good for me looking for job to do."

"Yes. Go away. And don't come back or I'll call the police."

"This is not . . ."

"I'm going to call the police," the coach said. Overlooking the precariousness of his situation, he picked up the phone and dialed 911. He started to say hello when Mr. Samonovitch reached over, severed the connection, and left without saying another word.

Coach Coneybear sat quietly in his office for a long time, astounded at what he had just done and wondering what the devil to do next. Should I call Max, he wondered? What the hell's going on here? he asked himself several times over. Perhaps I should wait to see what happens. Maybe this Smith dude will simply go away and never come back. Boy, didn't I call his bluff? I've got to get in touch with Mani, though, first thing. He called, but Mani was watching a movie and had turned off his cell phone. Well, no matter, the coach concluded. He would catch him later. He suddenly felt very good about himself for having shooed the big goon good-bye.

Gregori Samonovitch had problems of his own. As he walked through Mrs. Six's outer office, he lifted a moth orchid, tipped it upside down, and smashed it in the middle of her desk. He was in an ugly mood. The long hearty stem of the orchid, though flat on the desktop, held fast to its gorgeous white flowers, but the shredded bark spread over the desk and onto the floor.

Mr. Samonovitch walked to his illegally parked car, took off his coat, loosened his tie, and drove to a spot where he could park in the shade. There he lit a cigarette and reflected on his situation. He would do more legwork before making his next move, but of this he was sure. He would not go home empty-handed.

Chapter 8

Although Victor Malakhov had alerted Gregori Samonovitch to a possible contract in Plattefield, Wisconsin, he had been stingy with the details. He said merely that he had been given a tip that Coach Lawrence Coneybear might be willing to pay to get rid of a blackmailer named Basim Hachem. The nature of the blackmail was not disclosed, despite Samonovitch's pointed hints that without such information, he wouldn't take the trouble of going to Wisconsin. Pumped for information, Mr. Malakhov shrugged his shoulders, said little, and stared. His eyelids closed infrequently, lazily, like those of a lizard. Not a word passed his lips in regard to rigged football games, for he himself hoped one day to turn the dross of uncertain outcomes into the pure gold of manipulation.

Gregori Samonovitch had taken pains to hide his subsequent movements, for he had been well schooled in treachery. He bought a fake driver's license and other counterfeit documents from a crooked fellow Russian émigré. To avoid the ubiquitous video cameras at airports and to save money, for he and his family were near penniless, he took a bus to San Jose and swiped a car. He then swapped license plates with a reveler inside a tavern and drove no faster than the speed limit to Denver, where he rested for the next long haul to Milwaukee. Before leaving Denver, he stole another car and again switched license plates with an unsuspecting Colorado motorist. In Milwaukee, he stayed at a cheap hotel in a disreputable neighborhood. His plan called for driving to Plattefield, daily if necessary, but he would leave nothing behind in his room that could be used in an identification, just in case something went awry and he had to flee.

Now, in the shade of a linden tree, smoking a second cigarette and sweating profusely, he wondered if Victor Malakhov had played a dirty trick. Unlikely, he concluded, and he thought some more. He thought until he thought he had it figured out. Coach Coneybear had lost his nerve: that's what happened. He had decided it was better to pay blackmail than have his blackmailer killed. He has cold feet, Samonovitch concluded triumphantly.

What about blackmailing a blackmailer? Samonovitch wondered, slowly coming around to a new possibility. But then his mind leapt to an even better idea. Middlemen, after all, are so antithetical to Marxist-Leninist philosophy. So—eliminate the middleman. With Basim Hachem out of the way, he could deal directly with Coach Coneybear. Samonovitch grinned with satisfaction at his new strategy and wondered why he hadn't thought of it before. Now what he had to do was find out just what it was Hachem had on the coach and to estimate the maximum amount of money the coach would pay to avoid exposure.

He checked out the Coneybear residence (very expensive) and by chance saw a woman (must be the coach's wife) drive away in a white Mercedes coupe. His eyes narrowed. They are rich, he thought. Fat capitalist pigs. I aim to eat well, too, he thought, and grow fat. "Khyru, khyru," he grunted piggy sounds in Russian. He laughed wickedly.

From the University Faculty and Staff Directory, which he found at the student union, he got Basim Hachem's address and home telephone number and learned that Hachem's job description was Custodial Worker I, Physical Plant Division. When he called Physical Plant and asked to speak to Mr. Hachem, he was told Mr. Hachem reported to work at Johnson Hall. His work shift starts at two in the afternoon, a lady said, so he might be at home still. She asked if he wanted Hachem's home telephone number, but he said no and hung up. He checked out Hachem's house at 112 Cowslip Lane. The next day he waited ten minutes after a man in work clothes left the house carrying a lunch bucket. Then he made his move.

A skilled picker of locks, he walked to Hachem's front door, glanced right and left, and tried the door. It was locked. He withdrew a ring of prods from his pocket and set to work. In less that a minute, he was inside. The house was dirty and poorly furnished. The stink of garbage tinctured by something else hung in the air. Something chemical. Gas? He couldn't quite make out what it was. He did a quick walk through on the assumption he would have plenty of time for a more thorough search of each room later. He was amazed by what he found right off. A small bedroom contained an enormous quantity of dynamite. The closet was filled with rifles, machine guns, two grenade launchers, and boxes of ammunition. Most puzzling of all, though, was the large propane gas tank in the kitchen. Was it filled? And if so, why was it inside the house? How had Hachem managed to get the thing inside? Ah, maybe through an oversized patio door, Samonovitch decided. The door looked as if it had been added long after the house was built, possibly to facilitate moving the tank inside. The question remained, though: why inside the house?

Samonovitch returned to the main bedroom, sat at a scarred office desk, and started examining Hachem's papers. He grinned when he came across newspaper clippings in a plastic bag. This is what I'm looking for, he thought. He read clippings about Lawrence Coneybear. Someone had taken the trouble to underline in red the most significant passages. Ah, he thought, good, good. He put the clippings in a coat pocket and went on with his search. He wasn't worried that Hachem might return. He had a handgun with a silencer. If Mr. Hachem came home unexpectedly, he would exit the world to the sound of a quiet zing. He was destined for a short life anyway.

But Gregori Samonovitch was not the only one interested in Hachem's house that afternoon. Mani Malakhov had been sitting on a step at Johnson Hall watching the lot where Hachem parked his car while at work. When Hachem's car turned into the lot, he rose quickly, turned his back, and walked a few blocks to a public parking area. He climbed into his borrowed Buick and headed for 112 Cowslip Lane. Over the past few weeks, Mani had not wanted to be too conspicuous in his surveillance of Hachem. He had searched out a number of places in Hachem's neighborhood where he could safely park his car. Today he chose a spot behind leggy shrubs one of which had died of neglect and old age. He looked through the gap in the hedge at the front door to Hachem's house, sure it was locked, regretting his unfamiliarity with breaking and entering. Well, I'll smash a window if I have to, he thought. He got out of the car and looked around, thankful for a neighborhood overgrown with trees and shrubs. There wasn't a soul in sight.

Mani Malakhov had never burgled a house before, so naturally he was nervous. He hurried to the front door and, in the off chance the door was unlocked, tried the knob. To his amazement the door opened. Ever so carefully he stepped over the threshold into a small foyer and gently closed the door behind him. He stood very still, sniffed the fetid air, and looked about. Was it just his imagination, or did he hear a noise? He tiptoed to the kitchen and stood astonished before an enormous tank of some kind, right where you'd expect a kitchen table and some chairs. Heavy footsteps on a carpeted floor stood his hair on end. Because the front door was beyond quick reach, he ducked into what proved to be a small kitchen pantry stocked with canned goods, breakfast cereals, and other household supplies. He pulled the door mostly shut and peeked through the crack. A huge man crossed his vision. Good god, he thought. He breathed deeply hoping against hope that he wouldn't faint. Beads of sweat wet his forehead. After a few moments he heard what sounded like a glass clacking against other glasses followed by the sound of running water. Mr. Big's getting a glass of water, he guessed. But who the hell is he? What's he doing here? Oh god, he prayed, I hope he doesn't open this door. Pray to god he doesn't open this door. But suppose he does?

Mani reached toward the canned goods. His heart thumped

when he made a noise, but his hand seized something heavy. Somewhat reassured, he hoisted it up into the air and waited, just in case.

When Samonovitch opened the pantry door, wondering if he had heard a mouse, he was stunned first by what he saw, a terrified man holding a jar of mayonnaise in the air, and then by a blow to his forehead. The blow set him back a peg, but he didn't fall down. What he needed was a moment to regroup his scattered senses, but this was a moment he could ill afford. The second blow to his head drove him to his knees. The third knocked him out cold.

Something in his hand then spilled onto worn linoleum. It was a contraption of some kind with a clock and several wires. Good god, Mani thought. A bomb! A time bomb! He stood frozen with fear, certain that he would soon die. Nothing happened, which gave him a moment to think. And of course it came to him immediately. The man on the floor was a terrorist in cahoots with Hachem. It was *so* obvious.

He had to call Coach Coneybear posthaste to find out what to do, but he couldn't just dash off and leave a terrorist on the floor. The terrorist might come to and escape; god only knew what damage he might do. And the plans to capture Hachem would surely be compromised. Mani desperately searched kitchen drawers until he happened across a roll of duct tape. He grabbed the tape, found a sharp kitchen knife, and set to work. Soon the terrorist was bound hand and foot. A strip stretched across his mouth and around his head. Mani took one last look around the kitchen and ran to his car. He drove downtown to a kiosk with a payphone, called his partner in homeland defense, and breathed a sigh of relief when the coach said hello.

The coach listened to Mani's breathless and incoherent account and told him to slow down for chrissake. He made Mani repeat himself. He asked questions for clarification. Satisfied with his understanding of what Mani had uncovered, the coach thought hard. Ugly visions of 9/11 came to mind, but the only building in Plattefield worth bombing, as far as he could think, was the Babcock Cheese Factory. Did Al Qaeda plan to punish the infidels by threatening their supply of cheese? The coach willed himself to override the effects of two blue pills so he could make the right decision. No matter what the consequences to himself might be, he concluded, the authorities had to be notified immediately.

"Call 911, Mani," he yelled into the phone. "Do it now."

"But what about you, Coach? What if they find out about you?"

"I'll just have to take my chances, won't I? Call, damn it. Call now."

"But what shall I tell them?"

"Er, a, I know. Say you're a burglar. Say you broke into the house at 112 Cowslip Lane and discovered a nuclear bomb or something like that."

"What the devil is *like* a nuclear bomb? I can't think of a single thing that's like a nuclear bomb. I don't even know what a nuclear bomb looks like."

"I do," the coach replied. "I saw a photo of one of the bombs dropped on Japan. It reminded me of the pot-bellied stove my grandparents used to have in their cabin in the Sierras. You know, it was all fat and black, and it had fins on it. Well, not the stove. I mean the bomb." The coach was vaguely aware that this was not the time to get into such matters, but his young friend had raised the question, and he wanted to share.

"You want me to call 911 and describe your granddaddy's pot-bellied stove? Oh my god, I just remembered. I did see something like that in Hachem's house."

"No kiddin'."

"Yeah. It was enormous, like a tank of something. In the kitchen. Maybe it *was* a nuclear bomb, or maybe it was some kind of chemical bomb."

"Mani, um, maybe it would be better if you didn't get into all that. Maybe you should just say you saw lots of dynamite."

"Yeah, yeah. I'll say I found sticks of dynamite. Boxes of the stuff. I've seen that stuff on TV. And I could say I saw a poster of Bin Laden, too. Boy, would that get their attention or what?"

"It sure as hell would. Hey, are you using Hachem's phone?"

"No, no. I'm calling from a payphone. I forgot my cell phone at the motel."

"Good. OK, call 911 and don't talk too long. Just say what you have to and get the hell out of there. Go back to your room and stay put."

"OK, boss. We'll team up later."

"Right."

"Nine-one-one," the dispatcher at the Plattefield Police Station said.

"Hello, is this 911?"

"Yes, this is 911."

"OK. Listen. I'm a . . ." (Wait, thought Mani Malakhov, remembering his speech impediment. It would be a dead giveaway! He'd have to use words with no "r's.") "A, a, a, I've just now come from Hachem's house, oops, I mean the house at 112 Cowslip Lane. I went into his house to steal things." (Mani talked not in a flow of words, but rather as if he were simply reciting words one at a time.)

"Cowslip? Did you say Cowslip Lane?"

"Yes. I, a, got in the house to steal his money, see, and found the house is full of dynamite and stuff and I saw a, a big photo of Osama bin Laden. Get the SWAT team out to that place soon as you can. You gotta stop 'em. It's Al Qaeda. You got that?" (Having gained confidence, Mani had begun to speed up.)

"Yes, I have that. May I have your name please?"

"What?"

"Your name? What's your name?"

"Hey, I'm not giving you my fwickin' name."

Darlene Darrympal did what she had been told. She hurried straight to Detective Phillip Moran's cubicle in the rat's maze of fiberboard cubicles housing the Plattefield police. Feet on his desk, leaning back in his swivel chair, the detective was shooting the breeze with an underling. Ms. Darrympal waited patiently for an opening in the conversation before reading what was on her notepad.

Detective Morn was stunned by this unexpected call to duty. His eyes glazed, his face flushed, and his mouth moved without making any sounds.

"Should I get the guys together?" asked his young colleague.

"Yeah, yeah," Moran said finally, jumping to his feet. "Get 'em. We gotta get the guns, too. And the bullets. Hurry up, goddamnit."

Pandemonium reined at the Plattefield Police Station as SWAT geared up to kill or be killed. One of the men suggested Detective Moran should have a secretary call the absent members of the team to tell them to suit up and get there butts over to 112 Cowslip Lane on the double. Calls for help were duly made. SWAT suits and bulletproof vests were donned. Kevlar helmets were strapped around ruddy jowls. Guns, ammunition, and grenades were loaded in the team's two jungle-green Humvees. In less than an hour, the Humvees tore out of the police station parking lot, headed for 112 Cowslip Lane.

"Hello. Basim?"

"Yeah."

"This is Pamela . . . . Pamela Schultz. You know. Your next door neighbor."

"Yes, yes. Want do you want?"

"I've been trying and trying to reach you, but the lady said you were someplace in the building, but she didn't know where. Listen, can you hear me?"

"Yes, yes."

"Well, speak up. I can hardly hear you. Some time ago I saw a man going into your house. A big guy. At first I thought he must be a friend, perhaps someone staying at your place. Then I began to worry it might be a burglar. Should I call the police?"

There was a momentary silence while Hachem processed this astounding information. Coneybear's behind this, he decided. I gotta stop him. To Mrs. Schultz, he said, "No, no. Don't call the police. He's just a friend. I must go to work now. Good-bye."

In the room where janitors ate lunch, took breaks, and, in the wintertime, hung up parkas and stashed thick gloves, Hachem had been pouring coffee from his thermos. After hearing what his next-door neighbor had to say, coffee was the last thing on his mind. He slammed down the phone, tore from the room, and ran full out toward his car, thinking as he ran that the guy invading his house was probably the same guy who tried to kill him. As he raced for home, he removed the handgun that had been artfully concealed under his seat. He thought about what he would do to the intruder. The handgun? That was just a backup. His preferred weapon was a blade.

Hachem got home just as well-armed men were spilling out of two Humvees. The men watched in amazement as he drove his car up over the curb, across the lawn, and up to the front door. He jumped out of his car and raced inside. None of the SWAT guys had the presence of mind to tell him to halt and stick his hands up, which he wouldn't have done anyway because he had work to do.

Basim Hachem was now in a mess of trouble. Of immediate concern, of course, were the men spreading out and threatening to surround his house. Some were likely headed around to the back. They had to be stopped, for it was out the proverbial backdoor that he hoped to escape. There was, in addition, a house full of evidence of his Al Qaeda connections and terrorist intentions. Under no circumstance must this evidence fall into the hands of the authorities. He had been a fool for disobeying orders, which were never to buy anything, do anything, or say anything that would arouse suspicion. Except for meticulously planned clandestine get-togethers with his leader, he was to lead the ordinary life of a hard-working American. Trouble was, he hated being in a sleeper cell. He was more an action figure. And he neither trusted nor liked his leader. He assumed, or at least hoped, that one day his Al Qaeda brothers would call on him to carry out some mission like 9/11, and when they did, he would be prepared.

Now he had to dispose of the evidence: that was the main thing. And although he had not followed orders to refrain from building up an arsenal, he had made plans to destroy the evidence, if it ever came to that, and it had come to that.

Once inside the house, he locked the front door and wheeled into the living room. He smashed a window and got off a round with his Magnum 45 in the general direction of the lead Humvee. Then he shot at a man heading around the south side of the house, causing the man to take cover behind a tree. The bullet tore off a chunk of bark. He fired a few more shots for good measure and raced to the kitchen. There he was momentarily discombobulated by a man bound by duct tape and lying on the floor. The man was struggling to speak. His face was purple with rage; his eyes threatened to pop from their sockets. Hachem noticed as well that a time-bomb he had been making was on the kitchen floor instead of where it belonged, in the deep drawer of his bedroom desk. But he had no time for riddles. He opened the tank of propane gas that he had taken such pains to haul inside his house. There was a terrible hissing of gas.

Then he ran out the backdoor, scrunching over to conceal himself behind a thick, ill-clipped hedge. He knew exactly where to go. The previous owner of the house had been a bricklayer by trade and had laid a brick path to an outdoor grill near the back boundary of the yard. There, under a shade tree, he and his family used to cook and eat meals on a small patio. The outdoor grill was a substantial piece of work, big enough to rotisserie an entire hog. It was behind this bunker that Hachem threw himself to the ground and waited for what he was sure would be the mother of all diversions. He didn't have long to wait.

"This is the SWAT team. Come out with your hands up. You will come out now."

Thus did Detective Phillip Moran, from behind the safety of a Humvee, warn the terrorists to surrender. Distorted by a bullhorn's amplification, his voice boomed and boomeranged around the neighborhood, causing some confusion. Pamela Schultz, in particular, living next door, fingered her curlers and muttered to herself that she couldn't go out looking like this.

When Hachem fired his handgun, by sheer luck putting a bullet through a window in the lead Humvee, Detective Moran ordered his troops into formation for Attack Plan DaH, the DaH standing for Destroy al-Qaida Holdout. The men heading for the back of the house now proceeded with considerable stealth, slinking from bush to bush and tree to tree. Soon, however, the officers had taken up secure positions that afforded views of the sides and back of the house, ready to open fire on anyone leaving through windows or the backdoor. Beady eyes surveyed the backyard for any sign of movement. Out front, the remainder of the squad took refuge behind the two Humvees and pointed their AK 47's and Heckler & Koch MP5 submachine guns. Detective Moran made ready to fire the SWAT team's single grenade launcher. When he was all set to fire, he again shouted into the bullhorn, this time warning that those inside the house had one minute to come out with there hands up, or the SWAT team would open fire. (Mrs. Schultz barely had time to do something with her hair.) The minute passed and the SWAT team opened fire. The hail of bullets was hair-raising. Windows, sashes, doors, moldy bevel siding, ancient plaster, floor boards, furniture and even the asphalt shingles on the roof began disintegrating into splinters and clouds of dust. The onslaught continued for about a minute, and then Moran fired a concussion grenade.

According to the instructions that came with the grenade launcher from the U. S. Army Surplus Ordinance Division, the objective of a concussion grenade, "is to stun and disorient suspects by way of a large noise and a flash." The noise and the flash precipitated by the grenade exceeded by several fold Detective Phillip Moran's wildest expectations. The propane gas, dynamite, and ammunition inside the house ignited in a flash. The explosion was the loudest noise the people of Plattefield had ever heard. For the tiniest of seconds, the house actually lifted into the air off its foundation, as if an unwieldy rocket headed for the moon. Then it disintegrated into flames, smoke, red hot gases, and specks of debris. A small mushroom cloud rose threateningly up into the air. Except where protected by goggles, the faces of the SWAT team turned red from the heat. Several moustaches were badly singed. A cameraman and a newscaster from WMPM-TV, tipped off by an anonymous caller, were knocked flat. Mrs. Pamela Schultz, having heard the command to come out with hands up, had been standing on her front stoop, uncertain whether Detective Moran's order applied to her or someone else. Though protected by a blue spruce, she, too, was knocked down and scorched. The spruce was reduced to a smoking ruin. All around town, people stopped to look at each other and ask what was that?

Of the people in the immediate vicinity of 112 Cowslip Lane, only Basim Hachem had expected the explosion and was prepared to act. The solid brick grill had protected him from the ball of fire that had inflated in all directions. When the heat diminished, he calmly walked the fifty feet or so to Second Avenue and turned right. Later, on a street downtown, a small crowd of people stopped to watch a squad car scream by. This must have something to do with the great boom, it was generally agreed. It would have taken a very adroit observer, indeed, a veritable Sherlock Holmes, to have noticed the bearded man who didn't stop, who merely glanced up and hurried on.

Chapter 9

The short-run fallout from the biggest bang in Plattefield's history was more-or-less what one might have expected, particularly since the informer who lit the fuse, in a manner of speaking, claimed to have seen a poster of Osama bin Laden. A poster of Osama? In Dairyland? What unspeakable treachery had been fermenting amid the dairy barns, milk plants, and cheese factories of Wisconsin? People wanted to know. The media descended en masse on the sleepy college town in a fierce battle for scoops, interviews with Hachem's neighbors and fellow workers, and man-on-the-street points of view. At a news conference, reporters jostled each other, shouted questions, and repeatedly interrupted Chief Smedegard as he tried to explain what little was known about Basim Hachem at what was obviously an early stage of the investigation. He promised to keep the media informed of all breaking developments, which did little to placate the mob. When the conference was over, hoards of reporters descended on the town's bars and taverns to drink and complain about Dullsville, where you couldn't get a decent martini if your life depended on it.

A keen interest emerged at the news conference in how it happened that the SWAT team and Hachem had converged at Hachem's house at almost the same moment. The chief said Hachem might have been tipped off. In interviews after the news conference, Detective Phillip Moran seconded this idea, claiming that Hachem *had* been tipped off, probably by another terrorist, possibly by a "mold" at the police station. He said it stood to reason. Unfortunately, Pamela Schultz, who could have shed considerable light on the subject, had suffered a severe concussion from the blast next door and had been taken to the hospital. A doctor said his patient didn't seem to know where she was and kept warning the hospital staff of exploding trees.

The improbable story of a terrorist cell in Plattefield, Wisconsin, fleshed out with excerpts from the news conference, was the lead story on all the major TV networks. At the end of Dan Rather's report on the CBS evening news, Chief Smedegard sat back in his well-padded chair and relaxed, confident that he had acquitted himself rather well in the manner of his handling the media. Mrs. Smedegard's effusions did little to mitigate his complacency. The chief's reaction to the CBS interview of his most senior detective Phillip Moran, on the other hand, had been decidedly negative, aside from a moment's schadenfreude when he realized that the color of Moran's face, bright as a cooked lobster, was not so much the fault of TV lights as it was a consequence of the blast on Cowslip Lane. He scoffed aloud when Moran recounted the day's victory by his SWAT team and said there was no question but what Basim Hachem, a suspected terrorist, had been killed. He watched with grim satisfaction when Moran was asked about progress on the war on terrorism and replied that at the end of the day Americans would have to face up to the bottom line. The interview had been conducted against the backdrop of a singed hole in the ground where Basim Hachem's house had once stood.

Several hours were required for federal authorities to take over the investigation. The annihilation of a terrorist cell could hardly be trusted to a bunch of hick cops from a place called Plattefield. A bevy of FBI agents arrived, and a team of FBI engineers set to work. A backhoe and three dump trucks were rented to remove to a storage center pulverized concrete, doorknobs and nails, twisted steel from what had been household appliances, and bits of god knows what. The debris would be raked, sifted, and sorted. It was hoped that some scanty remains of Basim Hachem would be recovered for his DNA.

Attorney General John Ashcroft held a news conference on the day following the big bang to snatch what credit he could for the killing of a terrorist. He stressed the importance of his promoting vigilance on the part of every citizen concerned with homeland defense. Thus did he trumpet the Bush administration's war on terrorism. Wherever you go, he said, keep your eyes open. He did not go so far as to suggest breaking and entering as a means of spying on suspicious characters.

Mr. Ashcroft's most surprising announcement, however, was the arrest of an Arab professor of Middle Eastern studies at the Plattefield campus on the charge that he had aided Al Qaeda and other terrorist organizations. Assistant Professor Suleiman Daoudi, whose application for U.S. citizenship was pending, had made contributions to several charitable Muslim organizations, including the Holy Land Foundation for Relief and Development, which Ashcroft had previously tagged a North American front for Hamas. It was reported, as well, that after speaking at a colloquy on Islam in the modern world, Professor Daoudi had been seen conversing with a mysterious man fitting the description of Basim Hachem (bearded, swarthy, hook-nosed, unkempt, etc.). Several foreign students in close contact with the professor had also been taken into custody, said Ashcroft. Their records were under scrutiny for infractions of the rules governing their stay in America, infractions that might justify their deportation. The community soon learned that two Pakistani students had escaped to Canada where they requested asylum. The university faculty was outraged by the actions of the Department of Justice. A committee was formed to raise funds for Professor Daoudi's legal expenses, even though the professor, charged with being an enemy combatant, had been spirited away to a federal prison and had not been allowed access to an attorney.

With law enforcement officers poking in every nook and cranny, Mani Malakhov decided the time had come to vamoose. Basim Hachem, after all, was no more, so why hang around. Coach Coneybear drove over to the motel where Mani was staying to say goodbye. He brought along some booze and some pills. The coach's farewell took a good deal longer than he had anticipated. In the evening, over fat sandwiches and French fries at a tavern more than forty miles away from Plattefield, following their usual precautions in regard to being seen together, the coach and Mani discussed once again the behemoth Paul Smith. The coach again remarked on how big and ugly the Russian hit man had been and at last Mani concluded that Smith and the man he had struck down with a jar of mayonnaise were almost certainly one and the same. This was a mystery that needed to be cleared up. On the way back to the motel, Mani had an inspiration.

"Hey, I know what happened," he said. "My papa didn't know I was planning to, er, take care of Hachem myself, so he sent someone else to do the job. The guy must have gone up in flames, with Hachem."

"Yeah, but why was he there? In Hachem's house?"

"Hmm. That's a good question. Maybe he went there to kill Hachem when he came home from work. Sure, that's what happened."

"Well, great. We got rid of a terrorist and a hit man in one fell swoop. God, we're heroes, Mani, and no one will ever know. I haven't felt this good about myself in years. Jeez."

"Jeez is white," agreed Mani, spitting a little.

Figuring that the airports at Madison and Milwaukee would be closely guarded, Mani indicated his preference for flying home from Minneapolis, and the coach agreed to drive him there the following day. He pressed Mani to accept $5,000 at least, but Mani would only accept money for the fare home, since, as he explained, he didn't have sufficient funds to buy a ticket on his own. But the coach thought of a way to reward Mani for his services.

"When I get home," he said, "I'll make sure the patio door is unlocked before going to bed. OK, you can slip into the house and take Cat Stevens's vest."

"Oh, my god, coach," Mani replied, "That would be so awesome. Are you sure it'll be OK? I mean, don't you want it?"

"Hell, no."

After dropping Mani off at his motel, the coach thought of a refinement that would give his plan a touch of class. His eyes crinkled as a grin spread from ear to ear. He would stay up to help Mani with the heist. He would add a new wrinkle for his wife's negative benefit, just to piss her off totally.

In the midmorning of the following day, Mani Malakhov checked out of his motel and drove to the UW campus where he picked up Coach Coneybear. Both men were hung over and drained from their early morning escapade; they changed drivers several times on their way to Minneapolis. The coach's drive home was hellish. Not only was he dog-tired, but it occurred to him that his situation was far from satisfactory. He was glad to be rid of a blackmailer, true, but he had come to like Mani and wondered if he would ever see the young man again. They had hit it off so well and had so much in common. There remained the concern over his falsified vita, however, together with new ones. Actively seeking a hit man to kill Basim Hachem was a capital offense. Might he be found out? Suppose the police got wind of Mani Malakhov. Suppose Jane collects insurance on the stolen vest. He'd be a party to a swindle. Mmm. And then there was the overarching catastrophe of his marriage. He simply didn't have all that much to be thankful for. He had made a mess of his life, no doubt about it, and he was stuck with it.

By the time he got home, his wife Jane was in her bedroom with the door closed. Figures, he thought. She's probably got the damned thing barricaded. He popped a frozen pizza in the oven, opened a beer, and sat down to watch TV. In less than five minutes he was snoring. Two hours later the smoke alarm went off with an earsplitting shriek. He sat up, rubbed his eyes, and wondered where in the hell he was.

"You left a pizza in the oven, you dumbbell!" It was his wife Jane standing with startled hair in the doorway to the family room. Her hands were on her hips.

"Huh?"

"The pizza in the oven. It's burned to a crisp. You had the temperature set at 500, for chrissake."

"Oh that. I must have fallen asleep."

"Duh! Where in the hell were you last night?"

"I went for a drive."

"Oh, sure. No doubt with one of your pompom sweeties. Well, I'm going back to bed, you bastard."

"How's Laura?" the coach asked, referring to the mustachioed director of women's sports.

"Oh, shut up."

The following morning, as the coach hurriedly ate a bowl of Cornflakes before rushing off to work, he heard his wife scream. He knew what she had discovered: that the framed vest worn by Cat Stevens at his 1971 concert in Liverpool had been replaced by Mani Malakhov's crusty skivvies. It was not a pretty picture. The coach grinned maliciously, but the slate was clean by the time Jane stormed into the kitchen, demanding to know what had happened to her Cat Stevens vest. The coach said he didn't know what the hell she was talking about, and she said she was going to call the police if he didn't return the vest, and he said kiss my ass.

Oh the way to the office the coach sang,

Zippadee-doo-dah. Zippadee-ay. My, oh my, what a wonderful day. Plenty of sunshine headin' my way . . .

God, he felt good. Something was happening to him. He didn't know what, but it was good.

Plattefield's fifteen minutes of fame reached Sneem, Ireland, at about the speed of light. Gathered round the little TV in the Delaneys' cabin, the Plattefield party was amazed. Mrs. Willgrubs wanted to know what the world was coming to. Delaney wondered whether he would be needed at home and even speculated on the necessity of cutting short his honeymoon. Emily said the FBI would be all over the case, and Delaney said that that was why he might be needed. The professor pointed out that they would be home in just a few days anyway, and remarked on the cost of changing the tickets. Much more was said largely because Delaney couldn't put the matter aside. Eventually the Willgrubs said good-night and returned through an English garden to their room in the hotel proper.

Emily got ready for bed while Delaney stayed glued to the TV, hoping to hear more news about the terrorist threat in Plattefield. Now and again he looked at Emily's face, puzzled by her expression. Suddenly it came to him. He had been acting like a jerk. He turned off the TV and sat on the edge of the bed.

"Emily," he said, "Come sit a minute."

She had been headed for the bathroom, but she stopped and joined her husband. He had hunched his shoulders forward and lowered his head.

"I feel so awful, Emily," he said. "I've been a total ass. First I was sick and then I started feeling resentful and sorry for myself. You know, about your uncle and aunt being with us on our honeymoon. I'm just so darned sorry for the way I've been behaving lately. Always glum and cranky. I haven't been myself, Emily. I'm better than I've been. You have to believe that."

When he turned to look at Emily's face, he saw tears that broke his heart.

"It's all my fault," she cried. "I could have kept them from coming with us. I could have found the right words."

"No, no. You did the right thing. Think of what they've done for you. And for me. I should have laughed and tried my darnedest to make this a fun family outing. No, once they suggested coming to Ireland with us, you had to agree. Why? Because that's your nature, babe. That's one reason I love you, Emily. There are so many others."

"Oh, if you start talking pretty you'll have me crying like a baby. What are we going to do?"

"We still have five days. Let's make them wonderful, Emily. Let's make them the best darn days of our lives. We'll see everything, do everything. We'll make our uncle and aunt laugh till their ribs ache." He turned to her and gently held her face in his hands. With his thumbs he wiped away the tears.

"Why do I have the feeling that tonight is going to be fantastic?" she murmured.

Among a crowd of people five days later, the Delaneys and the Willgrubs sat in a row at Gate 10 for an Aer Lingus jet that would take them from Dublin to New York City. The party from Plattefield was not in the happiest of moods. Professor Willgrubs's left arm was in a cast from elbow to finger tips. The doctor had said that his thumb was severely sprained and was to be kept immobilized as much as possible for at least a month. The professor felt badly for having been a great bother on their last day at Sneem, and now he faced the terror of flying over an entire ocean. Detective Delaney was downhearted, though he was almost overdoing it in the aren't-we-all-having-fun department, managing the rental car, carrying the heaviest bags, offering to buy coffee and rolls. But the last day at Sneem had strained a bit, but just a bit, not so anyone could notice, his promise to Emily to turn a new leaf. He and his party had spent much of the day in the doctor's office. And then there was the packing for the trip home. Emily was a bit glum because she knew, though she would never press the point again, that she had erred. Months ago she could have explained to her uncle and aunt that it would be best if they saw Ireland on their own, rather than joining her and Patrick on their honeymoon.

Among the party from Plattefield, Edna Willgrubs was the most cheerful. Her despondency, not that it was anything to send a postcard home about, was attributable to the end of a wonderful vacation. She had seen much of Ireland, bought pretty things for the house, and had taken many photos with her new aim-and-shoot camera. Although Patrick had been a stick in the mud to start with, he had brightened considerably in the last few days. Maybe he had finally got over his illness. And it was such a pleasure having him drive around on the wrong side of the road instead of the professor. On the one occasion the professor *did* drive, to spell Patrick, he scared the devil out of a guy on a motorcycle. Her regret on leaving Ireland was now giving way to the fun she'd have with neighbors and friends back home. There would be the photos and adventures to relive and she could explain that it hadn't been *her* fault that the professor had abandoned her and gone off to Howth Cove Beach and tripped over a piece of driftwood.

As they waited the professor leaned over to Delaney and muttered, "Do you see that gentleman with the blue carryon? The one over there near the corner? With the little moustache and his hair slicked back?" The professor nodded his head in the direction the detective was supposed to look.

"Yeah, I think I know the guy you mean," Delaney replied. "The one who just lifted a newspaper?"

"Yes. He's the guy who knocked me down . . . . On the beach."

"Knocked you down?" Delaney replied a little too loudly. "I thought you said you tripped."

"Er, I'm sure he didn't mean to," the professor said sotto voce. "It was just a bump you see. We neither of us was looking where we were going I'm afraid."

"Hmm," Delaney hummed his acceptance of this explanation. His eye was drawn to a family with two noisy boys, and when he looked back at the man who had bumped the professor on the beach, he was sure the stranger had been looking at him. He would likely have recognized the professor. In another minute, the man with the slick hair rose with his carryon and left the waiting area, which Delaney thought odd. Why would someone waiting for a flight from some other gate choose to sit here, where it was crowded?

"There goes your man," Delaney said to the professor.

"Good riddance," the professor replied.

Just then the announcer at Gate 10 called for the boarding of the First Class Passengers on Aer Lingus Flight 73 to New York City. The Willgrubs and the Delaneys were going home at last, and Detective Delaney was eager to get back to work and to discover what role he'd play, if any, in the investigation of the death of Basim Hachem. When the man sitting next to him rose, grabbed his carryon and took off, leaving behind the newspaper he had been reading, Delaney picked it up. The headline said, "Investigation of Fire at Reeks Animal Disease Research Center."

The adjoining article described the suspicious nature of the fire and quoted a Professor Williamson who warned of a possible leak of hazardous materials and recommended quarantining all farm animals in the immediate vicinity. Delaney had only gotten partway through the article when Emily and the Willgrubs stood up and began gathering together their carryons in anticipation of boarding. Though interested in the fire and its dangers, he decided against taking the paper with him. Mrs. Willgrubs had a great many parcels that needed to be distributed among the members of her party, carried on board, and stowed carefully, lest some of her figurines be damaged by some ruffian with a hard attaché case. As Delaney waited in line, it came to him that the professor quoted in the paper had likely been the same professor he had seen on TV the day before. The fire at Reeks Animal Disease Research Center appeared to be of considerable interest to Irish authorities, which made him wonder about disease research in America. Hadn't he read about trouble at some animal disease research center in New York? Oh, yes. The Plum Island Animal Research Center near Long Island.

Chapter 10

A bump, the professor had said of his collision with a man at Howth Cove Beach, but it had been more than a bump; more than a push. It had been a willful shove.

One evening after dinner in the Derrycross Hotel dining room, Delaney asked Emily if she would like to visit a pub. The Jaunty Crown is near the outskirts of Sneem, he said, adding that he wanted to sample night life in a Irish pub off the beaten track. In truth, he wanted to get away from the Willgrubs, get a little drunk, maybe, and then take Emily back to their cabin, scoop her up in his arms, carry her over the threshold, and ravish her with kisses and such. Alas, it was not to be.

"I'm sorry," Emily said. She put her hand on Delaney's hand. "I have a terrific headache. Too much wine, I'm afraid. Couldn't we just watch TV and go to bed early?"

"*I'll* go with you," the professor chirped. "Edna doesn't like pubs and she can keep Emily company. I would welcome the opportunity to talk with the young working people of Ireland, with those who ordinarily have little contact with Americans. I think having a pint of beer with the locals would be most informative. And pleasurable, too," he added.

Oops, thought Delaney. What have I done?

"You don't have to do that, Professor," he said, wondering what he had got himself into. He looked imploringly at Emily, but she was watching the waiter bringing plates of food to a nearby table. She could not come to his rescue.

"But I want to," the professor persisted. "It wouldn't be a burden at all. I'm very eager to learn more about the Irish. I mean the things about their culture that you can only pick up from person to person contact, not the things gleaned from travel books. The pub is just the place to get the young working person's point of view."

It was settled.

The Jaunty Crown proved to be a lively spot, even on a Thursday night. The place was small and dowdy with hard bar stools and not the slightest pretense of plushness. Even so the place was jammed with people. There was much talking, laughter, and music. Now and again howls of laughter issued from a small room off to the side of the bar, a room the Irish call a "snug," the professor explained to Delaney. The air was thick with smoke and sodden with beery breaths. There was only one vacant stool at the bar, which Delaney insisted the professor take. He stood nearby and they ordered pints of Guinness. The professor soon struck up a conversation with the man sitting to his left and in a little while both he and his new friend swiveled their stools around somewhat so they could involve Delaney in the conversation. When he wasn't too busy with other customers, one of the bartenders joined in the conversation as well, apparently interested in an Irish cop from America.

Several pints of beer later, after Delaney had excused himself to take a leak, a lull in the conversation gave the professor the chance to choose a topic to his liking and to seek advice.

"I'm very much interested in tide pools," he said to his new friends. (He had to speak up because the place was very noisy.) "Is there some place nearby that has good pools, pools with starfish, anemones, sea urchins, invertebrates: creatures like that? That's something we have very little of in Wisconsin, I don't mind telling you."

"Not close to Sneem," said the bartender.

At this point a second bartender, who had been lingering nearby, joined the conversation. "How about Howth Cove Beach?" he said. "There's some interesting sea life down there."

The two bartenders exchanged significant glances. "Oh, yeah," the first bartender said. "I forgot about that one."

"Is it close by?" the professor asked.

"It's only a few miles away," said the first bartender. "Almost within walking distance from here. Do you have a car?"

"Well, not really," the professor replied. "My friend Patrick and his wife have a car, but I hate always asking them to go where my wife, er, where I want to go. Is there a bus?"

"Where are you staying?" the first bartender asked.

"At Derrycross Hotel."

"You're in luck," said the second bartender. "There's a bus that stops right outside your hotel. It'll take you to the beach and beyond if you want to go further. It runs every half-hour."

"Oh, that would be very fine, indeed. I'm much obliged for your help."

Just then Patrick returned from the gents and ordered another pint and asked the professor if he was ready for another, too.

"Oh no, Patrick," the professor replied, with a flushed and happy face. "I'm afraid I've had too much already. The gentlemen here have just been telling me about a beach with tide pools that are abundant with sea life. Edna and I can easily get there by bus. That's what I'd like to do tomorrow, if you and Emily wouldn't mind. I know you have other plans. I hope Edna is up for a bit of exercise. Would that be OK, Patrick?"

The professor noticed at this point that the two bartenders were exchanging grins; one winked at the other. The professor wondered if he had missed a joke.

Professor Willgrubs got off the bus at what appeared to be a tiny village called Howth Cove. The few shops and cottages making up the village had been painted in pastel shades of green, blue, lavender, and yellow, as if decked out for a postcard. A wooden sign shaped like a hand with a pointed index finger read, "Howth Cove Beach." The professor turned right off the main road down a broad gravely path. Up ahead he could see the trail leading downward through twisted trees and giant boulders strewn in beds of bright green moss.

Although the professor had a monumental hangover from the night before, he did so want to sea the tide pools. He had worked up such a head of enthusiasm, in spite of the twinge of guilt he felt for having abandoned his family. He was glad to be on his own for the very first time on his trip to Ireland, which seemed so selfish on his part. Mrs. Willgrubs had expressed the desire to stay at the hotel for the afternoon, to read and possibly take a nap. She had insisted that the professor should not feel that he had to stay behind on her account, but was mildly disappointed when he finally agreed not to. Emily had offered to think of something they could all do together, but the professor had objected. Now he would go where he wanted without worrying about what the others wanted to do and whether he was dilly-dallying too long here or too long there. And he *was* keenly interested in tide pools. If only he felt a little better. It was surprisingly warm and although he had thought to bring along his nonallergenic sun screen, he had forgotten his hat.

Before long, the professor was overtaken by a long-legged, athletic-looking couple who stopped to chat. The man said his name was Fred, shook the professor's hand, and said his wife's name was Bernie. She shook his hand, too. Fred was a tall, big-boned man with a strong jaw, receding hairline, and ruddy complexion. His wife was big, too, but not in the least overweight. She had lots of fine reddish hair. Her smile was big and friendly and revealed missing teeth beyond the apex of her dental arch, leading the professor to suppose that she had not been a child of affluence. Bernie and Fred were both deeply tanned and freckled, with sun-bleached hair and eyebrows. They seemed remarkably friendly, and when the professor explained that he was going to the beach to enjoy the sun and the sea, they said they were going there, too, and that they should go together. The professor was enormously pleased by this opportunity to mingle yet again with Ireland's salt of the earth.

Not far down the path, though, he had to stop at a shady spot to rest on a bench. Bernie joined him. Fred sat on the grass, said the professor wasn't looking so good, and asked if he was well. The professor said he had a bit of a headache, that they should feel quite free to go on without him, that he would hate to slow them down. Bernie wouldn't hear of it and rummaged around in her handbag for pills she said would help.

"Is it aspirin?" the professor asked, a bit leery of taking pills offered by a stranger.

"I don't know what's in them," Bernie confessed, but they're wonderful for getting rid of headaches. She found the pills and offered two to the professor along with a freshly opened bottle of water.

The professor would have declined but for a really serious headache that seemed to have gotten much worse during a stretch of walk in the sun. His vision was somewhat impaired, which he knew was a sure sign of danger. Besides all that, he was thirsty, and he didn't want to show distrust of good, common Irish folk. In short, he took the pills, drank some water, and thanked the stranger for her kindness.

After a quarter mile or so, they came out of the wooded area onto the outskirts of the beach. The sand was warm and deep; there were bunches of sea grass several feet high. The professor would not have been sure quite where to go, but Fred and Bernie had obviously been there before and were prepared to lead the way.

The first thing that should have suggested to the professor that not all was as it should be was when Bernie said,

"Oh, its going to be so nice to be free of troublesome clothes."

She stopped and took off her halter top, thus baring her substantial breasts. The professor was too shocked to say a word; he could only stare in astonishment. In a moment, though, he came to himself and shifted his gaze to more suitable objects. He knew about topless beaches in Europe, but in Roman Catholic Ireland! he muttered to himself. What would the pope say? And oh, what a topic of conversation this will be at dinner tonight. At last, I'll have something to relate that might be a source of merriment, he thought. And the good lord knows my little family could use some merriment. Poor Patrick. To have his uncle and aunt along on his honeymoon. The professor had no inkling at this juncture on his way to the sea that at the end of the day, he would have more to conceal than reveal.

Soon he could hear the surf. There seemed to be ruckus of some kind up ahead, for there was much shouting and laughter. Then Bernie said,

"Wait a minute." She took off her shorts and handed them to Fred along with her handbag. "Would you keep these with your things, honey?" she asked.

Then, stark naked, she ran toward the sea as freely as a school girl with a kite. Fred followed suit, stripping, and running on ahead. He stopped to turn back.

"Come on, man," he said. "Take your clothes off. Do you play volley ball?"

"Er, I'm not very good at it," the professor replied. He began unbuttoning his shirt, but Fred had turned to run after his wife. The professor took off his long-sleeved shirt to reveal the T-shirt underneath, thus baring his white hairless forearms. Despite pills that had done wonders for his headache and made him feel rather strange, he hadn't the slightest intention of stripping off his clothes. When he came round the last of the great clumps of grass, all was revealed to him. He had fallen victim to a prank.

The bartenders at the Jaunty Crown had tricked him into coming to a nude beach. There, not more than thirty feet from where he was standing, was a volleyball game in progress. Without stopping the game, the teams loudly welcomed Bernie and Fred who joined the action by running to the opposite sides of the net. The professor stood in awe. Breasts swung freely this way and that. Male genitalia bobbed alarmingly. The nudists were mostly middle-aged and came in all shapes and sizes. Aside from the game, there were nudists everywhere, on blankets and towels, sitting in beach chairs, frolicking in the surf. The professor could look nowhere it seemed except at the sky and back at the way he had come.

Oh, my goodness, he thought. He was dreadfully embarrassed. He didn't want to appear censorious (for was he not a liberal man?), or worse still, voyeuristic. It would be so awful if Bernie and Fred thought he had come to the sea to look at nude women. So, trying to avoid eye contact with the nudists, he looked right and left and saw what appeared to be a rocky point jutting modestly out into the sea to his left. He would walk in that direction and ignore the nudity. He shielded his eyes as if better to see what lay in the distance, thus to assure the nudists he was not there to gawk. Hmm, he thought, there might be tide pools after all. Perhaps the bartenders at the Jaunty Crown had not pulled a fast one on him after all.

He walked toward rocks, afraid to look back let alone walk back. When he arrived at the rocky point he discovered several tide pools. There wasn't much to see in them, but he would look at them all the same. What were his options? Those tricky fellows at the Jaunty Crown, he thought: darn their hides. He had barely begun examining the pools for aquatic life when a large party of Japanese tourists emerged from a wooded area not far up from the water. They had come down to the ocean following a different path from that used by the professor. They were nicely dressed and seemed to be carrying on a lively conversation. The professor was mighty glad to see fully dressed Japanese and wondered, too, whether by walking up the new path he could wind his way back somehow to the stop where a bus would carry him safely home.

The Japanese soon invaded the modest tidal outcroppings. They peered into the pools of clear water, pointed, and made comments. They took pictures of the sea and its tide pools and of each other. Even though he had plenty of time, the professor decided to give it up, to write the afternoon off as total waste. As he headed for the escape route, he was intercepted by a pleasant looking Japanese man who spoke excellent English. The tour guide, the professor decided.

"Would you mind taking a picture of all of us?" he asked.

"I would be most happy to," the professor replied stepping up rather too closely to the stranger. He had put on his long sleeved shirt without buttoning the front, thus to encourage the circulation of cool air.

The stranger stepped back from the professor, handed him an expensive looking camera, thanked him, and began calling together his group. There was chatter and confusion as he endeavored to arrange them just so on a large flat rock outcropping. A problem then arose. People called to each other and some pointed up toward the path leading back into the woods. One of the ladies broke out a cell phone and made a call. After several minutes, the group leader approached the professor and explained that an elderly couple and their son were on their way down to the beach, but that it might take some time.

"Would you mind terribly waiting until they arrive?" he asked the professor.

"No, not at all," the professor replied. "I'm in no rush at all. I'll just enjoy myself until they get here."

He wondered about, biding his time and looking for something worth looking at. Now and again he glanced toward the woods and wondered what was taking the elderly couple so long. Further up the embankment, where the grass was rather short, he came across a plant he had never seen before. Was it an orchid? he asked himself excitedly. It might very well be, he answered. Mmm. He had read about orchids that grew in coastal sand, but had never supposed that he would find them growing here. How interesting. How totally fascinating. If I could find a flower with a bilaterally symmetrical flower structure with three sepals, he muttered to himself, then by golly I would know for sure. He began slowly making his way back toward the nude beach, sticking to the border of short grass and weeds. Without giving it a second thought he lifted the camera strap up over his head so the camera could hang from a shoulder. He maneuvered the camera around to his back so it would not interfere when he stooped over to examine the fauna at close range. When he saw what looked like a blossom in the distance, he stood up and hurried toward it.

His progress was halted by shrieks in a foreign language. He looked back. With the team leader in the vanguard, a hoard of Japanese were running full out toward him. They were pointing and yelling. The professor became confused. The hangover, the sun, and the pills had taken their toll. He thought he might faint. Are they coming after me? he asked himself. He began to run, occasionally throwing a worried glance over his shoulder, which seemed to infuriate further the mob bearing down on him. Good god, what have I done, he thought? The answer didn't occur to him until he'd made it back to the nude beach. The banging of the camera against his back was the clue. With a flush of embarrassment, he realized the Japanese were merely trying to retrieve the camera: that they judged him a thief. He stopped long enough to lift the camera up over his head and lay it on the sand. Then he took off again, running on ahead, but staying some distance from the water so as to minimize close encounters with naked people. He saw a well-groomed, fully clothed man partly concealed behind a tuft of grass and was shocked when the man suddenly lurched toward him and shoved him to the side. The professor fell awkwardly over a piece of driftwood and crashed to the ground.

He sat up on the sand. His head was in a whirl. He couldn't focus his eyes and was horrified that he would be sick. And why did his left thumb throb so? He looked at it and wondered whether it was broken.

"Here he is," the man with slicked-back hair said to the Japanese. "Thief!" he snarled at the professor. "You were trying to steal their camera, weren't you? They should cut off your hand with an ax."

In a daze, the professor looked up at Slick Hair. His moustache had been clipped to the width of a pencil line. "I am not a thief," the professor said indignantly, but he felt too ill to explain. He breathed heavily and wondered if he could get to his feet on his own. The small crowd that quickly gathered about was both a source of embarrassment and bafflement. A few onlookers jabbered in a foreign language. What language was it? He wasn't sure. Others appeared to be naked. Where in god's name am I? he wondered. Have I gone mad?

"He's hurt!" someone said. Then the professor remembered where he was. The woman who had fallen to her knees and gently touched the professor's arm was Bernie.

"Are you all right?" she asked.

The professor tried to reply, but could only emit a little squeak.

"Fred," Bernie called to her husband, "I think he's hurt."

The Japanese guide held up his camera for show and tell. "He was trying to run off with this," he said, addressing mainly, it seemed, the naked people.

"I saw him," said Slick Hair.

Finally, the professor was able to speak. "I hadn't intended to run off with their camera," he said to Bernie. "You see, when they started to chase me, I panicked and began to run away. When I remembered I had their camera, I placed it on the sand. I'm an American. I'm a professor of agricultural economics. I'm no thief."

"Well, of course you're not," Bernie said. "But are you hurt? Do you think you can walk?"

"I think I can," the professor replied. With his one good arm he proposed getting to his feet. Fred came to his rescue and helped him up.

"There you are," Fred said, once the professor was standing. "Do you think you can walk?"

"I believe so."

"Honey," Bernie said to her husband. "Fetch our clothes. I think we should walk the professor back up the path to town. He's not well enough to go on his own."

"Of course," Fred replied.

Over the professor's lame objections that evening at dinner, Mrs. Willgrubs and Emily insisted that in the morning the professor would be taken to see a doctor. The professor said maybe in the morning his thumb would be better.

After dessert, the party adjourned to the Delaneys' cabin to watch TV. As usual, Mrs. Willgrubs took control of the remote; as usual, Delaney chafed at this outrageous encroachment on a man's prerogatives. He was particularly interested in any news of the terrorist cell in Plattefield, but Mrs. Willgrubs was more interested in the weather forecast, fearful that a storm might blow in from the North Sea and interfere with their flight back to New York. She surfed the channels relentlessly for the Irish counterpart to the Weather Channel back home. The viewers were thus treated to a potpourri of TV ads and scenes from sitcoms and old movies. One segment catching Delaney's interest came from a local news show. A man, looking and acting very much like a professor, spoke from an office well-stocked with books and journals. A partial sentence made reference to the government's assurance that there had been no bio-containment breach.

"If there were any risks of pathogens in the air," the spokesman had said, "there would be a need to quarantine all animals in the area. If they are certain . . ."

Mrs. Willgrubs changed channels. Delaney forgot himself and gave her a mean look, but stifled the urge to say go back. By the time she found her way back to the channel, the segment would likely be over anyway, he thought. He laughed aloud when he saw Emily smiling at him. He willed himself to be easy, philosophic, pleasant, no matter what. He would be happy. He was on his honeymoon.

Chapter 11

A thunderstorm rumbled over Plattefield. The townspeople stirred in their beds, rustling sheets and sighing protests at the thunderclaps rattling their tired bones. Chief Eugene Smedegard woke and couldn't get back to sleep. In pajamas he sat in his recliner chair, resting his head against the headrest and listening to wind-driven rain spattering panes of glass. He was reluctantly coming to a painful decision that he couldn't go on, not like this. He would retire, buy a condo in Florida, and die of old age: and that would be that. Time to give it all up, said the niggling voice of defeat inside his wizened old gray head. If Detective Philip Moran becomes the new chief, so be it. He could see no way out, and the reality of it pressed him down. He would try to forget Plattefield and what he had tried to accomplish there, which was to achieve law enforcement with a bit of heart for the down and out, for people born in the wrong circumstances, for people who had never had much chance. The university folks and the community at large, being of a liberal persuasion, had held his work in high esteem for many years, but now there were growing signs of dissatisfaction. He heaved a sigh at the latest blow to his plan for preventing Moran from becoming the new chief of police. Some plan, he muttered bitterly under his breath—hanging onto your job until Moran falls on his own sword.

But Detective Moran had *not* fallen on his sword. On the contrary, he had brandished the damned thing with extraordinary effect, which explained the chief's insomnia. Killing Hachem and exposing an Al Qaeda cell in the nation's hinterland had made Moran a hero. He was in an ABC Special Report on terrorism. His photo and scripted comments appeared almost daily in the *Plattefield Gazette*, which repeatedly called attention to his push to organize a SWAT team over the chief's objections. One editorial said it had taken 9/11 to bring the chief to his senses.

In the chief's opinion, it was the loss of sense on the part of the townspeople of Plattefield that had made SWAT a reality. He held fast to his belief that the bombast of SWAT, though it made for spectacular TV, was a miserable substitute for traditional modes of law enforcement. He had read too many accounts of SWAT team assaults on innocent parties. And for all the kudos Moran and his team had received in the media, the chief had wondered exceedingly whether the whole matter could have been better handled if the 911 message had been turned over to a couple of smart detectives who, instead of putting on a great show, had instead moved with secrecy and stealth, one day arresting Hachem for questioning and then searching his house. If only I had been in my office at the time, he had been lamenting privately, so that the 911 message had come to me. I would have taken Basim Hachem alive.

Chief Smedegard listened to the storm rumbling off in the distance, knowing that he would never get to sleep if he didn't stop thinking about SWAT and Detective Moran. His thoughts drifted over to Patrick Delaney, off on his honeymoon in Ireland. What will happen to *him* if Moran becomes the new chief? he wondered. God help the boy. Maybe you should try to stick it out for a few more months, he thought. Wait until after this business of Basim Hachem and what he was up to are all sorted out. Maybe something will happen. The chief pulled himself up from his recliner-chair and went back to bed. He had decided that he'd not retire after all, at least not quite now; he fell asleep immediately.

Detective Patrick Delaney was roundly welcomed at the station on his return from Ireland. The women smiled broadly, wanted to be noticed by him, and envied his new bride. A few made interpersonal comparisons that reflected rather poorly on their husbands. The men at the station grinned, slapped him on the back, and thought, not always privately, that he was a lucky bastard to have married a runner-up in the Alice in Dairyland Beauty Contest. Officer Wade Johnson, whose humor nearly always centered on body parts and functions, said Delaney was looking rather peaked and inquired whether he was eating enough eggs. As often the case, Delaney was unsure what exactly Johnson was getting at, but knew better than to ask.

When in Ireland, on first hearing about the death of a terrorist in Plattefield, Detective Delaney had longed to be home and in the thick of things. On his return, he found himself on the periphery of things: that he was outside the loop and ignored in what was surely the biggest case the police department had ever had. With encouragement from Chief Smedegard, he set out to catch up, using all his free moments and by working overtime. He checked out files on the case, read everything, took notes, and asked questions. He thought about the case to and from work and while jogging. He often discussed the public information with Emily and the Willgrubs over dinner. In the weeks following his return to Plattefield, he came to know as much about the case as any of his fellow officers and a great deal more than most. He soon knew a lot about Basim Hachem.

What struck him and nearly all those with an interest in the case was Hachem's seeming ordinariness. He did his work, minded his own business, and smiled at fellow workers and next-door neighbors. He had an on-and-off-again relationship with a woman who worked at the Farmhands' Tavern. She told the FBI that he was a good man, but on the secretive side, which probably explained why she knew so little about him. He had a checking account, wrote few checks, and kept modest amounts on deposit. If he had been accumulating a hoard of money for some sort of terrorist attack, he certainly had hidden it well. He paid his taxes on schedule and had never been audited. His biggest investment had been the equity in the house at 112 Cowslip Lane, a house now separated into piles of splinters, dust, and twisted bits of metal on the floor of a rented warehouse.

Basim Hachem was born and reared in a middleclass Arab neighborhood in Dearborn, Michigan. In his early years, his classmates poked fun at his name, which apparently bothered him because he used to claim that Basim meant perfection in Arabic, which, though not true, went unchallenged. He stayed at home a lot and liked to watch movies on cable television. His high school years seemed uneventful. He participated in no extracurricular activities and had few friends. True, he took a girl to the prom in his senior year, but she really wasn't his girlfriend and they never saw each other after graduation. He was a slow learner. His grades were below average, and his classmates laughed at him when he said he was going to college.

His family, friends, and neighbors were Muslims, but there was no hint of radicalism anywhere. After graduation, he worked in his uncle's sporting goods store for three years, and a fellow clerk said Hachem was not one to run for prayers during prayer breaks. He wasn't into Muslim charities, neither, another chimed in. His mother died in 1989, and when his father died shortly after, Hachem moved to Milwaukee and became a welder. Eventually he settled in Plattefield where he found employment as a state employee at the University of Wisconsin.

There had been one chapter in his life's history, however, that few people knew about, and those who did were not ones to talk. When Basim Hachem quit his job in Milwaukee, he quite unexpectedly made a Muslim pilgrimage to Mecca. Before returning to the United States and settling in Plattefield, he spent two years abroad. In London, according to Scotland Yard, he became friends with Muslims at the Finsbury Park mosque where he prayed and studied the Koran under the tutelage of the radical Egyptian-born imam Abu Hamza al-Baskri. According to the Brits, much of Hachem's time away from America was unaccounted for, and there was speculation that under a forged passport he might have flown to Pakistan and made his way to Afghanistan for further religious instruction. If so, he most certainly would have come in contact with Al Qaeda. Delaney had to agree with the FBI and nearly everyone else: Basim Hachem had in all probability become a terrorist. But what had he been up to? Did he have accomplices? Who were they? Where were they hiding? The questions were urgent; the answers, unknown.

According to one of the files, Basim Hachem's sister Raida, who worked for a tailoring business in Detroit, insisted that her brother was not a terrorist, but it appeared she hadn't been in close contact with him for several years. She was unaware, for example, that he had spent time in London. She willingly volunteered a sample of blood for a DNA analysis she said would show the man who died in the blast at 112 Cowslip Lane was not her brother.

Hachem's file contained family snapshots and his high school yearbook photo. The most recent photo was for his security pass as a custodial worker at the university. As a high school senior, Hachem looked mature for his age. He was clean shaven except for a pencil-line moustache. Short hair had been neatly combed. The most notable aspect of Mr. Hachem's appearance as a custodial worker, on the other hand, was the overmuch of black hair. His head was big and bushy. The nose perched atop a walrus moustache hooked slightly downward at its tip, reminding Delaney of a hawk settled deeply in a twiggy nest, staring with hatred at the hidden camera that would dare take her picture. But there was something else about Hachem's photos that made Delaney chew his lip and rub his nose. Had he seen Hachem before, around town maybe, in a restaurant or grocery store?

Transcripts of interviews of people who knew Hachem—his neighbors, fellow-workers, and the people back in Dearborn who remembered him as a shy young man—were uninstructive. Most people expressed shock at discovering Hachem's true character. The few who wanted to impress the police said they always knew the guy was up to no good, but they were unforthcoming when asked for details.

Delaney muttered, "Aha!" when he came across the transcript of the interview with Joe Maidin, but "ho hum" would have been the more appropriate interjection. Mr. Maidin answered a series of stock questions and was dismissed. He said he might have seen Basim Hachem sweeping floors and such but had never talked to him and hadn't known his name. He had never been to Michigan, let alone Dearborn, and was not a devout Muslim. He was shocked that still another Middle Easterner had turned to terrorism. It seemed that half the population of Plattefield had been interviewed by the FBI, but no one had mentioned ever seeing Basim Hachem with Joe Maidin.

Of greater interest was the interview with Mrs. Pamela Schultz who on recovering from the blast at 112 Cowslip Lane provided useful information on why the SWAT team and Hachem had arrived at his house at about the same time. She had seen a stranger walking up to Hachem's house after Hachem had gone off to work, she said, but had not seen him leave. Worrying that Hachem might have had a burglar in his house, she called him and asked about it. There had been a considerable time lapse between her seeing the stranger and when she finally got through to Hachem. Investigators believed the stranger was the burglar who called 911. Mrs. Schultz could not provide much of a description of the man except that he was very big and had black hair.

Let's see, Delaney thought as he set out to jog a few miles at five one morning. A burglar walks up to a house in broad daylight and let's himself in. How? Picks the lock? He must have known the owner of the house was at work. Did he know Hachem's name? I think he mentioned Hachem's name in his call to 911. I should double check this. Did the burglar know Hachem? OK, so he rummages around inside for maybe an hour or so and finds evidence that Hachem was a terrorist. Had he been suspicious of Hachem in the first place? Is this why he burgled his house? He drives downtown to call 911. I gotta check the record carefully for the times of various events. The exact times could be important. Why didn't the burglar simply use Hachem's phone? His 911 message smacks of urgency. Very odd. I should listen to the recording of that call sometime, to catch the tone of the guy's voice. But why a burglary in that part of town? The houses there are all rundown. We have had no burglaries reported in that part of town since I joined the force, at least none that I can recall.

Later in the day, at his cubicle in the squad room, Delaney finally got around to reading the file on Professor Suleiman Daoudi, which gave him a headache. It was clear that Attorney General Ashcroft and company wanted either to put Daoudi in jail forever, or, at a minimum, deport him back to Yemen. Professor Daoudi was a devout Muslim and had been highly critical of US foreign policy. He had had the audacity to argue that the Gulf War, which came about because of Papa Bush's careless diplomacy, he said, had been the cause of 9/11. But Delaney saw major difficulties for US prosecutors once the Daoudi case hit the federal courts, where it seemed destined to end up. The only evidence against Daoudi came from Ahmed Hmimssa, a thirty-five year old Moroccan who had committed a string of felonies in several states that could have landed him in jail for 90 years. His sentence would almost certainly be reduced to a slap on the wrist in return for his allegations against Daoudi, one of which said Daoudi was planning to use a crop-duster to spread anthrax over Lambeau Field during a football game. There was no evidence in the record that linked Daoudi with Hmimssa, however. And why would Daoudi have passed along such information to Hmimssa, of all people, without having told anyone else about it? There was no evidence that Daoudi was a pilot, nor was there evidence that he had tried to secure anthrax.

On his way home from work, Delaney met Tom Willison at 112 Cowslip Lane. A fence had been erected to keep the curious and the scavengers at bay. Detective Willison unlocked the gate and the two detectives walked around the hole in the ground. Cracked, blackened concrete basement walls were about all that remained of Hachem's house. Willison had been over the site before and pointed to various things of interest that had not been carted off by the FBI, including the blackened trees, the devastated shrubs in the back yard, and the brick grill that had withstood the blast without much damage. As they walked about and kicked the ashes, Delaney was reminded of the detective stories he liked to read, stories where the protagonist comes across some bit of evidence that although overlooked by everyone else unlocks the mystery. He smiled at the silly notion that just such a bit of evidence was lurking somewhere here among the embers: that he would find it, crack the case, and become world famous. But as he and Willison walked over the torched vegetation on what had been Hachem's patch of earth, he found no telltale matchbook, no initialed cufflink, no overlooked bone or hank of hair.

A thunderbolt struck the Plattefield police the following morning. At an emergency meeting of his troops, Chief Smedegard explained that the DNA tests by the FBI had been completed. There is an 80 percent probability, the FBI report said, that the DNA salvaged from the scene of the blast is not that of Basim Hachem. The report said that a further search for DNA evidence would be undertaken: that possibly Basim Hachem had perished in the blast together with a coconspirator. A murmur of surprise and disbelief arose from the officers. Detective Moran spoke up, saying there had to be a mistake: that there was no way Hachem could have fled the house without being seen: that by the time he had disappeared inside, his men had already surrounded the house. The men who had been there said, yeah, that was true. The officer who had hidden behind a tree and knew better chose not to dampen spirits with a dose of reality, even after Detective Willison wondered aloud whether Hachem might have exited the backdoor unnoticed. He and Delaney had discussed just such a possibility the previous day after visiting the scene of the explosion, he said. He called attention to the stubs that remained of what might have been some fairly thick shrubbery. Could the shrubbery have provided cover for Hachem's sneaking out the backdoor, he asked? His speculations were quickly attacked by various officers and prompted one to ask why one terrorist, the one who had left behind his DNA signature, hadn't also tried to escape out the backdoor if that had been possible? No one could give a plausible explanation. The agreement was widespread that more than one terrorist had likely been in the house at the time of the explosion. Either that or the FBI analysis was faulty. It was concluded that the continuing search for DNA evidence would surely show that Hachem had been killed. Just as the meeting was about to break up, Detective Moran had an idea.

"We've been supposing," he said, "that the man Mrs. Schultz saw walking up to Hachem's door was the burglar who called 911. Maybe he was Hachem's coconspirator, the one who got blown up in the explosion. The unexplained DNA could have come from him, not Hachem."

The murmur of approval of this observation was caught up short by Detective Delaney.

"Maybe," he said, "but I wouldn't bet on it. Mrs. Schultz said she saw the stranger at about 2:30. The burglar called 911 at 3:49. SWAT arrived at 4:50 and killed the alleged coconspirator. Are we to suppose that the coconspirator went to Hachem's house and then left, and that while he was gone the 911 burglar came and left, and that the coconspirator then returned and was blown up? That's a lot of coming and going if you ask me. Otherwise, it would appear that the burglar and the coconspirator were in the house at the same time. The more likely case, it seems to me, is that the coconspirator came to the house after the burglar left, in which case the man Mrs. Schultz saw was the 911 burglar."

A murmur of, Oh yeah, passed through the ranks. And here it must be noted that for all his smarts, Delaney had been bested by his nemesis Detective Moran. But then, how could a bright young detective like Delaney have guessed that two men *had been* in Hachem's house at the same time: that a Bolshevik hit man from LA had been knocked flat by a Fred Astaire groupie, also from LA, wielding a jar of Mayonnaise?

"Well, I suppose that's true," said the chief. "Yes, yes. It seems likely that Mrs. Schultz saw the 911 burglar." (The chief was all too glad to support Delaney's criticism of Moran's hypothesis.) "If Hachem had a coconspirator, we've got to find out who he was and we should also find out who the burglar was. The burglar might have seen something or someone that would help us figure out this case."

"The idea of a coconspirator might explain the stolen car found on the street," Delaney ventured on, "the car stolen in Milwaukee. No one has ever figured out what that car was doing there. True,

Hachem could have stolen it, as the FBI seems to think, but maybe one of Hachem's fellow terrorists swiped it and drove here because some operation was about to be carried out. Some operation that was to involve stuffing explosives in a car along with a detonator. I wonder if the burglar saw the second terrorist coming up the front walk. You see, sir," Delaney added, as if talking mainly to the chief, "I've been puzzled by why the burglar called from a payphone downtown instead of simply calling from Hachem's house."

After the meeting, Delaney wondered whether his hard work playing catch-up might now pay off, whether he might be given a greater role in unraveling the mysteries surrounding Basim Hachem. His wish came true sooner than he imagined. The next day he was assigned to the joint FBI-Plattefield task force investigating terrorism in Plattefield, working under the direct supervision of Detective Tom Willison.

As he walked to the front door at 114 Cowslip Lane, Delaney waved at carpenters working on the right side of the house, presumably repairing damage done by the explosion at 112. He rang the doorbell and waited.

"Yes?" said Mrs. Pamela Schultz from the open doorway.

Delaney introduced himself, showed his identification, and asked Mrs. Schultz if she had time for a few questions. She said she did and ushered him in. She was an elderly lady who moved slowly, but her eyes conveyed the sparkle of a keen mind. She led him to a gloomy sitting room with dark walls, a worn carpet, and faded furniture. The voices of the carpenters outside filtered through gaps in the rough framing around new windows.

"Would you like a cup of coffee or tea?" Mrs. Schultz asked. "I'm thinking of having tea, myself."

"Yes, thank you. Tea would be very nice," he said, though he disliked tea.

After tea was creamed, sugared, and served with utmost politeness, and after friendly chitchat re house repairs and the pleasant weather, Delaney got down to business. He wasn't expecting to learn much beyond what was already in the record, but still, he had had experience with senior citizens, with Grandmother Delaney, in particular, before she passed on. He knew that sometimes, in a relaxed and friendly atmosphere, memories of things forgotten by the elderly can occasionally be resurrected. Thus, he started asking about Basim Hachem, what kind of man he was, what people in the neighborhood had thought of him, whether she had ever witnessed anything or anybody at the Hachem residence that seemed odd or maybe even suspicious. It wasn't until he got around to asking about the suspected burglar, however, that he was able to add a mere sliver of new information to the record.

"Mrs. Schultz," he said, "I know you've been grilled a number of times about the man you saw entering Hachem's house . . ."

"You mean the burglar," Mrs. Schultz interrupted.

"Well, possibly the burglar. We are interested in your description of the man. I'm new to the case, and I'm wondering if you would mind going over what you saw one more time."

"Well, as I told the FBI agents and some other detectives, I didn't get a very good look at him."

"Could you tell me where you were standing?"

"Oh, well sure. I was ironing you see, and I had set up the ironing board by the bay window. You know, so I could see good. That's where I usually do my ironing."

"Could you show my where you were standing?"

With an effort, Mrs. Schultz hauled herself up from her chair and walked over to the window. She stood facing the window and ironed an imaginary piece of clothing.

"Like this," she said, turning to see Delaney over her shoulder. "I usually stand like this with the ironing board in front of me. I looked up and there he was: this man walking up to Mr. Hachem's front door. But I didn't get a good look at him. Too many branches in the way."

"So you didn't see much of his face?"

"No, not much, but enough to lead me to think I hadn't seen him before. He didn't have a beard. He wasn't like Mr. Hachem in that regard. Anyway, I knew Hachem had gone to work, so I watched to see the stranger walking back to his car."

"Did you see his car?"

"Oh, no. That's what I explained to the FBI men. I just assumed he had one. Only he never returned to the street. He never walked back down Hachem's front walk. I figured he must have gone into the house. It was while I was ironing a blouse that I thought maybe he might be a burglar. That's when I tried to call Hachem. I had a dickens of a time getting through to him. I left a message, you see, but he never returned my call, so I called again."

"As you've explained before, Mrs. Schultz, you thought the burglar was a big man."

"Yes, yes. Very big. Oh, excuse me a minute. I'll close the door. My grandson has turned up the volume."

Mrs. Schultz was referring to the thump of hip-hop music coming from the outside, possibly from behind the house. The music reminded Delaney of that Emily played while doing aerobics in their basement rec room.

"How tall would you say he was?" Delaney asked when Mrs. Schultz again sat down. "Over six feet?"

"Easily over six feet. You see, my Albert—he passed on a few years ago—was a little over six feet and the burglar was much taller than that."

"So, would you say, maybe six-foot-five?"

"Taller. When I was younger, I used to like basketball. My husband and I went to nearly all our home games. Maybe that's how I learned to appreciate the heights of men. Now that I think of it again, I would judge that the burglar was in the neighborhood of six-foot-seven."

Wow, thought Delaney. This guy is one big guy.

"What about his build?" he asked. "Was he fat?"

"No. I would not describe him as fat. Muscular, heavy-shouldered. He might have had a paunch, but most men do, don't they?"

Delaney laughed and said, "I'm afraid we do."

"Oh, I wasn't speaking of you, Detective Delaney. Was there anything else?"

"No, that about wraps it up."

Delaney picked up a tray of dishes and tea things and followed Mrs. Schultz across the room. She opened the door and led him through to the kitchen. The thump of hip-hop grew louder. Delaney put the tray on a kitchen table and looked out the patio door. What he saw explained the music. An absurd pantomime horse seemed to be practicing a dance routine. Mrs. Schultz looked on. Because of a misstep on the part of the horse's rear end, the pantomimists stopped and started afresh.

"My grandson and his girlfriend," Mrs. Schultz said. "They've just started. Fred—he's my grandson—seems to think there might be some money in it. I don't know. I wanted him to be a doctor, not the front end of a horse."

"It could be worse," Delaney said, smiling. "He could have been a horse's rear end."

There was a pause in the conversation until Mrs. Schultz laughed and said, "Oh, I see what you mean."

We're looking for a guy who's six-foot-seven, Delaney wrote in his handy-dandy notebook after getting back to the squad room. The FBI report said the man seen by Mrs. Schultz was big. There's big, thought Delaney, and there's six-foot-seven. This guy's a giant. And we should catch him. He saw inside Hachem's house. He could have vital information. Delaney checked out a file he had gone through before; it was as he remembered. Some several seconds prior to the 911 call from the public phone at the corner of Gardner and Seventh Street, there had been another call from that very same phone. The first caller might have seen the second, the burglar, in which case he certainly would remember a man who stood six-foot-seven. He might be able to give a good description of the guy. How many six-foot-seven men would there be roaming around Plattefield? Finding the first caller could be tough, but finding out who he called would be easy. He wondered why this hadn't been done already. He checked with the local phone company. Within the hour Detective Delaney knew that the person who called just prior to the 911 call had dialed Coach Lawrence Coneybear.

Chapter 12

Mani Malakhov had been warmly received getting back from the Midwest. Even his father seemed glad. Ever mindful of his son's interest in sissified pursuits, not to mention his always hanging with half-naked beach boys, he asked if Mani had met any nice girls while he was away. Not wanting to disappoint, Mani said he had, a nice Swedish girl as a matter of fact. He observed as well that Minnesotans drank milk and seemed to be mostly fair-skinned and overweight, details he thought might strengthen the pretense of his having stayed in Minneapolis. His mother noted that he had received a letter from the University of Minnesota and said she was dying to know what it said, whether he had been accepted. Grandma Malakhov again inquired about hockey, and Mani, remembering his father's frowning at his stated interest in figure skating, said that if he went to college he would be much too busy for sports.

Except for frequent phone conversations with Coach Lawrence Coneybear, Mani soon fell back into his old routine. He chopped red cabbage till he was blue in the face, watched the chefs prepare Russian specialties, and partied with his friends. Turning on affection and charm, he soon convinced his girlfriend Genna Woods to forgive his having not called as often as he had promised. They had no sooner kissed and made up than Genna suggested going shopping. Laughing gaily and horsing around, they ambled out of her apartment to the yellow convertible Volkswagen that had been Genna's high school graduation present.

"You drive," she said, throwing him the keys.

"OK. Where are we going?"

"Let's go to Eileen Fisher at Century City. You can help me pick out charmeuse pants. I saw an ad in the paper."

"Oh, honey, charmeuse pants are so ten-minutes-ago."

"Really? We could buy new matching sunglasses."

"Yes, yes. Those new square rimmed glasses the Dutch architects are wearing. I wonder who sells them."

In the weeks that followed, both Mani Malakhov and Coach Coneybear lived under the apprehension of being arrested for this, that, and the other thing: for conspiracy to murder Basim Hachem, stealing Cat Stevens's vest, and defrauding American Family Insurance out of $10,000. The coach of course suffered the additional burden of a lying vitae that might come to light at any moment. Wooo-eee, he often thought as his little friends took effect, overlaying the more somber shades of his life with the brighter hues of the rainbow.

"Hi, Mani. Larry here. How're you doing?"

"Have they found Hachem's DNA?" Mani asked, cutting straight to the chase.

"No, but they've matched the DNA found earlier with DNA found in the stolen car. They think Hachem had a coconspirator, someone who showed up after you took off. They're gonna try to find out who this new guy was sure as shit. Jeez, Mani, things aren't looking good for me."

"For us, Coach, for us. I'm in this thing too, you know. But look, how are they going to find out who this guy was? OK, so they got some strange guy's DNA. They don't have anything to match it with. And the description of him by Hachem's next door neighbor, Mrs. What's Her Name . . ."

"Mrs. Schultz. Pamela Schultz."

"Yeah, whatever. Her description of the guy was certainly vague, at least from what I've been reading in the papers."

"Yeah, but I keep telling you he came to see me. My secretary saw him for chrissake."

"Oh, yeah. I forgot about that, but she hasn't linked the two, has she? You know, the guy who came to see you and the guy who walked into Hachem's house. After all, there must be a lot of big crooks wondering about the place."

"How many guys do you know who stand six-foot-seven? I ask you. And remember the timing. It wasn't long after the guy showed up at my office that he was spotted going into Hachem's house."

"Yeah, I see what you mean. We do have a problem. So what will you tell the cops if they put two and two together?"

"Well, I'll just say what I was able to get out of my secretary. You know, support her story. The guy's name was Paul Smith. He came to tell me my star quarterback made a pass at the wrong time and the wrong place." (Unbidden, a Cole Porter tune popped into the coach's brain. He sang a few bars.)

"What?"

"Oh, nothing."

"But, it's so damned odd. Why would a guy who came to you to complain about a gay football player end up burgling a terrorist's house?"

"What the hell else can I say if they ask me? What am I going to say, for chrissake? I've gotta say something. I sure as hell won't say he was a hit man from LA."

"I wish I could think of something, Coach. Hey, wait a minute. I got it. You could say he wanted money to keep his mouth shut, you know, to protect your star quarterback. Yeah, yeah, that's it."

"Yeah, well, maybe. I'll think about it."

"About the stolen car. Anything more on that?"

"No, just that it was stolen in Denver. And I've told you about the DNA. The cops think the terrorists might have been planing to fill the thing up with explosives and drive it into the Sears Tower garage or something."

"This reminds me, the hit man my papa sent might have stayed someplace other than Plattefield, perhaps to stay clear of the scene of the crime."

"Well, I think that's what happened, else some innkeeper here in Plattefield would have told the police by now about a big goon who checked in but not out. I just hope to hell they don't find where he was staying. He might have left something behind in his room. Thank god there was nothing in the car. Hey, I've got to go. I'll give you a call later."

"OK, Coach. Bye."

Detective Delaney was enjoying a day off. He had tried to reach Coach Lawrence Coneybear both at home and at his office, but the coach wasn't around it seemed, for he had not yet returned the call. Well, he'd keep after the coach, but not on his day off. Delaney sat alone in the living room of the small house where he lived with Emily, who, before bicycling off to register for the fall semester of her senior year, had handed him a list of home projects that needed doing. Delaney wasn't sure he liked the idea of such lists, but figured it was something he'd just have to get used to.

With stockingfeet atop the coffee table, he drank coffee, read the paper, and tried not to notice Emily's list. He was a contented man. He and Emily would start a family as soon as Emily got her degree, found a job, and worked a year or two. They were making plans for furnishing their new three-bedroom house, getting a lawn started, and planting a vegetable garden (Emily's idea). He kept telling himself to get off his fat butt and get to work, but he was in a lazy mood. So he half-heartedly read the sports page and drank tepid coffee.

After several minutes, he rose to refill his cup and remembered what Willison told him the previous afternoon: that the FBI's search for evidence that Pit Bull Peter had run down Michael Patriarca had turned up zip and that Pit Bull Peter's DNA was not found in the stolen car. The FBI's failure to find a mob connection with the hit-and-run on Greenbriar Road now turned Delaney's thoughts once again to Joe Maidin and whether there was a connection between the man from Cairo and the man from Dearborn. He wondered if *Hachem's* DNA should be checked against that found in the car that killed Patriarca. By golly, we ought to do that, he decided, surprised that he hadn't thought of it before. He poked around in a messy drawer below a kitchen desk for a legal-sized writing pad and pencil.

Again comfortably settled on the sofa, he sucked a swallow of hot coffee before picking up the pad and pencil. At the top of the page, he wrote, "Dots." He smiled, recalling his complaint to Emily that he was sick to death of the expression, "connecting the dots." Since 9/11 every guy and his brother were babbling about connecting dots, he told her. Under the heading, he wrote, "Dot 1. Basim Hachem was a terrorist. Why Plattefield?" Delaney chewed his pencil and thought about possible answers; none seemed promising. Had Hachem planned to blow up a student dormitory, he wondered? Mimicking the Oklahoma City bombing? Was he just hanging out in Plattefield? Waiting for a call to duty elsewhere? Mmm, somehow "duty" didn't seem quite the right word.

He sucked up more coffee and then wrote, "Dot 2. Two people killed in Hachem's house." Hachem and someone else. But who was the someone else? No one had reported a missing person. Had a terrorist come from Denver or some other city? Or some other country? Had an attack been near at hand?

"Dot 3. No suspicious bank records or phone calls. No suspicious friends, according to FBI." Hmm. If Maidin had been in on the plot, he had been extremely careful. And what the devil could they have been up to?

"Dot 4. The 911 call from burglar is odd." What would a burglar hope to find in the house of a man as poor as Hachem? In broad daylight? And why call from a payphone? This is driving me kind of nuts.

"Dot 5." But Delaney could think of nothing more to write down. He felt useless and bored.

And then it came to him out of nowhere. The photo of Basim Hachem had reminded him of someone, and now he knew who it was. It was the man with the funny nose he had seen at the Dublin Airport, the man the professor said pushed him. The photo Delaney remembered was not the most recent one, where dark eyes stared from a tumbleweed of black hair. It was rather the photo taken for Hachem's senior class yearbook. There he had smiled a bit. His hair had been slicked back and the hooked tip of his nose was plain to see. Could his fellow officers have erred in thinking Hachem had not escaped the house? As Tom Willison had suggested? But the very idea that Basim Hachem had had an encounter with Professor Willgrubs in Ireland, of all places, and had been at the Dublin Airport at the very same time he and Emily and the Willgrubs had been there was totally absurd. The coincidence would have been staggering. The man at the airport couldn't have been Hachem. Hachem is dead. What am I thinking? Delaney muttered to himself in disgust.

But then a new dot came to mind that brought him to his feet. Why had he and Emily chosen the Derrycross Hotel in Sneem? Because Caroline Maidin had suggested it: that's why. She said that's where she met Joe Maidin: that the Maidins often stayed at the hotel while vacationing in Ireland. If Maidin and Hachem had been fellow terrorists, Hachem might have known about Sneem—and the Derrycross Hotel, too. If Hachem *was* the man at the airport, there would then be a connection between Hachem and Maidin. But why had Hachem been at Sneem?

And Hachem could have been the man who killed the wrong person on Greenbriar Road, Delaney thought, his mind returning to an old suspicion, straying in a new direction instead of answering his self-posed question. Caroline Maidin could never have mentioned the Derrycross Hotel if Hachem had run her down. The real coincidence might well have been Michael Patriarca's deciding to jog down Greenbriar Road on the very day Hachem had planned to kill Caroline Maidin. After that, events followed one another as dutifully as trunk-to-tail elephants in a daisy chain. OK, Delaney muttered to himself, I've got to cool it. I'll first call the professor and arrange to meet him at the police station. We'll look at the Hachem photo together, the one in the yearbook, not the one that's been on TV and in the papers. I won't say anything about my suspicions. Let him come to an unbiased opinion. See if he sees what I see. Whether he does or not, by golly, we're going to check Hachem's DNA against all the

DNA found in the car that killed Michael Patriarca. I've got two ways of connecting Hachem and Maidin, the hotel and the car.

"Hello?" Edna Willgrubs answered the phone.

"Hi, Edna. Patrick here. Is the professor there?"

"Oh, I'm sorry. He left some time ago for Green Valley Farm. He wanted to visit the marsh again. You know how fond he is of wood ducks, and with his new camera, he's taken to photographing everything in sight. Well, it's too bad the professor doesn't have a cell phone. Otherwise you could call him. I've been after him to buy a cell phone, you know, but you know the professor. He's very set in his ways. He says if we had a cell phone he might start using it while he's driving, and you know how he feels about driving and talking on the phone at the same time. By the way, did you know the Olsons had to move out of the house at Green Valley Farm? The professor talked to Mr. Olson about it and I don't think he was very happy about it. I guess Mrs. Olson's in a real snit. Apparently the Maidins are moving in, you know, as a second house. You know how rich people . . ."

"I'm sorry to interrupt, Edna. I'm in a bit of a rush here. If he happens to call would you ask him to call me at my cell phone number right away. Good-bye."

"But Patrick, all I wanted to . . . Patrick? Patrick? Well, I mean really!"

In Delaney's mind, Green Valley Farm had become a dot as big as a bull's-eye. He had gone back to the question of a motive for Hachem's being in Sneem. "Farm animals and bioterrorism: that's what this is about," he said aloud. There had been a fire at some kind of animal disease research center near Sneem. It came back to him in a rush. He had seen just part of the report on TV because Edna had changed channels in search of a weather report. But there was the front page article in a newspaper as well, at the Dublin Airport. There had been concern about the escape of pathogens. Now there were other dots, and the connecting line segments sketched a nasty picture. A terrorist cell had developed in the heart of Dairyland to infect the nation's dairy cows with a contagious disease. Yikes! thought Delaney, mad cow. Yussef Maidin's wife had come into the possession of Green Valley Farm through a bizarre accident. Accident my butt! Delaney fumed. And Green Valley sells cows all over the nation, according to the professor. Caroline *was* the object of a staged accident on Greenbriar Road. Yes, yes. Hachem had run down the wrong person. This is all about mad cow disease.

But another thought sent Delaney running for his cell phone and his .40-Glock pistol. The professor was headed for Green Valley Farm, Edna had said. And what was that about the Olsons no longer living there? That the Maidins were moving in? Something about a second house? If Basim Hachem were hiding out there and the professor saw him, he would never live to tell about it. In minutes, Detective Delaney was in his car racing toward Green Valley Farm. If only I had a squad car instead of this piece of crap, he complained, pushing his Honda Civic to the limit.

He broke every traffic law on the books. Horns honked; drivers shouted; hoisted fingers implied buggery. He waited until traffic thinned before getting on the phone. Sergeant Chad Hutton was the officer on call at the station.

"Listen up, Chad. Delaney here. This is life and death. I've just discovered there is an Al Qaeda cell at Green Valley Farm. I think they're planning some kind of bioterrorist attack against the nation's dairy herd. This could really be important. Professor Willgrubs is headed there now, but he doesn't know what he's getting into. His life might be in danger. I'm driving to Green Valley Farm now, but you've got to send a backup pronto. You got all that?"

"Yeah, sure. I'll get right on it. Al Qaeda. Green Valley Farm. We'll be on our way pronto. You bet, by god."

"Go, go. I'll call back."

Delaney was going to pass a car that had stopped without pulling over, but had to slam on his brakes and get back in line to avoid a head-on collision. He swore under his breath a half-mile further on when he arrived at a railroad crossing just as the arms banged down. An AMTRAK train glided majestically over the tracks as if the engineer hadn't a care in the world.

"Goddamn!" shouted Detective Moran when he was relayed Delaney's message. He couldn't believe his good fortune. He and his entire team had just suited up for a weekly practice run on a make-believe Al Qaeda holdout. They were armed with live ammunition. They had planned to burst into a deserted house intended for demolition. They'd rush from room to room and shoot up a storm. But now! But now they'd shoot actual terrorists, not those silly damned cutouts of Osama bin Laden supplied by the FBI. He took a few seconds to drink in the glory that would be his. He would receive national recognition. He would appear on national news and morning talk shows. There would be write-ups in magazines and newspapers. Now if offered the job of chief of police in Plattefield, he might or might not accept, depending on his other options. Some big place in Texas would be good. Some place like Dallas. He had always liked Texas justice. He was keen on killing killers. Too bad Delaney is the one who discovered the cell, he thought, but SWAT's gonna get the glory all the same. He'd see to it. He'd push the wet-behind-the-big-ears Delaney aside easy as cowflaps.

With more excitement than coherence he explained the new mission to his team and told them to break out more ammunition, that they were going to need it. For several minutes the station was a hubbub of shouting and running about. The secretaries and the officers not on the team did what they could to help. They yelled encouragement. It wasn't until he was in the parking lot, ready to go, that Moran suddenly realized he didn't know where Green Valley Farm was.

"Hey, wait a minute," he barked to men about to climb into the department's two Humvees. "Where in the hell is Green Valley Farm? We gotta figure out how to get there."

"I know where it is, sir," replied Danny Christensen. Danny was a fresh recruit from the Madison Area Technical College and looked no more than 18 years old. He had only recently begun shaving every day. "My dad's farm is out that way," he added by way of explanation.

"Great," Moran replied. "You sit up front with me so you can show the way. OK guys, climb in. We're pulling out, goddamnit."

One of the secretaries who had come outside to wave the brave SWAT team on now rushed back inside to the ladies room where she broke out her cell phone to call her friend.

Meanwhile, out at Green Valley Farm, Professor Myron Willgrubs was in the fight of his life. He had had time for only the most fleeting of thoughts about someone's coming to his rescue, but had known deep down that no one would, that he was on his own, that his chances for survival depended on his own paltry resources. And there was more at stake than his wretched life. Oh, so much more.

The professor had called Troy Olson several days ago about coming out to photograph wood ducks at Green Valley Marsh.

"You're welcome to visit the marsh as far as I'm concerned," Mr. Olson said. "But I should tell you I don't live there any more."

"But who's taking care of the farm?" the professor asked.

"Oh, I'm still doing most of the work there," Mr. Olson replied, "with the help of a couple of other guys. It's just that me and my wife had to move out. The Maidins decided their big new house in Plattefield wasn't enough for them. They had to have a summer house, too, and they're going to redecorate the place and snazz it up. Well, the work was supposed to start a month ago, but I don't see any action around the place. Well, it's their property. They can do what they want with it."

"Perhaps I should call the Maidins to make sure it's all right to walk across their property to see the marsh?

"Oh, I wouldn't bother them if I was you. Hell, it's no big deal. If anyone gives you any flack, you can tell 'em I said it would be OK."

"Well, if you're sure, Mr. Olson. Many thanks."

The first thing the professor did on his arrival at Green Valley Farm was knock on the door of the gracious old yellow brick house. He saw no evidence of someone's being there, but he hoped to greet the Maidins none-the-less. If they *were* there, he would introduce himself and shake hands. He would double check whether it would be permissible for him to walk over their property to see the marsh. He would talk a bit of shop, perhaps drop a comment or two on the current price of cheese, thus to make a valuable contact. Foreign students at the university often desired to see firsthand US farms and talk face-to-face with real live farmers as opposed to professors of agricultural economics who were forever talking about production functions, cost curves, and profit maximization. Green Valley Farm would be an exemplary example of US agriculture, the professor believed. As he waited for someone to answer the door, he noticed a foundation bed of perennials overrun by weeds, but he resisted the temptation to pull a few while he waited. He knocked again, but still no answer. Giving up, he turned and walked away, noticing that like the garden the great lawn wrapped around the old farm house, with its colonnade of black trunks supporting the green canopy far above, was also in need of care. The lank grass was over six inches long at least and looked malnourished. Thistles had begun taking root. The professor disapproved of this of course and wondered if the Maidins were up to the task of running a big farm like Green Valley. Maybe this would *not* be a suitable place for foreign student visitations after all, he began to suspect.

He started across a barnyard stubbly with mowed grass and weeds, heading for a gap between two service buildings that opened onto the snowmobile trail to the marsh. A door to the service building on his left hung open, and he thought he'd stop to see whether someone was inside who should be greeted. Maybe the open door was a mistake, and if he could so determine, he would close it. He veered left unaware that he was under surveillance.

From an upstairs window in the farmhouse, Basim Hachem had been watching an unexpected visitor who seemed familiar. As the visitor approached the house, Hachem caught glimpses of his face through the branches of trees. As the visitor walked away, he was struck by the pear shape, the thin stooped shoulders and apple-shaped bottom. He decided to act when the visitor poked his head into the open door to a barn and hesitated a moment before walking in. He would go after the snoop and find out what he was doing here. On the way to the barn he checked to see if the visitor had by any chance left the keys in the ignition. He had.

"Hello. Is anyone here?" the professor called.

His voice was swallowed up by the dark, cavernous interior of the barn. An eerie silence was the only reply. A musty odor of hay, uneaten corn silage, and rotted manure reminded the professor of his youth on the farm, an odor that was at once offensive but somehow reassuring. He walked in, a bit curious to know what the barn was used for and to ascertain, if possible, whether the door had been left open on purpose. It had been his experience that barn doors were to be kept closed at all times. It took a moment for his eyes to adjust to the dim interior. There were no milking parlors or other equipment for the milking of cows. Hmm, must be the heifer barn, he decided. Yes of course, this is the feeding alley. Curiosity carried him still further into the barn. Near the far end of the alley, he found empty horse-stalls on his right.

He turned back toward the open door when he heard a noise. The figure of a man loomed black and ominous against the glare of the outdoors. Embarrassed and startled, the professor started toward the stranger who flicked on the overhead lights. Instinctively, the professor resisted the propensity to introduce himself at close range and to offer a hearty handshake. Inexplicably, the hair on the nape of his necked bristled.

"Hello," he said. "I'm Professor Willgrubs. Mr. Olson has been kind enough to give me permission to walk over to see the marsh. Have we met?"

"What are you doing in here?" Hachem demanded.

"I'm here to visit the marsh," the professor said, thinking, This face, this face. I've seen this face before. "The door was open," he added, "and I . . . I know where I've seen you before. You were the gentleman at Howth Cove Beach, the gentleman who pushed me. I want to assure you again, sir, that I had no intention whatever of stealing the Japanese gentleman's camera. Remember? And then I saw you again at the airport. I was with my family from Plattefield."

The professor was going to comment on what an extraordinary coincidence this was when other recollections came to mind that caused him to ease backward toward an open door on his left. There was a resemblance of this man to the photo of the bearded Basim Hachem on TV. The suspicious fire at an animal disease research center near Dublin tickled his antennae. Dear me, he thought, I might be in danger here. His pale blue eyes, already magnified by thick glasses, grew to the size of saucers when he saw the stranger trying to withdraw a handgun from his pants pocket. The gun caught on tight folds of cloth, which gave the professor a split second to act, which was all he needed. He ducked through the open door to his left as a shot rang out. A bullet lodged in the door frame with a thud. The professor slammed the door shut behind him and looked desperately about what he perceived was a feed room. He required some means of securing the door, but the only thing near to hand was a scoop shovel. The professor grabbed the shovel and braced the handle up underneath the latch on the door. Perhaps this will hold him whilst I make my escape, he thought.

The feed room had a door to the outside, which he opened and closed quietly behind him, hoping the terrorist would neither see nor hear his egress. He started trotting across a smallish pasture in the direction of a thick woods on the far side. A woods would provide plenty of places for a person to hide, he thought, if only I can get there in time. Two shots sent bullets zinging by his ears. When he turned to see how close his attacker might be, he tripped and fell down, hurting his shoulder and losing his glasses.

He struggled to his feet and put his hands up. The man with the gun approached and said, "You know too much. Now you must die."

The professor's heart tried to stop, but was he the kind of man to give up hope? And now the professor noticed something that both he and the terrorist had been overlooking, namely a one-ton-plus Holstein bull Mr. Olson once said was mean as hell. Instantly the professor knew where he was. He was on ground belonging to Burley Smokes. The bull, apparently standing off to the side, had been watching the action and was now on the move. Sooner or later, the professor reasoned, Mr. Hachem would turn to see the behemoth that was picking up speed behind him, and when he did the professor would act. But he needed time, time, not much, just a little! Please, dear god, he breathed a prayer as he walked up to the would-be killer. He had a plan.

"See here, sir," he said on the premise that no one was ever shot in midsentence. At least this was the case on the British mystery shows he liked to watch with Mrs. Willgrubs on PBS. It's as if—the thought raced through his mind—there were some immutable law stating that once begun a sentence is entitled to an ending, with a period in written material, or a pause in conversation, not unlike a convict's entitlement to a cigarette before the bullets are loosened. The professor only hoped the same law might be stretched to include a small paragraph, providing the intended victim was a fast talker, which he could be in an emergency, jumping with alacrity from one sentence to another, thus minimizing those dangerous lapses.

"There's something you very much need to know," the professor said. "It just so happens that on my way here I stopped at the Plattefield Police Station to speak with my nephew-in-law Detective Patrick Delaney. He and several of the officers there know that I was driving out to Green Valley Farm. Suppose I go missing. They know I'm here. Where do you think" (Dear me, he thought as he talked, the bull is moving rather fast. Can't the terrorist feel the earth shaking? Is he deaf or something?) "they're going to start looking for me when I go missing, which means they're going to come out here. You'd better think about what you're going to say when the police . . ."

When Basim Hachem turned to see what was galumphing up behind him, the professor made his move. He stepped forward and with all his might struck the hand that held the gun. The gun popped free, flying up into the air and landing several feet away near a clump of milkweed. Hachem looked at the professor and then back at the bull. Then he started running across the pasture in the direction of a tree. Two considerations decided the professor against running. First, he could not outrun a bull. Second, he could always wait and at the last second, hopefully with a bit of panache, make like a matador and step aside. If the professor had not lost his glasses, he would have known a third reason for standing still. Burley Smokes's mean yellow eyes were trained on the man in motion. The professor breathed another prayer.

Do mean Holstein bulls, like elephants, never forget? Did Burley Smokes remember both the man who had once bounced a stone off his ribs and the man who had once shown him a kindness and scratched his ears? Are prayers really efficacious? Perhaps it was no more that just a case of a bull excited more by a moving target than by man standing still with his mouth agape. Whatever it was, Burley Smokes brushed past the professor in a fury.

Mr. Hachem won the race to the white oak at the center of Burley Smokes's pasture. With skills he didn't know he had, he climbed to a sturdy branch fifteen feet up at least. There he caught his breath and watched the enraged bull milling around down below, occasionally peering up at him with cruel eyes. After a time the bull clawed at the earth with his big cloven hooves and bellowed his deep frustration. After more time still, he noticed some inviting leaves of grass and began to nibble, as if forgetting his quarry up a tree. Through branches of oak, Hachem saw Professor Willgrubs down on his hands and knees in the distance, no doubt looking for his glasses.

Professor Willgrubs *was* down on his hands and knees, and he *was* looking for his glasses. What he found instead was Hachem's gun.

Chapter 13

Danny Christensen was a nice young man, nice but not real smart. A light complexion set off startlingly his bright blue eyes. His cut-short brown hair stuck up around his cowlick like a tuft of exclamation marks. He was always talking and laughing and fooling around. He was well-liked, but had become aware that his abilities were not always respected: that some of the older cops figured he was a dufus. When the other SWAT guys seemed impressed by his knowing where Green Valley Farm was, his face glowed with pride. He was thrilled to be riding in the lead Humvee, telling the driver where to go. The entire mission rested on his key knowledge. Now, like a poor poker player throwing good money after bad, he couldn't bring himself to admit that he didn't know exactly where Green Valley Farm was. He knew where it was more-or-less, that it was somewhere in the neighborhood now flying past the windows of a speeding Humvee. He kept looking for a great farmstead bright with fresh paint, bristling with blue Harvestores, and festooned by black and white cows with teated bags. Farms whizzed by one by one, but none came even close to his expectation. And, as far as he could recollect, the gravel road they were on would soon T at Highway 68. And then he'd have to say to turn back.

Finally, he saw a driveway worthy of a prestigious farm. It had been recently built or redone and rose high above the adjoining fields. It was wide and well graveled. Gently graded ditches on either side facilitated the runoff of summer rains and provided ample space for plowed snow in the wintertime.

Unfortunately, the driveway ran up a hill blocking from view the presumed farmstead at its terminus. Danny Christensen was worried, but what could he do? If this isn't the right place, he told himself, wiping a sheen of sweat from his forehead and glancing nervously at Moran, someone here will be able to tell us where Green Valley Farm is; it can't be far from here. Thus, did Danny Christensen draw to an inside straight, not knowing the deck was stacked against him.

"Turn here," he barked. "Up here on the right."

The Humvees tore up the hill, raising dust and spraying newly spread gravel. Danny's heart sank when the buildings came into view. In dire need of paint, the small clapboard house stood depression gray in a dusty yard overrun by red chickens, reminding him of the Ma and Pa Kettle movies he'd seen on TV. The barn leaned precariously toward the east, a standing witness (but barely) to a great storm that had blown in from the west in the summer of 1949. Its siding was only marginally better than that of the house. Several outbuildings were collapsing in slow motion. A broken-down corncrib looked like rat heaven. Danny decided that when the Humvee stopped, he would bail out and run to the front door. He wouldn't listen to orders. He'd run, and he'd ask if this was Green Valley Farm, and if it wasn't, he'd ask where it was. No one would get pissed just because he was a few miles off.

Inside the house Harriet Hoffnagel stopped peeling a potato when she heard the sound of engines out front. She was suspicious, for she and her husband Elmer never had visitors, not counting their son Derrick who sometimes brought his family down from Ashland for Christmas. Though not in recent years, he hadn't: the ungrateful skunk. She wiped her hands on a dirty apron before twitching a dusty lace curtain to see who it was. What she saw in the yard set off alarm bells: two of the strangest vehicles she had ever seen in her life were disgorging men in suspicious uniforms, helmets, and goggles. They were carrying alien guns. One seemed to be running toward the front door. And then it came to her. It was just as Elmer had been predicting for years, warning about them black helicopters that flew over once in awhile taking pitchers. The United Nations was taking over America sure as the dickens, and be darned if she was going to let them get the family farm without a fight. She locked the front door and ran to the pantry where her husband kept his two-barrel, twelve-gauge shotgun. She picked up the gun, put a handful of shells in the pocket of her apron, and struggled up stairs, getting dizzier with each step and ignoring the knock at the front door. Someone was yelling in the yard, but she ignored that too. She opened a window in what had been her son Derrick's poky room, stuck the gun through the rusty screen, and pulled the trigger. She hadn't counted on the recoil of a twelve-gauge shotgun, however, which pushed her backward and threatened to knock her over. Striving to catch her balance, she inadvertently pulled the second trigger. Two blasts in rapid succession reverberated off the old gray barn. Sparrows in nearby box elder trees scattered like birdshot. Pigeons in the barn's hayloft wheeled into the sky and escaped south in a winged formation. The first blast of buckshot killed three chickens. The second tore a huge hole in the ceiling of Derrick's room and knocked Mrs. Hoffnagel off her feet. She landed on the floor with a thud. Stretched out flat on planks of oak, a smoking gun at her side, she lay perfectly still.

"Danny," screamed Detective Phillip Moran, "get your ass back here. OK, guys. You know what to do."

Boy, did they ever. With the demolition of Basim Hachem's house under their belts, they knew exactly what to do. As heavy shelling commenced, the Hoffnagel residence, having survived wind, rain, and hail for the seventy years of its life, began settling toward the ground. Lucky for Mrs. Hoffnagel, Detective Moran had forgotten to bring his grenade launcher. After five minutes, to save ammunition for a possible further fight, he signaled the shelling to stop. The air was thick with the smoke of burned cordite. Hot brass bullet casings littered ground where, minutes earlier, chickens had been pecking for grit. The men looked with satisfaction at a job well done and waited impatiently for Moran to give the signal to storm the house; to charge from room to room and wipe out any surviving terrorists.

A popping noise caused the team to wheel around toward the barn. There they noticed for the first time that a large sliding door on the side of the barn was open. Had it been open all the time? Or had it been slammed open just a second ago? Alone among his teammates, Danny Christensen knew the door was wide enough to accommodate a manure spreader. The men approached the barn cautiously, thinking not so much about manure spreaders as about a fast moving get-away vehicle with Tommy guns blazing from every window a la *Bonnie and Clyde*.

Detective Moran manned the bullhorn to demand surrender of anyone inside, but there was no response. A second summons fared no better. Because he feared the remaining ammunition was insufficient for decimating an entire barn, Moran knew *someone* had to go inside. But why me, he thought? He didn't want to lose face by asking someone else to do what he was afraid to do, which meant he had to do it himself.

He handed the bullhorn to a nearby officer, drew his handgun, and ran to the side of the barn. He inched his way toward the open door and stepped inside.

"Anyone in here?" he yelled.

There was no reply, and he could hardly see a thing. The barn had only a few glass windows. Broken ones had been boarded up. Interior walls further restricted what light passed through panes of glass clouded by decades of fly specks, cobwebs, and the spray from cow tails dipped in watery manure. Trying to breathe in as little as possible the abominable air, Detective Moran waited for his eyes to adapt. He saw something in a corner, but couldn't quite make out what it was. He advanced cautiously.

"Hands *up*?" he said in a quiet, uncertain voice.

Something spotted and moving fast struck him in the thighs and sent him sprawling. His handgun discharged with a sharp bang. Outside the men looked on in astonishment as a billy goat dashed out the open door, slued around the corner of the barn, and disappeared.

"Help," cried Moran from inside. "I've been shot."

His team responded in a rush. Inside the barn they spread out, ready to blast to kingdom come any terrorists lurking among the stanchions or in the mangers. Danny Christensen, mindless of danger to his person, rushed to Detective Moran's aid and discovered the injury appeared to be in the detective's right foot. With the help of another officer they carried him out into the yard and set him down on the ground not far from the Humvees.

"Oh, oh," he wailed, "Take it easy. Jesus Christ does my foot hurt. Who shot me?"

None would say what all feared was true. Their fearless leader, felled by a goat, had shot himself in the foot. A moment's uncertainty hung in the air as the men shuffled about. Their embarrassment was alleviated by the sound of an approaching tractor. In a few moments, a rusty green John Deere putt-putted its way at max speed up to where the men had gathered round their fallen comrade.

A grizzly old farmer in bibbed overalls climbed down from the tractor and said, "What in tarnation's goin' on here?" He spat a brown splash of tobacco juice contemptuously.

"Sir, is this Green Valley Farm?" Danny Christensen asked. His fellow officers, city slickers all, were shocked. It hadn't occurred to any of them that the Hoffnagel farmstead, due death by bulldozer for thirty years at least, was other than that of Green Valley Farm. What did they know of farming?

Arrested by the crack of timber as the house settled another half-inch, Elmer Hoffnagel turned away from the men to look at the house. "What's happened to the house?" he squawked, no longer interested in the men from outer space. "What's happened to the missus?" Slowed by an arthritic limp, he loped toward the house like a lame horse. The SWAT team looked on with grave apprehension. Had they got the wrong place?

Burley Smokes had exerted himself excessively in the pursuit of a bioterrorist. A dizzy spell came over him as he nibbled grass. The spell was not altogether displeasing, rather like a buzz from a strong cigarette, except of course Burley Smokes had never enjoyed a cigarette despite a lifetime of frequent ejaculations. Beyond the shade of the only tree in his pasture, the great bull lay down on the sweet warm earth, closed his yellow eyes, and died. He had lived his life.

Time passed, and Basim Hachem slowly came to appreciate the new situation. While the professor crawled around on his hands and knees looking for his glasses, Hachem came to understand from his perch in the tree that the infidel bull had died. He shinnied down the tree and withdrew from his pocket a switch blade. He would cut the throat of this beast. If the bull's heart were still beating, he would witness a flow of blood. His intention to thus glorify Allah was arrested by the sight of Professor Willgrubs scampering toward the heifer barn. Knife in hand, Hachem ran after him. It was essential the professor be killed before he could summon help.

Professor Willgrubs beat a shortcut through the heifer barn to his car. Bother that his driver's license restricted his operating a motor vehicle without corrective lenses, he would drive to a neighbor or to Hunters Point. He would alert the authorities forthwith. True, he had Hachem's gun, but what good was that without his glasses. He might aim at Hachem, but hit the broadside of a barn instead. And suppose there were other terrorists about. No, he must not stand his ground. He must flee. When he got to his car, he couldn't believe his faulty eyes. Hadn't he left the keys in the ignition? Just in case someone had to move his car while he was at the marsh? To make way for some big piece of farm machinery? He had figured it was unlikely that that might happen, but one never knows; and one would have hated to have been a bother. Now he searched his pockets in vain. His keys weren't there, either.

Oh dear, he thought, I must have lost them in the pasture when I fell. What to do? he dithered. Oh, what to do? I must summon help, he decided: that's the imperative. I'll walk for help. He took off briskly down the driveway.

Basim Hachem had his knife, but he wanted his gun, too. So he stopped to look for it. Professor Willgrubs wasn't going anywhere. And since the house was locked, the professor wouldn't be using the phone either. Still, he wanted the professor dead and the sooner the better. A few minutes elapsed before he realized the professor might have already found the gun. He would take extreme care. He snuck into the barn, brandished his knife, and looked about. He could neither hear nor see anybody. Then he heard a car door slam. He raced to the open barn door and peaked out. He saw the indefatigable professor hurrying down the driveway with the gun in his hand, probably to get help. He smiled to himself at the plan that sprang to mind. He waited until the professor had walked the length of the driveway and turned left. Then he ran to the car and climbed in.

Professor Willgrubs hurried down a gravel road, but stopped when he heard a car coming from behind. Good, he thought, I'll hail a ride. He peered into the greenish gauze of distance, made a stop sign with his hand, and waited for the vehicle to appear. When it did, he was struck by two thoughts in rapid succession: first, this car is familiar, and second, someone is endeavoring to run me down with my own car. With remarkable agility for a man his age and musculature, he skipped over the shoulder of the road and flung himself into the ditch. The car dug a track in the soft gravelly shoulder of the road, careened back onto the roadbed, and, almost sailing into the left ditch, skidded to a stop.

Hachem cussed at having failed to run the professor over. He backed up in the hope of another try. Perhaps the professor might climb back onto the road, he thought. If not, perhaps he could simply drive the car right down into the ditch and nail him there. True, the professor had a gun, but he had a car.

Never in his wildest dreams did Professor Willgrubs ever suppose that he might one day find himself in his present predicament, out on a road in open countryside with someone trying to run him down with a car. He had thought about it, however, in connection with the movies he had seen. He had in fact groused to his lady more than once about movie directors who would have one believe that any protagonist in his right mind, running for his life from someone driving a car, would be so stupid as to run down the road or anyplace else, for that matter, where a car could follow. The man would obviously look for an escape route inaccessible to a villain in a motor vehicle, he had explained to his wife. The professor was now confronted by the necessity of heeding his own advice. The problem of course was the absence of crowded parking lots, open doorways, or narrow alleys between buildings. There were no small lakes or rivers one might ford, or rocky gullies a car could not traverse, or woods thick with trees and brush. But one thing was clear to him. He wasn't simply going to run down the road, or, for that matter, along the bottom of a nicely carved ditch traversable by a motor vehicle. All these ideas passed quickly through his mind before he noticed what he was pretty sure was a cornfield. Ah, a place to hide, he thought. He climbed up the far side of the ditch and ran for a field.

He soon found himself among stalks of corn over seven feet high. It was like a jungle. His first thought was simply to lose himself in the field—it would be so easy to do—but then a more aggressive strategy came to him, for there was more to this chase than his own life, much more. He ran down a furrow between two rows of corn, scuffing the soil with his feet from time to time to make obvious his path of escape. Then he backtracked several feet before stepping through a row of corn. He sat on the ground and fine-tuned his position to see however blurry anyone following him. He took the gun from his pocket, undid what he was pretty sure was the safety catch, and waited for the man he knew would follow. He didn't have long to wait.

When he saw the dark blur of a man running toward him through the corn, he held the gun with both hands, aimed, and pulled the trigger at close range. The shot was followed almost instantly by a cry of pain as the stranger fell backward to the ground. From a safe distance, the professor looked down on the man. Blood stained his midsection. The professor stumbled out of the cornfield back onto the road. He was afraid he was going to be sick, that he might pass out. He sat down on the shoulder of the road, curled his legs to one side, and supported his upper torso with his arms. Saliva filled his mouth and he swallowed. Then he threw up, unmindful of a car that had skidded to a stop nearby.

"Professor, are you all right?"

The voice was that of Detective Delaney. It was all too much for the professor. His nose became snotty and he began to cry.

Driving hell-bent-for-leather toward Green Valley Farm, Detective Delaney had cautioned himself more than once to slow down to avoid an accident: that the professor's life might hang in the balance, not to mention his own and those of startled farmers on their way to town. His cell phone rang from time to time, but he refused to pick it up. He would wait until the traffic thinned. Well beyond the town limits of Plattefield he called the station a second time to make sure there had been no snafu, that indeed a backup force was on its way. Then he called Detective Willison and learned that Willison had been trying to reach *him*. In a police cruiser, with sirens screaming and lights blazing, Willison said he was also headed for Green Valley Farm and that two ambulances were not far behind. He said Sheriff Summerfield had been alerted too: that he and a few deputies were planning to rendezvous with the SWAT team at the farm. Because Delaney wanted his fellow officers to know what *he* knew, he gave Willison a quick overview, explaining why he figured Hachem was alive, why Hachem and Maidin were part of a terrorist cell, and why it was imperative to arrest Joe and Caroline Maidin immediately. Willison said he'd organize the arrests pronto and hung up.

Detective Moran had also been trying to reach Delaney, and when he finally succeeded, he barked,

"Delaney? Moran here. Now, what . . ."

"Where are you guys?" Delaney asked.

"We're about ten miles out of town. Now, there's . . ."

"Do you guys know were the farm is?"

"Well, what the fuck do you think? That we'd just go for a

drive in the country and ask around? Now listen up, goddamnit, you're not to go near the farm until we get there."

"But Professor Willgrubs's life could be in danger!"

"Tough tits, kiddo. We're talking about the security of our nation here, and we ain't going to let some dumb-ass professor fuck it up. Now you listen to me, and this is an order, you're . . ."

"Hey, say again. You're breaking . . . I didn't . . ."

Delaney brushed the mouthpiece of his cell phone across the dash board.

"Don't pull this bullshit on me," Moran screamed.

"What? What? What was . . ."

Delaney brushed the phone against the dashboard some more and then turned it off. It was just as well, for he could see the first turnoff coming up fast and after that he would be on country roads and didn't want to be on the phone anyway. And screw you, Phil, he muttered under his breath. Then he had to concentrate on how best to approach the farm. Go in with his horn blazing? Park by the road and go by foot? Drive into the yard, walk up to the door, and say he was a salesman from Duffy Feeds? In baggy shorts and a faded blue T-shirt? He elected to sell feed despite his clothes. He would tuck his handgun under the waist band of his shorts above his backside. And he'd turn off the safety catch, too, by god, bother the risk to his bum.

When Detective Delaney saw the professor sitting on the shoulder of the road, with his car half in the ditch and a door hanging open, he figured there had been an accident. Though far from his articulate self, the professor explained how a man had tried to kill him, how a Holstein bull he had once assisted had returned the favor, and how in the cornfield, just beyond the ditch, he had shot a man, a man he believed was Basim Hachem.

"Can you show me where the man is?" Delaney asked.

The professor started getting to his feet. Delaney lent a hand and steadied him by holding onto his arm. The professor walked slowly to the leafy entrance between two rows of corn and pointed. "He's in there," he said. "He's in a bad way I'm afraid."

Delaney walked slowly forward into a green pool of shadows and leaves. In thirty feet or so, he came upon Basim Hachem, left arm stretched out toward stalks of corn, right arm at his side. He lay perfectly still. His face was the color of ashes. His eyes were closed. Above his navel, a stain of blood had seeped through his shirt to the shape and size of a plate. Was he dead? Could he somehow be helped? Delaney leaned over to look for signs of breathing and was startled when Hachem's eyes blinked open.

In a flash, Hachem thrust a knife, but strength failed intent. He had wanted to hit the heart, but his knife struck a rib and glanced off. His arm fell back.

For a moment Delaney could not breath for the pain. Then he groaned and, holding his side, stood up and kicked Hachem's knife away from his opened hand.

"Allah, be praised," Hachem murmured. His eyelids relaxed. His eyes became cloudy even as a little smile played across his face.

"Fool," Delaney said, but then, in a kind of prayer, wondered if god, at least, suffered fools gladly.

He walked slowly out of the field into the sunshine, holding his side. The professor was again sitting on the ground.

"You've got to help me," Delaney said.

The professor looked up and leapt to his feet when he saw the blood seeping through Delaney's T-shirt. "Oh, Patrick, my boy," he said. "What's happened?"

"I was careless. He got me with a knife. I don't think it's bad. Just a flesh wound. I've got to get to the hospital."

And then it was the professor's turn to help the detective. Together they moved slowly down one side of the ditch and up the other onto the road.

"I'll drive," the professor said, as they headed toward Delaney's car. "You'll have to help me since I've lost my glasses. I can see the side of the road OK, which I'll stay close to, but you've got to keep a lookout for oncoming traffic and road signs."

"No, wait," Delaney murmured, leaning against the car. "The cell phone. Get the phone. On the front seat. I've got to call Willison."

"Willison?" Delaney spoke into the phone.

"I've been trying to reach you. Where in the hell are you? What's happening man?"

"I'm hurt, Tom. I think Hachem is dead now, but he got me with a knife. We're a quarter mile or so from the farm, on the side of the road. We're close to the driveway to Green Valley. The professor's here. He's going to take me to the hospital, but I've got to . . ."

"No, no! Goddamnit Delaney, stay right where you're at. The ambulance will take you in. They're going to be there in a minute. Now let me make sure I've got this right. You're parked on the side of the road not far from the driveway to Green Valley Farm. Hey, I think I can see you guys now. I'm calling the ambulance."

"Tom?"

He was too late. Willison was on the radio to the lead ambulance. Delaney had wanted to ask about the SWAT team. He had wanted to say how important it was for the SWAT team to seize control of Green Valley Farm as soon as possible. He could hear the siren in the distance now, coming ever closer, which made him wonder why Willison and the ambulances were arriving ahead of SWAT.

Chapter 14

Chief Eugene Smedegard and his wife Gertrude sat in their pine-paneled family room watching TV and waiting for the five-thirty news on ABC. They were joined by a fat tabby cat splayed on the sofa with an eye trained through a window to the backyard. Mrs. Smedegard sat next to the cat and now and again gave him a little pet. He rippled furry hide in appreciation without losing for a moment his concentration on songbirds chittering about a birdfeeder. In rather high spirits, the chief sat in his favorite chair armed with the remote for the VCR. For the second time in his life, he would appear on national TV, and there would be further appearances, he was sure, before he retired and decamped for Florida.

Over dinner he would tell his wife all, of his plan to retire and to recommend Tom Willison for the new Chief of Police. What a great sendoff this will be for us, he had been thinking since arriving home late from work. And what a capstone for my career. He wanted to jump up in the air and click his heels, but knew better than to try, lest he end up at the Plattefield Memorial Hospital where two of his detectives already lay abed. Contributing to his consummate bliss was the parting gift he would leave to the good people of Plattefield: the maggoty carcass of Detective Phillip Moran, hoisted on a pike for crows to peck. When symphonic music swelled, the chief depressed the red record button, settled back, and waited for Peter Jennings to speak, which he did:

In an astonishing new development today, the terrorist Basim

Hachem, thought to have been killed earlier, was shot to death in a cornfield near Plattefield, Wisconsin. The Plattefield police now believe that an Al Qaeda cell has lain dormant in Plattefield for several years planning a bioterrorist attack against the nation's livestock industry. The plan involved infecting dairy cows with a highly contagious disease, possibly mad cow or foot-and-mouth. The suspected ringleader, Joe Maidin, previously known as Yussef Maidin, disappeared before the Plattefield police could arrest him. He is now the subject of a nationwide manhunt. Joe Maidin's wife Caroline Maidin is in police custody and is said to be cooperating with the authorities. Now, live from Plattefield, here is Clyde Morrison with the latest report.

One of those awkward pauses occurred while Mr. Jennings and the camera stared at each other as they waited for Mr. Morrison to appear, which he did momentarily, though not before Mrs. Smedegard was able to say, "My word, Eugene! Why didn't you say something?" Mr. Morrison stood before tasseled stalks of corn. He spoke into a handheld microphone and told the extraordinary story of a professor of agricultural economics at the University of Wisconsin-Plattefield who had teamed up with a Holstein bull named Burley Smokes to thwart and kill the suspected bioterrorist Basim Hachem, and how Hachem, near death, had stabbed Police Detective Patrick Delaney. He went on to explain that it was Detective Delaney's investigation that had unraveled the terrorist plot, but that a key member of the cell, its probable mastermind, had disappeared: that a nationwide search was now in progress to apprehend Yussef Maidin and any other terrorists who might have been involved.

Mr. Jennings reappeared. According to his further report, Dr. Mirza Paracha had been arrested in Ireland on charges of arson and terrorism. It is believed, he said, that Dr. Paracha had supplied Basim Hachem with vials containing deadly animal viruses. He explained that Detective Delaney had come across a crucial piece of evidence while on his honeymoon in Ireland with his wife Emily and his in-laws Professor Myron Willgrubs and his wife Edna Willgrubs. (The chief was pretty sure he detected a telltale grin on Mr. Jennings' face, but it was so subtle and fleeting that it was hard to say for sure.) Originally from Pakistan, Dr. Paracha had received his Ph. D. in Veterinary Medicine at Iowa State University, according to Mr. Jennings, who went on to say that no other suspected terrorist had yet been arrested in Ireland. He said that Detective Delaney was taken to the Plattefield Memorial Hospital where doctors said he is in a satisfactory condition and will soon be released. Mr. Jennings then introduced still another bit of tape, this one covering a news conference called by Plattefield's Chief of Police Eugene Smedegard.

It became clear that it was the chief's opening statement and his answers to follow-up questions that had provided the information previously reported both by Peter Jennings and Clyde Morrison. Repetition is forgivable in cases such as these, however, and there was one item worthy of national attention that had not been previously reported. Not far into the question and answer period, a reporter shouted a question about Plattefield's SWAT team and whether the team had raided the wrong farm. The chief had known it was coming. A little voice inside him had said, I thought you'd never ask. His manner was serious. His expression was troubled and sad. There was no trace of the mirth that roiled his gut and threatened to evoke a burst of laughter. With staid composure, he said:

This afternoon the Plattefield SWAT team, under the leadership of Detective Philip Moran, raided a farm owned by Elmer and Harriet Hoffnagel who we believe had nothing to do with the terrorist plot. Their farmhouse was apparently wrecked beyond repair. More importantly, Mrs. Harriet Hoffnagel, in the house at the time of the assault, was knocked unconscious and is now under a doctor's care at the Plattefield Memorial Hospital. Detective Moran was also wounded in the raid. It appears that he was knocked down by a goat and accidentally shot himself in the right foot. He, too, is recuperating at the hospital. Because Detective Moran is responsible for the SWAT team's raid on the wrong farm, I have relieved him of his duties pending a further investigation. He will remain on the payroll for the time being.

The chief knew Harriet Hoffnagel might have taken a couple of shots at the Humvees, but he declined to comment on that. His silence on the matter could be justified, he believed, should a justification later prove necessary, by his saying that he wanted to be absolutely sure of his ground before charging, or even hinting, that Mrs. Hoffnagel might have fired on the police. Dead chickens on the ground and spent shotgun shells on an upstairs floor clearly require investigation, he would say, were he forced to say something more.

"Coach, did you catch the news? My god, it is *so* fantastic! Do you realize we've changed the history of the world?" (Mani Malakhov had rung up Coach Lawrence Coneybear.)

"I do, indeed, my friend, and for the better. We're heroes, Mani. We're heroes."

"But what about this Maidin character? How did he get away? Do they know yet?"

"What I'm hearing is that he was in our main library and overheard some coed yakking away on her cell phone, telling her mamma about the SWAT team's going to raid Green Valley Farm, saying that the news had just been on the radio. When questioned by the FBI, she said she saw a man who looked like Maidin running down a stairwell. Well, who knows what really happened?"

"He must have had an escape plan. You know, like Hachem. Do you think they're going to catch him?"

"Oh, yeah. They'll nail his ass good. There's going to be a reward sure as shit. We're the ones who should get an award. Jeez."

"You didn't know him, did you?"

"Hell, no. And Hachem never mentioned him, either. Those guys were keeping their cards mighty close to their vest. What's worrying me, though, is the goon that got blown up. Now more than ever they're gonna want to know who he was, where he came from, who his friends were. See what I mean? They'll be looking for accomplices. They won't rest until they figure out who the goon was."

"This Delaney who got stabbed: isn't he the cop who called you? Maybe he'll forget about whatever it was he wanted to ask you. If I were you, Coach, I wouldn't return his call."

"I'm not. If he asks about my not returning his call, I'll say I didn't want to bother him 'cause of his injury. I'll be so goddamned noble. What I can't get over, Mani, is the great service we've done for our country. We're unsung heroes, you and me. I hate being unsung."

"So do I, but what can we do? My god, if we stepped forward, they'd throw our asses in jail forever. Oh, I almost forgot to tell you. My papa said something interesting at lunch yesterday. It seems one of his Russian acquaintances has gone missing. I asked him what the guy's name was, but he just hunched his shoulders and said it wasn't important. As soon as we find out who's missing here in LA we're gonna know who the guy was who went up in smoke."

"Just so the authorities don't know. Jeez, what a mess we'd be in if they find out his name. This whole thing could blow up, Mani. This whole damned thing."

That afternoon, at work in the kitchen at Petrouchka's, Mani Malakhov remembered a word the coach had used, "unsung." The word slipped in and out of his consciousness as he washed and chopped heaps of leeks and beets. All the while a thought was fomenting in his brain that he knew nothing about. And when it came to him, it came full-blown, like a rose bud unfolding before a time-lapse camera. It opened in all its beauty just like that. The coach should chuck coaching, move to LA, and become a cabaret singer. With that fine tenor voice of his? No problemo. He could sing his own songs, too. Like Bumper Car Baby. Hey, maybe he could write a ballad about us and what we've done for America. Awesome. I could help him develop a style. I could become his agent!

"Stop daydreaming to get work finished," Victor Malakhov admonished his son.

How would you like if I shove leek up your fucking potato

nose, Mani thought. Was Mani Malakhov at last getting ready to break away?

Detective Delaney was enjoying the dubious luxury of a private hospital room with a view. He was feeling no pain. Drip by drip, the IV that administered a doctor's brew of electrolytes and nutrients included a narcotic for good measure. When he woke up from one of his innumerable catnaps, he turned his head to see if Emily was there. She wasn't, but her book was, lying on the side of his bed. She would be back. He pressed a button to raise the top half of his bed so he could see out the window. His room was in a new addition to the hospital and he could see newly landscaped grounds: bright green grass, scrubby shrubs, and saplings supported by steel posts and ties. Beyond the grounds were fields and beyond the fields, in the far distance, faded blue hills. Only vaguely aware that his euphoria was the product of a narcotic, he drank in the view, confident that everything would be OK: that the world was a really swell place. He heard someone in the hall and turned his eyes toward the door. When Emily came into the room, he was one of the happiest men alive, which is saying something.

"Hello, copper," she said. She bent and kissed him full on the mouth. "How are you feeling?"

"Just fine, baby. Just fine."

"The doctor said you can come home tomorrow, or the next day at the latest, but that you mustn't think about going back to work for at least two weeks."

"Good. It'll be like a second honeymoon."

"Oh? Maybe I should invite my auntie and the professor to stay with us during your convalescence."

"I'll wring your pretty neck."

"When you're feeling better, honey, we've got to have a long talk about your carelessness. You should have checked Hachem for weapons."

"I feel pretty stupid about that. I'll be more careful from now on. Promise. Have they caught Joe Maidin?"

"Not yet, but they will. Everyone's looking for him."

"Yeah, except me."

"And whose fault is that?"

"Oh, Emily, don't be so hard on me."

If he hadn't said her name, she would have been tough as nails. She had been steeling herself to be tough as nails. She would learn to take in stride her husbands' being away at odd hours and that he would sometimes be exposed to danger. And she had spilled tears lavishly before learning that her husband's injury had not been serious. Now, when he said her name, she remembered what that had been like, of not knowing whether he would survive, of not knowing whether she would live her life without him. She took his hand, raised it to her face, and wiped away fresh tears.

Delaney was taken off his IV the following day, and reality made him frown and look for hangnails to chew. Detective Tom Willison stopped by to cheer him up and tell him the latest news.

"We didn't find a damn thing at Green Valley Farm," Detective Willison said when Delaney asked about it. "There was no computer in the house, no documents, correspondence, nothing. It was clear Hachem had been staying there, of course."

"What about Hachem's billfold?" Delaney said. "Didn't he have a billfold?"

"Yeah, I was coming to that. Get this. He had stolen the identity of a man in New Jersey. About five years ago there was a break-in at the main office of FalEast Healthcare Alliance in New York City. The names, addresses, telephone numbers, birth dates, and Social Security numbers of about 50,000 patients were stolen. You see the information was on laptops and computer hard drives that were taken from the building. A lot of the records included credit card numbers. OK, this information would be valuable to people who wanted to use other people's credit cards and invade their bank deposits. But here's the odd thing. As far as we know, no one has peddled the records to would-be thieves. No one has used the records to steal from FalEast patients. So, why the theft? The FBI guys worry that the theft was the work of terrorists who wanted new identities, not to run up purchases on credit cards, but to allow easy access to passports and to be able to move freely anywhere in the world. And you see they could search for identities that suited their purposes. Well, Hachem's billfold showed that he had stolen the identity of Abdulaziz el-Atriss, if I'm pronouncing the name right, from Union City, New Jersey. The real Mr. el-Atriss had no clue because Hachem had never used the stolen identity to steal. El-Atriss's credit card statements and credit reports were always in order, so there was no way of knowing what was going on."

"Well, I suppose Joe Maidin also had access to false identities. If he isn't caught soon, he'll slip out of the country. What of Hachem's movements? Have they been traced?"

"We know he flew from Kennedy Airport to Dublin on a round trip ticket. He paid for it using traveler's checks made in the name of el-Atriss. Presumably, Hachem bought these checks using cash. This happened two days after his house was blown up. You probably know from TV that the Brits have taken into custody a Pakistani who worked at the Reeks Animal Disease Research Center in Ireland. It's just as you thought, Pat. The fire was a cover-up. The Pakistani Mirza Paracha was a researcher with a Ph. D., and he's admitted to the theft of several vials of livestock serum laced with foot-and-mouth-disease virus."

"Does it kill the animals? Is it mainly a cow disease?"

"I'm no expert, but from what I've read thus far the disease is highly contagious. It affects most cloven-hoofed animals. It doesn't kill mature animals ordinarily but it does seriously restrict meat and milk production. You see, the animals get terrible sores in their mouths and won't eat. Hey, just a minute."

Detective Willison was interrupted by his cell phone. He had a brief conversation before saying he had to scoot.

Fame had been foisted upon Professor Myron Willgrubs, who proved to be a most reluctant recipient. The very idea that a milquetoasty professor of agricultural economics, whose life history excluded military experience, had brought down a terrorist single handedly was a story the mass media found irresistible. Newspaper and TV executives went berserk. An army of reporters descended on the professor. They called, sent telegrams, flooded his email, and filled the mailbox at the end of his driveway. They trashed his lawn and gardens, peeked in the windows, bribed neighbors, interviewed university colleagues and students, and harassed the professor's niece. The chancellor of the Plattefield campus arranged for Professor Willgrubs to take a paid leave until the whirlwind spent itself, which allowed the professor and his wife to hunker down inside their little house. The professor found solace looking through the Encyclopedia Britannica for articles of particular interest, which he then read and often shared with his wife. The Willgrubs's attorney read a prepared statement urging reporters to respect the professor's desire for privacy, but in the question and answer period, the reporters demanded to know what the professor was really like.

The basics of Professor Willgrubs's life history and work for the university and the story of how he came to shoot a terrorist became common knowledge across the nation and, indeed, the world. Several New York Book Publishers began intensive explorations as to just what kind of deal they could offer the professor to get his story in his own words. Those who perused his textbook on agribusiness management, written fifteen years earlier for sophomores majoring in agricultural economics, were disheartened, and there was talk of ghost writers and creative editors.

Emily Delaney also attracted considerable attention after appearing on CNN News. Her great looks, poise, and cool demeanor and the heartfelt manner with which she explained the professor's preference for privacy, which she inadvertently pronounced the way the Brits do, which came about because she often watched mysteries on PBS with her uncle and aunt, not to mention that she was nervous, raised a buzz of excitement among Hollywood agents. This kid's got talent, it was said all around. She should dump her hubby, take a few acting lessons, and get bigger boobies.

But then a bomb fell, and all the possible book deals, TV deals, and Hollywood-screen-test deals fell through. It was discovered that Professor Willgrubs, while in Ireland, had slipped away from his family to visit a nudie beach and had tried to steal a camera from a Japanese tourist. What was *that* all about, people wanted to know? Was Professor Willgrubs a dirty old man? And a thief? Had he tried to steal a video camera to take pictures of naked women playing volleyball? Oh, how disgusting. How humiliating. Would there be film clips on TV? Pop preachers and right-wing politicians waxed sanctimonious. With slight variations, the cable news channels ran the story every hour on the hour until the sensation they had helped create could no longer be sustained. Then the story faded away like an outbreak of flu that had run its course.

When the story first broke, Mrs. Willgrubs burst into tears, for she knew right off that it was untrue. Sitting side by side on their bed, the professor explained to his wife what happened, about how he had been hoodwinked by Irish bartenders and had taken pills he thought were aspirin, but which must have been something quite else. He said he had been embarrassed: that he had never been wise to the ways of the world and was sorry for being such a naïve fuddy-dud. Mrs. Willgrubs gave her husband a bone-crunching hug and invited the Delaneys over for fried chicken.

Delaney, now out of the hospital, though still not back to work, remembered vividly the conversation he had had with the professor in the Jaunty Crown regarding the alleged tide pools at Howth Cove Beach. He remembered, too, the sly manner of the bartenders as they went about their business, laughing and winking at each other. The bloody buggers, he thought. The Willgrubs's attorney was called upon once again to make a public announcement.

To jog the memories of the bartenders at the Jaunty Crown and, if necessary to urge their telling the truth, for the professor's story was sure to be checked and rechecked, Delaney called the pub and talked to one of the bartenders in on the joke. The bartender was delighted to hear from the detective and immediately admitted the prank. In no time at all the story spread throughout Sneem. The couple who had given succor to the professor after his injury confirmed the professor's story, though they said nothing about the illegal pills he had been given. They said they were sure the professor hadn't planned to steal the camera. Although they hadn't actually seen the professor getting pushed, they remembered the man who did it. They told everyone that it was they who had escorted the professor back to the bus stop at Crawly and Thurston. For a while, they were the toast of Sneem.

All this was in time reported by the press, but by then most people had already decided that the professor was a dirty old man and had moved on to other sensations that passed for national news. The Jaunty Crown became famous, of course, and was soon overrun by tourists, forcing the locals to look for new, less expensive watering holes.

The lives of the Delaneys and the Willgrubs returned slowly toward normal in the days following Hachem's death. Eventually Detective Delaney returned to work. High on his "To do" list was interviewing Coach Lawrence Coneybear.

"Hello," he said to the coach's secretary. "I'm Detective Delaney and I'm here to see Coach Coneybear." (He flashed his ID.) "Is he in?"

Irma Six didn't bother to look at the ID. She recognized Delaney as soon as he walked through the door. Hypersensitive to reports of police discrimination against blacks, Mrs. Six would not have liked Delaney for simply being a policeman. That he was a famous policeman served merely to increase her antipathy.

"May I ask what this is about?" she said. Icicles dripped from every word.

"You may, but I'm afraid it's confidential."

"I'll see if he's busy," Mrs. Six sniffed after a pause. She had thought about insisting that the policeman make an appointment for later.

Delaney was shown in, shook Coach Coneybear's hand, and took a chair.

"I'll get right to the point," he said to the coach. "On August 14th, you received a call at 3:49 in the afternoon. The call came from a payphone downtown. Can you remember who called you?"

"No, not off hand," the coach replied.

"The call is important, you see," Delaney continued, "because seconds after that call, another call was placed from that very same payphone. The second call was from the burglar who dialed 911 and reported that Basim Hachem was a terrorist. Have you read about this in the papers?"

"Yes, I have."

"Good. The reason why this is important is because the person who called you probably saw the burglar and could possibly give us a description of the man. So, any idea who might have called you?"

"No, none at all."

"OK, could you check your calendar? To see if perchance you made some kind of notation that might jog your memory."

"Sure." The coach paged back through the Success calendar on his desk, looked at the page for August 14, and said, "Nope, there's nothing here that helps."

"OK. If anything occurs to you, would you give me a call?"

"Sure."

"Thanks. Here's my card."

Delaney shook the coach's hand, but he didn't want to leave quite yet. His radar had picked up strange vibes. The blinking of the eye, the color of the cheek, the vibrato of the voice: Delaney wasn't sure what it was about the coach, but there was something. He turned to go.

"One other thing," he said from the doorway. "According to Irma Six's interview with the FBI, someone broke into your desk last spring, and I believe you later confirmed that that indeed was the case. Any thoughts on what the thief was after?"

"Well, as I told the FBI, the only thing I could think of was that maybe someone thought they'd find a description of our plays, or maybe notes on our football strategy. Perhaps someone wanted to make some bets and was after inside dope." The chance choice of words struck the coach as funny and he grinned. He started playing with a pen on his desk. "I know it seems ridiculous," he added, "but what else could it be?"

"But why did you keep the drawer locked if it contained nothing of value?"

"Well, um, when I first came here, I did keep valuable information in that drawer: notes on prospective players, valuable contacts, game strategies, stuff like that. But now all that stuff's in the computer. The drawer was locked and the key somehow got lost. It might even be in one of the other desk drawers right now. I'm afraid I don't keep a very tidy desk. Anyway, it simply wasn't important to me. I more-or-less forgot about it."

"Is that why you never reported the break-in?"

"Yes."

"One other thing, was your desk ever checked for fingerprints? I'm wondering if Basim Hachem was the one who broke into your desk. Did you ever think of that?"

In a remarkable display of dexterity, the coach had been twirling a pen horizontally with the fingers of his right hand. The pen now fell on the desk. He had goofed a twirl. To guilty eye, cheek, and tongue, thought Delaney, add nervous fingers. This guy's hiding something.

"No," the coach replied. "That never occurred to me."

Coach Coneybear stood at a window in his office, looking down on a parking lot where he and the other coaches parked their cars. He had already spotted a booger green Ford he hadn't seen before, a ford with ugly black wheels. He had guessed right. It was the detective's car and when Delaney drove away in booger green, the coach grabbed his cell phone and headed for a small campus park where there were benches. He called Mani Malakhov and for the first time in several weeks the conversation did not begin with a hearty round of self-congratulations.

"Mani, Detective Delaney was just in my office and you can't believe what he asked me. He wanted to know who called me on August 14th at 3:49 in the afternoon."

"Was that me?"

"You bet your sweet ass it was you."

"Well, what did you say?"

"I said I couldn't remember of course. That seemed to satisfy him, but there's more. The cops know someone broke into my desk."

"Yeah, I know. You already told me that."

"Yeah, well Delaney's guessing that the guy who broke into my desk was Hachem."

"Great balls of fire. That sounds bad, Coach. That's not good at all. Listen, do you have a few minutes?"

"Sure, shoot."

"Now, this is important. Don't dismiss out of hand what I have to say. You've got to get the hell out of coaching. It's just a matter of time before someone takes a really close look at your record and discovers you've never played college football. When they do, you'll have to quit your job. Quit now. Maybe no one will poke around in your past. Even if they do, you'd be long gone. I say quit now, while you're ahead."

"Yeah, but . . ."

"Let me finish. Resign your position. Say you don't like the pressure. Make up some excuse, pack your bags, and move back to California."

"How in the hell am I going to make a living in California?"

"That's not going to be a problem. There's lots of opportunity out here. You could easily become a top-notch cabaret performer. You could become a keyboard driven one-man band, bringing old-school craft and soul to the world of jazz. You'd be a sensation. This is just so damned exciting. And you could perform your own works."

"I don't know, Mani. God, I'm thirty-eight years old. It's a helluva late time to get started in show business. I mean, you've got to get your body pierced from your eyebrows to your dickey.

You've got to look like your pubes came in yesterday afternoon. I mean, Jeez."

"I had an ear pierced once."

"No kiddin'."

"Yeah, I came home with lavender hair and an earring. My papa had a ministroke, but the doctor insisted it wasn't my fault. I was only a junior in high school. Jeez."

"Well, I ain't ever going to get my body pierced, period, end of report."

"Well, who said anything about body piercing? But you *would* have to develop a look. You have a great bod and you'd have to show it off. What I see is a big black grand piano. You'd be wearing faded jeans without a belt and a perfectly tailored brown silk shirt tucked in. Rich brown. An it wouldn't kill you to wear a little earring just to tell folks you're cool."

"No way."

"Well, you could wear a chain and unbutton your shirt halfway, couldn't you?"

"What? In public?"

Late that afternoon, after the staff had headed for home, Coach Coneybear started thinking about leaving his wife and moving back to California. He had no relatives there. His parents had died years ago. His little sister lived in Texas, and they didn't even exchange Christmas cards anymore. From his briefcase he extracted a flask of Scotch and four lavender pills. He rolled his chair to a position where he could lean back and rest his head against the wall. He sang in a soft velvety voice;

If you're going to California,—Be sure to wear some flowers in your hair.—If you're going to California,—You're gonna meet some . . . some . . . some gentle . . .

A sharp pain caught him in the throat. For the first time in twenty-one years, Coach Coneybear began to cry. His voice faltered. He couldn't sing his song.

Chapter 15

Ms. Sally Holmes sat at the beat-up desk that was the main piece of furniture in the Madison office of the People for the Ethical Treatment of Animals, known as PETA by those with an interest in such things. Not only was she the driving force behind the local chapter of PETA, she was also a stalwart member of Wisconsin Citizens Concerned for Cranes and Doves, an organization that had taken on white males in a fight to outlaw the hunting of mourning doves. "Chalk up one more victory for white testicles," she muttered contemptuously when she saw on TV that the mourning doves had lost. But Sally Holmes was not one to give up. One morning her fight for the humane treatment of animals was fired up by an article in the Wisconsin State Journal. The paper said that the World Dairy Expo, originally scheduled in Madison for early October, though later cancelled, had been rescheduled to begin on November 8th.

Ms. Holmes was so excited by the article's lead paragraph that she could only skim what followed, which explained how the Expo's board of directors had come to its decision. From behind bars in Ireland, Dr. Mirza Paracha had confessed that the terrorist cell trying to decimate America's livestock industry had consisted of only three men, none of whom remained a threat. Dr. Paracha would likely be incarcerated for the rest of his life. Basim Hachem was dead. Yussef Maidin, having eluded US authorities, had been reliably spotted in Morocco. A fourth possible terrorist, perhaps unknown to Dr. Paracha, had been killed in the explosion at Hachem's house. That, at least, had become the conventional wisdom. The danger of concentrating in one place prize-winning dairy animals from all over North America had passed, or so it seemed. So why not proceed with the World Dairy Expo? That was the question put before the Expo's board of directors, and the answer was, why not, indeed.

Although dairy farmers would flock from all over the world to observe and to learn, Sally Holmes's intention was to be observed and to instruct. She had earlier harangued her little group into organizing a demonstration at the Expo in October; now she had to rethink the entire matter. Should she get on the telephone and call key people like her useless boyfriend Ralph for their input on whether a meeting of the executive committee should be called? If the committee were to vote for a November demonstration, they would need organize a fund drive. Posters would need be designed and constructed. Flyers would need be printed for distribution. Who would provide the transportation to and from the coliseum? How many members could be rousted from their classes for the demonstration? Problems, problems. But there was opportunity, too, she thought, opportunity that should not (could not) be passed over. She didn't want to think about how far she had fallen behind in her classes at the university. She would simply have to work harder and sleep less. Too bad, though, that the money collected for the October Expo had been squandered on the free-the-mink project, which had been a total disaster. But she didn't want to think about that either.

Ms. Holmes was vivacious and bright. She was delicately framed and ate no more than a sparrow. Her large dark eyes had an elfin quality. She looked as if she might at any minute blow pixie dust into the air and disappear. Her black hair had a bit of natural curl, was cut short, and rarely brushed. After showering she simply fluffed it with a towel. Always pressed for time in the morning, she pulled on her clothes and, out of a nervous habit more than anything else, combed her hair with her fingers. The secondhand clothes she wore seemed foreign, like those of a waif from some poor land far away, an island off the Irish coast, possibly, or maybe where the rainbow touches the earth.

Sally Holmes was from no farther away than Minnesota, as it happened. Her father and mother had once owned a rundown resort there on Jack Pine Lake. Even as a little girl, she evinced a strong empathy for animals. She fed and petted the family dog and cats. Her mother laughed whenever her daughter rescued moths inside the house and rushed them outside and when she scolded anyone who would dare roll up a newspaper for the purpose of swatting. She cried and stamped her foot whenever her father refused to take an ailing pet to the local veterinarian, which he invariably refused to do until the pet was practically dead and beyond saving, which then reaffirmed his disbelief in the efficacy of veterinary science. The circularity of his logic didn't fool his precocious child one bit.

John and Margaret Holmes never had any money to speak of. To supplement profit from the resort, Mr. Holmes one fall started driving a school bus. He then moved on to driving trucks for the Rushville Cooperative Creamery, picking up the milk produced by farmer-members for delivery to the butter-powder plant in town. Later still, he became the cooperative manager, thus joining a long line of managers who understated the weights of milk deliveries from members in a desperate effort to keep the cooperative afloat. It was largely the need for money that prompted Sally Holmes's only sibling, her older brother Vincent, to trap wild animals for their pelts, and it was this venture that steered an animal-conscious little girl toward a lifetime fight for the prevention of cruelty to animals.

One autumn, when Sally was only five, Vincent invited her to come with him to check a trap he had set in a hole next to a pile of brush. The brush had been built up at the edge of a woods as part of a land-clearing project to make way for crops. With little appreciation for what trapping involved, she was pleased to be asked to do something with a big brother who liked to tease and be mean. Thus, she was in high spirits as they left the house. As they approached the cite, Vincent yelled,

"Hey, I got somthin'."

And he did. A badger had stepped in the trap. Iron jaws had snapped tight around one of its forelegs. Tethered to a steel stake, the wretched animal, in a fight for its life, had swept clean the swath of land allowed by the length of the trap's chain. All the twigs, weeds, and leaves had been chewed and pushed to the perimeter of its prison yard. But the worse part, oh, the part that would haunt Sally Holmes for all her life, was the badger's bloodied leg. The flesh had been ripped aside. The steel jaws held fast to bare bone. The badger hissed at the creatures who had come to kill him, but Vincent was not deterred. He found a good sturdy stick and beat the badger's head in. Sally watched the animal's death throes in stunned silence. Vincent stepped on the trap's spring to free the leg, picked up the badger by the back legs, and headed for home, eager to show his prize to his dad and to inquire how much money the pelt might fetch. He was startled when his little sister threw herself against his back, beating him with her fists.

"Hey, you little shit," he hollered, "cut that out. What do you think you're doin'?"

That evening Sally Holmes ran a fever and wouldn't eat her supper.

"Tell him to stop, Mama," she whispered when she was put to bed early.

"Yes," Margaret Holmes replied. "I'll talk to father about it."

As she walked downstairs Mrs. Holmes realized how thoughtless she had been, letting her tender-hearted daughter go with Vincent. She knew Vincent's trapping wasn't making much money. It's a cruel sport, she now knew, cross with herself for not seeing it sooner. Why not stop him? By god, she would stop him, and that's all there was to it. The decision was made before she reached the bottom step. It was Sally Holmes's first victory in her fight for animal rights.

Though she often thought of the trapped badger, she never spoke of it anymore. Once, though, when she was sitting in the study hall at Rushville High, already depressed because a boy she liked had taken up with the banker's daughter, she remembered the badger's torn leg and to keep from crying bit her thumb till it came close to bleeding. Afterward, when she looked at the hideous back and blue marks on her skin, she came to the hard-nosed realization that it wouldn't do to give in to emotion: that in the fight for what's right, you have to be cool-headed and calculating. Now, a major in psychology at the University of Wisconsin-Madison, she rarely thought of the animal in the trap, but took a philosophic view whenever she did. If women could only see what I once saw in a northern Minnesota woods, she assured herself, they would not wear furs.

There were so many don'ts in Sally Holmes's life. Don't eat netted tuna. Don't eat foie gras. Don't eat Kentucky Fried Chicken. Don't eat Broad Breasted White turkeys. Don't go to zoos. Don't patronize entertainment involving trained exotic animals. And don't consume dairy products until dairy farmers guarantee the humane treatment of calves.

On a crisp, cool November day, Professor Myron Willgrubs drove from Plattefield to Madison to attend the opening day of the World Dairy Expo. Mrs. Willgrubs sat up front. Emily Delaney was glad she had insisted on sitting in the back when the time came to leave. She was aware that her wish had met with only polite resistance. Mrs. Willgrubs volunteered sitting in the back on the argument that she had quite gotten over getting carsick from riding in the back. The journey got underway after a late morning breakfast, thus allowing Emily to join the outing without skipping a class. The professor had been excited by the prospect of seeing first hand what the exposition entailed, for he had never attended one before. His lady had fretted over what shoes to wear, fearing that if the professor insisted on their visiting the dairy barns, which seemed likely, she might step in something vulgar.

Emily was thankful for a drive in the country. As a bonus, she would see her husband at work, although he said all he'd be doing is standing around looking for suspicious characters. She was delighted by the passing countryside: pretty farmsteads with gardens gone to seed, fields of corn in varying stages of harvest, and blue ponds with icy edges set off nicely against the autumnal background of old gold and bronze. Exams, term papers, lectures to attend, books to read and understand, all the tasks that cause stress in the life of college students, soon fell away. She was asleep before they reached the halfway mark to Madison.

As his family drove south, Detective Delaney strove to study however briefly all the drivers and passengers flowing into the Alliant Energy Center Coliseum's enormous parking lot. He had not been surprised when Chief Smedegard had agreed to lend him to the Madison Police Department to assist in thwarting a possible bioterrorist attack. Many state law enforcement officials were concerned about such a threat and had at the outset opposed rescheduling the Expo so soon after Maidin's escape to the Middle East. Other than FBI agents who would not be present, Delaney was the only officer who had both seen and talked with Joe Maidin. It had been the chief's idea to have Danny Christensen drive Delaney to Madison and help with surveillance, for Christensen had been quite down in the mouth over his part in the SWAT raid of the Hoffnagel farm.

While Detective Delaney and other officers scrutinized the incoming visitors to the coliseum, Officer Christensen roamed freely about the grounds, poking his head into buildings housing livestock, visiting a store selling homespun arts and crafts, and stopping in the coffee shop for coffee and donuts. Of main interest was the coliseum itself, with its cavernous arena that could seat over twenty thousand people. In a grand loop, the main concourse ran entirely around the arena at ground level. Corridors admitted spectators to sections numbered in the 200s. Dogleg stairs led to the second concourse where spectators could then pass through to sections numbered in the 300s reaching up to the steel rafters of the coliseum's umbrella-shaped canopy.

Danny Christensen had visited the coliseum once before,

when he was a member of the Hunters Point High School hockey team. The school had arranged for the team to attend a non-conference game between the Wisconsin Badgers and the Winnipeg Bears. As he walked along the main concourse, he was struck by the contrast between then and now: between a game of fun and a game of life and death. In stalls cluttering the main concourse, salesmen hawked dairy equipment, feed, farm implements, and the consulting services of veterinarians, breeders, and farm management companies. How could all these stalls ever be adequately policed, he wondered? As far as he could tell, there wasn't another policeman in sight. Just for the heck of it, he walked up a stairway to the second concourse, entered the arena and then climbed to Row R, the highest row of seats in the arena. That's where he and his hockey teammates once sat. He took a seat and thought back on that night, how he and his buddies whooped and hollered as the badgers eked out a five to four victory. To celebrate, they sang dumb songs going home in the bus. Funny, he thought, how something like that sticks with a guy for so long. For a few minutes, Officer Christensen's naturally happy temperament gave way to melancholy as he reflected on youth's passing, even though he *was* only twenty-five years old.

At the entrance to the coliseum's parking lot, security requirements were causing delays. Two lines of entering traffic needed screening. Drivers showed their licenses. Armed officers looked at passengers and examined car trunks and the cargo spaces of vans and pickups. Detective Delaney moved from one line to the other in an effort to see as many of the visitors as possible. It was not possible to see them all. As the day worn on, his mission seemed increasingly futile, but he strove to stay watchful, to look carefully at all the young men. Even as he did, he worried about other entrances that might not be closely guarded. And what was to stop a terrorist from simply climbing over the fence? What about the place within view where scrubby trees and shrubs had grown up close to the fence? Couldn't someone have slipped onto the grounds during the night and hidden himself in one of the service buildings housing the animals? For all anyone knew, a virus might have been loosened in the cattle barns already. This whole thing is a helluva mistake, he kept telling himself.

A bit of excitement occurred before lunch. A small but determined group of protestors, having been waived through onto the coliseum grounds, had formed a thin gauntlet just inside the gate. The subsequent visitors were accosted by raucous calls for animal justice. Posters were waived in their faces showing calves in steel cages. There were threats of a nationwide boycott of veal, butter, and cheese. Some of the messages were couched in language ill-suited to the very objectives the protestors had hoped to advance.

The members of PETA were treated with hostility. Guards wanted to arrest them, but the top guns at the Madison Police Department said no: that as long as protestors were peaceful, they were to be left alone. Farm men snarled and opened the windows of their vehicles and swore. Farm wives signaled agreement by mean faces and stony silences. Teenagers who had skipped school catcalled and made obscene gestures. Despite the unsympathetic response to their protests, the chanting and waving of posters continued until noon, when the protestors broke for lunch.

Emily Delaney and her aunt and uncle arrived later in the day and missed the excitement. Waiting in a lineup of cars, Emily saw her husband before he saw her and glowed with a mixture of pride and affection as she watched him moving from one vehicle to the next, bending over to look at the occupants. He smiled and seemed embarrassed when he finally noticed the professor's car. When the professor stopped to pay the parking fee and popped the trunk, car windows were lowered to allow greetings. Emily induced a trill of Patrick's heart strings when she made a little kissy-poo with her lips, flicked her eyebrows, and smiled suggestively.

"You saucy minx," he said to her through the open window.

She laughed for she knew her charms had had the desired effect.

Once parked, the Willgrubs party went first to the coliseum. An enormous bank of doors opened onto the brightly colored carpet of the lobby. There the professor picked up the schedule of events and learned that the next event in the arena, to start in forty-five minutes, was the judging of bulls. This gave his party time to visit the barns where farmers from all over the country were housing there best bulls, cows, and heifers. The visit to the dairy barns was such a success that the Willgrubs party almost missed the judging of Holstein bulls.

Professor Willgrubs led the way into the arena from the main concourse and found seats close to the pending action. A few minutes passed before the parade of bulls commenced, each led by a leash attached to a ring in his nose. Attention was momentarily drawn to the west end of the arena where a man in a cowboy outfit played a guitar and sang into a microphone. The sound system was not the best, or perhaps it was the acoustics, but for whatever reason a few moments passed before Emily realized that the faux cowboy was singing, "I'm in the moo for love," which made her laugh. It was something she could tell her husband that night, along with the misstep in the dairy barn and the good-looking rustic who had cleaned her shoe.

The bulls were led into a semicircle and the judge set to work, examining each of the animals and making notes on papers held by a clipboard. When the champion was announced together with the farm of his origin and his owner's name, there was a scattering of polite applause.

While the spectators waited for the finalists in the competition for best Jersey bull, a deep voice over the loud speaker system announced the entrance of Seamuffin, the world's most famous dancing horse. A murmur of curiosity rippled through the crowd. A famous horse was quite unexpected. There was no mention of it in the program. All became clear when a pantomime horse with a smile on his face trotted gaily into the arena. The announcer asked for a round of applause, which was warmly given. The horse stopped in front of the audience and bowed deeply, center first, then right and left. When the Andrews Sisters began singing, "Don't Fence Me In," the horse began to dance. When the song and dance were over, the pantomime horse bowed to the applause and trotted out the way it had come in. As it approached the exit, however, the part of the costume covering its behind fell down around its hooves, revealing what seemed to be the rump of a young woman in a flesh-colored body stocking. A cow's tail had been affixed to the stocking, thus assuring the spectators that what they were then seeing wasn't really a mishap, but rather a pantomime of a pantomime. Given the handicap of a fallen costume down around its back hooves, the horse's rear end followed tolerably well the horse's front end out of the arena to a hearty round of applause. In a moment a young couple appeared for a second bow, carrying with them their pantomime horse clothes. The man was tall and slender; the woman in the body stocking was short and had bushy hair.

By closing time, Sally Holmes had become depressed. Except for Lily Siskind, the other protestors had gone. The two remaining sisters-in-arms sat on folding chairs at card tables that had seen better days. The brown vinyl coverings were coffee stained and torn. Duct tape covered the more serious rips. On the table were stacks of flyers that had been prepared for the occasion, spelling out the offenses against dairy calves and pleading for reforms, particularly in specialized veal-calf operations. Exactly two flyers had been picked up. The remainder rested under a stone to keep the wind from blowing them away. Perhaps they could be used at next year's Expo, Ms. Holmes thought, or maybe at the Dane County Fair.

No wonder she was depressed. She had missed a day of classes, and for what? The reaction of farmers and farm input suppliers had been hostile at best. The flyers had been a waste of time and money. The turnout of animal rights supporters had been much less than she had hoped for. Her boyfriend had said he wouldn't be able to come until after lunch, but in the end, he hadn't shown up at all. Once the bag lunches were consumed and the hot coffee ran out, protestors drifted away, and Ms. Holmes could hardly have blamed them. Her suggestion that they take up the protest signs and mingle with the crowds moving about the barns and into and out of the coliseum lost credibility when the first of the protestors to give it a try was relieved of his poster and pushed around. First, the free-the-mink disaster, Sally thought, and now this. Is it all worth it? Well, she thought, there is one silver lining I can cling to, too distraught to recognize her confused metaphor. She gave thanks for their new recruit, Lily Siskind.

But even Sally Holmes had to admit that Lily Siskind was odd. She used a lot of makeup and always wore one or another of her three Lands End outfits. Her countertenor voice reminded Ms. Holmes of Dustin Hoffman in *Tootsie*. She had shown up in response to a university campus flier asking for volunteers and financial support. She came into the office, read over the materials, checked out the website for the People for the Ethical Treatment of Animals on an old office computer, and said she was interested in joining. She asked how she could help the cause. Her contribution of $100 was a godsend. After signing up, she had come to the office every day to man the telephones and greet the few prospective members who wandered in off the street. She was a very private person, though, in Sally Holmes's opinion. Ms. Holmes couldn't get much out of her except that she was from New York City, that her father ran a food catering business, and that she no longer had much to do with her family. Had there been some kind of family rift? Ms. Holmes wondered. Could it have been over a man? Lily had no boyfriend that Sally knew of and quite frankly didn't seem much interested in men. She didn't seem much interested in animal rights, come to that. There seemed to be no real passion in her gut. Her involvement in the movement seemed so—so mechanical. She seemed merely to be going through the motions. Ms. Holmes decided that Lily Siskind simply wasn't one to wear her emotions on the sleeve of one or the other of her pastel cotton sweaters. But for all that, here she was, still keeping the protest vigil after all the others had abandoned the effort.

"If you want to go, Lily," Ms. Holmes said, "please do. Nothing much seems to be happening here and its getting cold."

"Oh, I won't abandon you, honey," Lily replied in her beautiful low voice. (Her diction was always perfect.) "Before I leave, I want to visit the coliseum and see what all is there. I have my car, so you don't have to wait for me when it's time to go. I'll help you load the van and then you can leave."

"Are you cold, Lily?"

"No, not a bit. Oh, but maybe *you* are. Could I fetch a blanket or something?"

"No thank you."

That's Lily Siskind for you, Ms. Holmes thought. Always ready to lend a hand.

Just when she decided to give it up for the day (the grounds were nearly deserted), a young woman who had been talking with friends some distance away approached the table, inquired what the protest was about, and asked for a flyer. She was polite. There was something classy about the way she walked, talked, and looked. There was something familiar about her, too, but Ms. Holmes couldn't quite make out what it was. She couldn't quite recall that Emily Delaney had appeared on television in connection with the hoopla following the death of Basim Hachem. Ms. Holmes didn't notice Lily Siskind's nervousness in handing the woman a flyer.

When the pretty woman returned to her group, a man who was there put an arm around her and drew her up close. Sally Holmes suddenly felt alone in the world. He must love her so much, she imagined, to hold her like that. She had never had a lover who would hold her like that, someone who would watch over her, like the man Roberta Flack longed for in that Gershwin song. She was looking for someone like that, and she decided then and there that Ralph Baker was not that man. She would give him his walking papers, even if it meant getting another student loan to help pay the rent.

"So, are you about to join the fight against cruelty to animals?" Delaney asked his wife, almost as a joke. He was taken aback when she frowned and replied,

"Yes, Pat. We really should join. The trouble is there are so many worthy organizations, one must make hard choices."

The detective was further surprised when the professor said, "We aren't members, but we make annual contributions to help fund their programs. They do a lot of good work."

"They do, indeed," said Mrs. Willgrubs. "Cruelty to animals is so unchristian."

"It looks like the last of the animal rights people are packing up to leave," Delaney said. "I'm afraid they weren't treated very kindly here today," he added, feeling contrite about a few of the jokes he had shared with his fellow officers, jokes made at the expense of the protestors.

"There was something very odd about the tall woman who handed me the flyer," Emily said to her little group. "She was wearing a ton of makeup. And I think she was wearing a wig, too. You wouldn't expect an animal rights woman to fix herself up like that, would you? How odd." Emily laughed out of a nervousness for having poked fun at the looks of a total stranger.

Detective Delaney was tired and it took a while before what his wife said registered. When it did he walked briskly over to an old Dodge van where one of the women was pushing a folded-up card table into the van through the side door. When the table had been stowed, she turned and the western sun shone in her face. She wore no makeup. The other woman, the tall one, had walked off toward the coliseum at a brisk clip.

"I'm Detective Delaney," he said to the woman packing

up to leave. He flashed his ID. "The woman who's walking to the coliseum, have you known her long? This could be important."

"I've seen you on TV," Ms. Homes said with a bright smile.

"The woman," Delaney said in a brusque voice. "The one walking to the coliseum. Have you known her long?"

"No," replied Sally Holmes, now wide-eyed and serious. "Not long at all. She just joined our group a few weeks ago."

Delaney starting running after the woman headed for the coliseum. When she turned and saw him, she looped her handbag over a shoulder and started running too.

"I'm a police officer," Delaney yelled. "Stop, or I'll shoot."

But the woman did not stop, and Delaney did not shoot.

Danny Christensen had exited the coffee shop with two large coffees to go. When he saw Delaney and heard him yell, his eye was drawn to the woman running toward the coliseum. "What's this?" he said.

"Hey, Danny," Delaney yelled. "Stop that woman."

Christensen looked back and saw the woman pull open a door to the coliseum. He threw lidded cups of coffee to the ground and ran full out, beating Delaney to the coliseum by several rods. Inside the deserted lobby he paused to look this way and that, but could see no one. Stalled by indecision, he was caught up by Delaney.

"I don't know which way she went," Christensen said.

"OK, I've called for a backup," Delaney replied. "She isn't going to hide. This place is going to be swarming with police. She's got to keep on the move. She's going to try to get away. OK, you go to the right. I'll take the left."

Officer Christensen ran to the right, flying past a wide flight of stairs leading to the second concourse. Was he going the right way? In the distance, three men in work clothes seemed to be involved in a conversation. Would the suspect have risked running past them? Indecision slowed his pace. Quite suddenly, a strange equine apparition trotted out an open door, a pantomime horse.

Music with a hip-hop beat issued from a room tucked in under the upper part of the arena. Christensen could hardly believe his eyes when the horse began to boogaloo. He was momentarily discombobulated. Could a pantomime horse be part of a terrorist plot? Impossible.

"Hey, I'm a cop," he said to the horse. "Did you see a woman running in this direction?"

Over the course of his thirty-some restless years, Fred Schultz had gotten to know the police rather well, but the reason for the acquaintance boded ill for his cooperating with Officer Christensen. In addition to his dislike for the police, this had been a really bad day in the life of the pantomime horse called Seamuffin. The new costume that Mr. Schultz had designed and sewn together had not been a success, although his idea of letting its hindmost part fall to the ground as Seamuffin exited the arena had drawn a good belly laugh. But the off-white canvass with tie-dyed blacks spots had proven to be a bad choice. People who hadn't heard the announcement of Seamuffin the horse thought Seamuffin was a Holstein cow with a really long neck. His girlfriend Goodie Fortuna, the horse's rear end, had complained about the tail, too. Ha! he had snorted. As if she could have done any better. And then after muffing dance steps time and time again, she bitched fiercely just because he insisted they practice until she got it right.

The pantomime horse's front end stopped dancing in response to Officer Christensen request for help. The rear end stumbled, stopped, and said, "Oh, shit." It seemed to Christensen that the damned horse was smiling at him. He was totally pissed when the horse said,

"Fuck off."

Without giving the matter a second thought, Christensen gave the horse a terrible wallop upside the head. The blow did no real damage to Mr. Schultz, since it merely glanced off a hardened part of his outfit, but it did upset his balance, and with no arms to steady himself, he fell over, taking with him the horse's behind.

"Eee-iiii," cried the horse's behind.

"Jesus shit," declared the horse's head. "She ran up the steps, for chrissake. The ones you just passed."

Christensen backtracked and tore up the steps two at a time. On the second concourse, he looked both ways but could neither see nor hear anything. Out of desperation he pushed aside a red curtain signaling a closed section and walked out into a vast arena that was dimly lit and ominously quiet. He walked along an aisle to his left. It all seemed so hopeless. Was he screwing up once again? If only he could catch the suspect and thus make amends for his Green Valley Farm mistake. A noise drew his eye to a room numbered 317 just below the rafters. A pressroom, he guessed. When a door opened, he started running up the steps. In a moment a man staggered out and collapsed.

In navy blue work clothes, he lay on the floor just outside the open door. Christensen turned him over gently. A security pass on a string hang from his neck. The man put a hand over his bloody chest.

"Hey, what happened?" Danny asked.

"She stabbed me with a knife," the man replied quietly. "I think I'm a goner."

"Hold on," Christensen said. "I'll call for help."

He broke out his cell phone and dialed the emergency number he and Delaney had been given on their arrival that morning.

"She's up on a catwalk," the downed man said.

"Officer Danny Christensen here," Christensen said to the woman taking his call. He talked as he hurried into Room 317. "Emergency, there's a badly injured workman just outside the press box numbered 317. It's on the south side of the arena up near the rafters. Got that? . . . Good. Now listen, call Detective Delaney and tell him the suspect we're after is up on the catwalks above the arena. Got that? . . . Good. I gotta run."

Christensen climbed up a steep, narrow stair that led to a labyrinth of steel catwalks spanning in all directions. He walked out on one of them and said, "Sweet Jesus," when he looked down and saw how far he was above the seats below. Ahead, he strained to see through the superstructure of steel beams and rods that supported the coliseum's roof, but no suspicious lady was in sight. She's hiding up here somewhere, he decided. Maybe she's lying down somewhere on a catwalk, hoping I'll go away. Maybe she didn't count on the injured man spilling the beans. Well, by god, I'll flush her out. Where is that fucking Delaney, anyhow? Damn.

Christensen started toward the center of the arena where several catwalks joined in a hub above a giant scoreboard hanging forty feet at least from the ceiling. A third of the way out, he heard footsteps, wheeled to his left, and saw the suspect running on the outer most catwalk along the periphery of the arena. Ah, he thought, now I'll get her. He retraced his steps and turned right. "Stop, or I'll shoot," he yelled.

The suspect kept on running. Christensen aimed his gun and pulled the trigger. The pop was enormous, like the time he set off a firecracker in an empty corn silo and scared his dad half to death. The bullet struck a steel girder and ricocheted four times before falling silently to the sawdust covered floor of the arena.

Good god, he thought, a guy could shoot himself in the butt in this place. And there's Delaney. Well, it's about time. Did he stop somewhere for a hotdog? Damn.

"Hey Delaney," he shouted. "She's coming your way. Up on the catwalk."

Detective Delaney had entered the arena from the second concourse, having received Christensen's message through a police operator. He heard his partner's warning and could see the suspect running toward him. He rushed up steps to Row R and drew his gun.

The suspect saw him, hesitated, and looped her handbag around her neck. Her next move was extraordinary. She grasped a nearby rod and swung her body off the catwalk, dangling precariously above the rows of seats far below. Her intention was clear. Support rods positioned in X-patterns had been bolted to steel beams running both up and round the great canopy. By moving down the rods in a zigzag fashion, going down hand over hand, switching from one rod to another, she could get close to the floor at Row R. If she could make it that far without falling to her death, she could then simply drop down 10 feet or so to the floor and run for an exit.

The suspect acted accordingly. Using her legs and her arms, she hung below the rod monkey-style. Hand over hand movements, letting her legs slide, carried her down from one rod to another. Her speed was remarkable.

Christensen could see that Delaney was too far away to either intercept or shoot her. "Oh shit," he said aloud. "I'm not going to like this." He, too, grabbed a rod and swung himself off the catwalk. He, too, made like a monkey, with an agility that easily matched that of the suspect.

By the time Christensen was able to drop to the floor, the suspect was racing down the steps toward an exit. He aimed his handgun with both hands and pulled the trigger. Damn, he thought. I've got to practice more. And then the suspect got lucky.

Sally Holmes walked out of a corridor into the arena. She saw Lily Siskind coming straight at her from not more than six rows up. Behind her, at the top of a long series of steps, a man held a gun, a man who must have fired the shot. Everything seemed to be happening so fast. Ms. Holmes was momentarily confused and in that moment fell into the iron grip of Lily Siskind.

"If you try getting free," Siskind snarled in a man's voice. "I'll slash your throat."

She pressed the knife against Ms. Holmes's throat, drawing a trace of blood. Then, in a violent lurch, she twisted Ms. Holmes about to face the cop with the gun.

"Stop, stop," the suspect shouted, "or I'll slash her throat."

The voice was again that of a man. The female impersonation had outlived its usefulness.

Goddamnit! Christensen swore under his breath. Now what am I going to do?

Chapter 16

Emily Delaney and her aunt and uncle had watched, with color-coded alarm turning from yellow to red, as Patrick first hurried to the old van and then ran after a woman, drawing his gun and yelling that he would shoot if she didn't stop. Good god, they thought in unison. They were further alarmed when he shouted something at Officer Christensen who then threw what looked like food-to-go on the tarmac and joined in the chase. After the suspect and the two officers disappeared inside the coliseum, Emily said,

"The woman with the wig: she must be a terrorist! She's a man in disguise!" She started toward the coliseum, but Professor Willgrubs grabbed hold of her arm.

"No, no, my dear," he insisted. "Your going into the coliseum at this critical juncture would be an egregious mistake. You are unarmed and untrained, my dear. You might get in the way. You must let the police manage this."

"What on earth is the world coming to?" lamented Mrs. Willgrubs.

"But what are we going to do, Uncle?" Emily said. She held a tight fist to her mouth and began to cry.

"Now is no time for tears," the professor said in a stern voice. "We've got to do our part. Didn't you bring your cell phone with you?"

"Yes, it's in my purse."

"Get it quickly. I'll call 911. Patrick has in all likelihood already called for a backup, but we must make doubly sure."

The professor dialed 911 and said, "My name is Professor Myron Willgrubs. I'm calling from the Alliant Energy Center Coliseum. I have every reason to believe that a bioterrorist is on the loose in the coliseum. Two police officers are already in pursuit. Get this message to the police immediately. The officers will need a backup. Hurry."

The professor stayed on the phone a few moments longer before saying good. Then he said good-bye and handed the phone back to Emily.

As they wondered what to do next, the PETA woman at the van suddenly dropped a folding chair. It banged against the tarmac. Then she, too, ran toward the coliseum.

"Shouldn't we stop her?" Emily asked.

"Goodness gracious no, child," Mrs. Willgrubs said, finally getting into the spirit of homeland defense. "She might be armed. Goodness gracious, she might take us hostage. Perhaps we should disable the van, though, just in case the terrorists break free from the officers and try to drive away."

"Capital idea, my dear," said the professor. "Let's see what we can do."

With that, the threesome hurried over to the van. The back door on the passenger side had been left open. Emily poked her head inside and then ran around to the driver's seat.

"Look," she said, holding up car keys. "They were in the ignition."

"If we could get the hood up," said Mrs. Willgrubs, "we could smash the engine. What we need is a big rock." She looked fiercely about for something really heavy.

"Now wait," said the professor. "We can't be sure this van belongs to a lady terrorist. The second lady, the one who stayed behind, might be the owner, and it appears that Patrick judged her innocent, else he wouldn't have run off and left her with what could have been a getaway vehicle. She must have said something that convinced him of her innocence. Ah, and what about that car over there? Might that be the car owned by the questionable transvestite? Let's take a closer look."

The threesome checked out an old Chevy Lumina, but its doors were locked. Mrs. Willgrubs complained that if they couldn't get the hood up, they couldn't smash the engine, but the professor had a better idea anyway.

"We'll use our car jack and take the back wheels off," he said. "A terrorist would have a tough time making a quick getaway if she had to put the wheels back on, particularly if we keep the wheel nuts."

"Yes, yes," Emily said. "And when we're through with that, we'll move the van. We'll hide it somewhere. Why not hide it behind one of the cow barns? No one would ever think to look for it there."

"Yes, behind the barns," agreed the professor. "Or maybe we could find a good spot amongst the choppers and vertical feed mixers. A van wouldn't be very noticeable among an assortment of machinery like that, and we could keep the keys, too."

"Hurry up, my sweet," said Mrs. Willgrubs to her husband, her big fleshy face flushed with excitement. "Bring our car over here. I'll help you with the back wheels."

"I'll move the van right away," Emily said.

"No, no," cried Mrs. Willgrubs. "I've seen enough movies to know that we should all stay together."

Somehow, in the excitement of the moment, her observation passed for sound judgement, which it might have been had Emily Delaney been a teenage sweetie in a slasher movie, scantily dressed, suggestively posed, and saying to her friends, "Maybe I should, like, go to the basement to check the fuses." Be that as it may, acting in unison, the threesome did disable one vehicle and hide the other. Then they watched from inside the Willgrubs's car, ready to spring into action in the event a terrorist broke free from the coliseum.

"We'll call 911 in the event a terrorist breaks free," the professor said, "and we can always evade a terrorist by driving about the parking lot at the minimum required speed."

After their run-in with Officer Christensen, Pamela Schultz's grandson Fred Schultz and his girlfriend Goodie Fortuna took a time-out. In puddles of pantomime horse clothes, they sat on the concrete floor of the main concourse. Ms. Fortuna called Fred a jerk. Then she said,

"Why didn't you simply answer the cop's question?"

"Ha! He didn't show me his badge," Schultz replied. "How do you know he wasn't a rapist?"

This quieted Ms. Fortuna for a few moments. Perhaps Fred hadn't been a stupido after all, she thought. Perhaps. Then she complained that she was tired and wanted to go home.

Fred Schultz knew that if Seamuffin were ever to turn a decent profit, he and Goodie would need develop great prance and dance routines. They'd need become professionals, which would require an enormous amount of hard work. He had told her this many times before, but now he needed a new inducement. So he said,

"I know you're tired, honey. And I'm really sorry about the bruise on your hip. So I'll make you a deal. Let's just go around the concourse one more time. I have an idea for a funny gallop, and our canter could use more work, too. When we're through, we'll go home, clean up, and go out for Chinese food. My treat."

"Can I order an umbrella drink?"

"As many as you want."

"OK, let's go."

Thus did Seamuffin begin working his way around the main concourse, little knowing that he would soon canter through the porthole to fame and fortune: that conventions, sporting events, and state fairs would become passe: that he was headed for a new children's program on network TV!

Sally Holmes had been dumbfounded by Delaney's reaction to Lily Siskind. Faces came back to her as she thought about it. Delaney was the very detective who had been instrumental in exposing a fiendish bioterrorist plot. That's why his face was familiar, but what was he doing here? And the pretty woman who had asked for a flyer was his wife. She had been on TV, too. Ms. Holmes did the math: 1 disguised man + 1 alarmed cop + 268 pampered dairy animals = bioterrorism. The immensity of her unwitting culpability, of having provided cover for a terrorist with god knows what in her handbag—well, it was just too much. She was overcome by a fierce determination to assist the police, which explained why she had run pell-mell toward the coliseum. She would help catch Lily Siskind, or die trying.

Ms. Holmes had been momentarily immobilized, however, when she looked up into the upper reaches of the great arena and saw a man with a gun. In the same instant, she saw Lily Siskind coming toward her. She would grab hold of Lily and not let go, she decided, but of course it hadn't worked out that way. Before she could react, she found a strong arm around her waist and a knife pressed to her throat. When she struggled to get free, Siskind's knife cut.

"Stop, stop, or I'll slash her throat," Ms. Siskind had shouted in a man's voice.

Christensen had worried for a moment about what to do. Now he acted, "Don't," he yelled back. He stopped and lowered his weapon.

"OK, throw the gun away . . . . Do it, or she'll die."

"Don't drop your gun," Ms. Holmes screamed at the man she now assumed was a cop. "Shoot, shoot. No matter what. Don't let her . . ."

The blade went deeper. Ms. Holmes thought she would faint. The rows of seats sweeping round the great arena moved like waves in a foggy sea.

"Look, lady," Christensen yelled. "If you kill her, I'll shoot you dead. Your scheme will come to nothing."

"She ain't no lady," Ms. Holmes whimpered.

"Throw the gun," warned Ms. Siskind. "This is your last chance."

"I'll make you a deal," said Christensen. "Now, listen. If you kill her, you'll die, too, and all your plans to get even with America will go down the drain. So, we have to make a deal somehow.

You've got to give me a chance at least of catching you, and I have to give you a chance of getting away. We've gotta compromise. I've got it. If you let the girl go, I'll count to ten before I come after you. That'll give you a chance to get away."

"Throw the gun. I'll count to three, you donkey. One . . ."

Danny Christensen tossed his gun away.

"Now, I'm taking the girl hostage," Ms. Siskind said.

Holding fast to Ms. Holmes, Lily Siskind backed out of the nearby exit onto the second concourse. She loosened her grip some so she could move more quickly down stairs to the main concourse. When the scream of distant sirens came within earshot, she inadvertently loosened her grip a bit more. Ms. Holmes wrenched free and ran for her life. Ms. Siskind paused to think what to do, give chase or run for an exit to the parking lot. She chose to run for an exit.

It was now Lily Siskind's turn to be unnerved by the sight of a pantomime horse coming toward her in smooth long strides. Because of booths, displays, and tables, there wasn't much room for passing. Lily Siskind moved closer to the inner wall to avoid the horse, but she did not reduce her speed. Speed was of the essence. It was just a matter of time before the whole place would be crawling with cops.

As Ms. Siskind was about to run past the smiling horse, Fred Schultz looked out of the horse's mouth and saw a crazed woman with hair askew running toward him. She was carrying a knife. Was that blood on its edge? he asked himself at the last second. Whoa, he thought. He shied to the right, throwing the horse's behind off balance. It all happened very quickly.

Goodie Fortuna was furious. With her head inside a horse's gut, she could hardly see a blessed thing. It was the third time in less than an hour that Fred had moved erratically, thus throwing her off balance. The first time, he had been struck for not cooperating with a probable policeman. The second time, while they were trying to develop his absurd idea of a gallop, he had moved too close to a table and she had struck her already bruised hip against a corner. It had hurt like the devil. It still did. Now, he was shying to the right again, for reasons she couldn't fathom, since she could only see the floor and his ridiculous hooves. To avoid a third injury, she jerked to the left as hard as she could. She fell over directly in the path of the fleeing Lily Siskind, who collapsed on top of her. Schultz fell over too, all arms and legs sprawling more or less on top of Ms. Siskind. Because the costume had pulled to the side, he, like Goodie, could no longer see a thing. He struggled to get his arms out the slits of his costume, but couldn't find where the hell they were.

At the bottom of the tangle, Ms. Fortuna was pretty sure that her partner had cuffed her on the head, which was just the last damned straw. When her hands came across what felt like a leg, and it certainly wasn't her leg, not that she could tell for sure, it was all *so* confusing, she took hold of it and bit it.

"Ahhhh," a man cried out.

Was that Fred's voice? Ms. Fortuna wondered. Didn't sound like him. How queer.

Ms. Siskind finally disentangled herself from the disarray of a fallen pantomime horse and jumped to her feet. Detective Delaney stood no more than seven feet away. He was holding a gun with both hands. It was pointed at her heart. She held fast to her knife, thought about life versus death, and leapt toward death. The sound of Delaney's shot was deafening. Lily Siskind's wig fell away. Yussef Maidin lay dead on the floor.

Doors burst open in a moment, and three cops rushed forward. A two-way radio crackled, and an officer said, "Yo, Cole, we've got 'em. Delaney's here. The suspect has been shot. We're on the main concourse. Get the medics up here on the double, and don't forget the guy up in the arena. That damned pantomime horse is here too. It must have fallen on its ass."

Danny Christensen was a bit late to the scene because he had to find his handgun, and the lighting was bad. When he did arrive, he saw the suspect lying in a pool of blood. A tall gangly man, holding on to a horse's head, talked to an officer with a radio. He seemed to be explaining something. Delaney was talking to a short woman with hair that reminded him of one of his dad's old haystacks. Officers swarmed everywhere. He looked about but couldn't see the girl who had risked her life telling him to shoot. She had been injured and might need his help. He wanted to find her and knew just where to look, for she was the PETA girl by the rusty old van. She had handed him a brochure and smiled up at him. A darned pretty smile, it was, too.

Several squad cars and ambulances stood in the parking lot with their lights whirling. Officers had fanned out in a loose circle around the coliseum. They were joined by several farmers and farm workers who, while tending their stock, had been attracted by the commotion in the parking lot. A helicopter whooped overhead with a searchlight moving over the scene. You could hear faraway sirens as still more cops raced toward the coliseum. It was like a war zone. Where did all these guys come from, Christensen wondered? He hurried toward where the van had been parked, but found it was no longer there. Mrs. Delaney and the Willgrubs were talking with two cops not far off. He trotted on over, calling as he drew near,

"Mrs. Delaney, did you see the animal-rights woman drive away in her van?"

"Oh, gosh," Mrs. Delaney answered. "I'll have to tell you about that."

Officer Christensen listened to her explanation and then headed back toward the coliseum. That's when he saw Sally Holmes in the distance, sitting on a bale of straw with her back resting against a livestock barn. He ran to her, dropped to his haunches, and looked up at her sympathetically.

"Are you OK?" he asked.

"Someone stole my van," she cried, not bothering to wipe the tears rolling down her cheeks.

"No, no. Some friends of the police moved your van. They were afraid a terrorist might use it to get away. The police will want to keep the van anyway. You know, for evidence. Please, don't cry. Everything's going to be OK. Now, let me see your neck."

Sally Holmes had pressed a tissue against her neck to stem the flow of blood. She removed the tissue and Christensen studied the wound.

"Good," he said. "You've stopped the bleeding, but we've got to get you to a doctor. You'll likely need stitches and maybe some shots. Here, use my handkerchief. It's clean. Hold it against the wound. Gently does it. There, good. Can you walk? The detectives are going to ask you a million questions. I'm afraid it won't be fun, but first we've got to get you to a doctor."

"Yes, I can walk. I'm OK, really. Couldn't we just sit here for a minute? Tell me what happened, officer. Please. I'm so wretched."

Talking quietly with Sally Holmes some distance from the war zone sounded just fine to Officer Christensen. He had done his part after all; he wasn't needed anymore, except to stay with a valuable witness, a witness who had risked her life telling him to shoot. What kind of girl would do such a thing? He wanted to know more about her. He moved a bale of straw so he could sit down and look at her. He leaned toward her. And then he did a very impolite thing. He took her free hand and cupped it gently in his two strong paws.

"The suspect has been shot," he said. "She wasn't a woman, was she? I heard her voice. I'm pretty sure she was Yussef Maidin."

"I think so, too. That's why I ran to the coliseum. I wanted to help catch him, but all I did was get in the way."

"It's OK. You did just fine. If you hadn't appeared when you do, he might have gotten away from me. His grabbing hold of you turned out to be a big mistake. You might have saved the day."

"Oh, do you really think so?"

"I read your flyer. I got it right here in my pocket." (He extracted from his pocket a flyer that had been folded in quarters.) "I agree with you, Sally. That's your name isn't it? Sally?"

"Yes, Sally Holmes. Do you honestly think farmers should take better care of their calves?"

"Absolutely. I was raised on a dairy farm myself. Me and my pa always took good care of the calves. Have you ever taught a newborn calf how to drink?" he asked after a pause.

Sally shook her head no.

"Well, that was one of my favorite jobs when I lived on the farm. You see, what you do is you put milk in a bucket and then you give your finger to the calf to suck." (In total innocence, Christensen held up the naughty finger of his right hand for illustration.) "And while the calf sucks, you lower your hand into the bucket, so the calf starts getting the milk, see. Then, when the calf is getting milk, you try to ease your finger out of its mouth. You mustn't do it too fast, else they'll butt the bucket and get milk all over you. But if you do it just right, pretty soon the calf learns he doesn't have to suck, he can just drink. Calves become very dependent on you when you do that. I guess they kind of look on you as their mother or somthin'. Sometimes when I crossed our pasture, young stock would come running, thinking maybe they'd get a handout or somethin'. I used to like that, having young stock following behind me, licking my clothes and butting me gently, as if wanting to play. Isn't it extraordinary that wild animals have given themselves over to our care. I think we have an obligation to be good to them."

Sally Holmes looked at this young cop who would talk of weaning calves when her whole world seemed to be falling to pieces.

"I think I'd like that, too," she said softly. "Having friendly calves licking my clothes." She looked up at a windswept sky, dark now, except for a few sun-gilded clouds rolling away into the night. "Oh, I wish we could go somewhere for a cup of coffee," she added, shivering.

"We can't do that now. The paramedics will take you to a hospital. And later, when the doctor says its OK, we'll need to find out everything about Maidin, how he worked his way into your group and things like that. It's nice just sitting here and talking, but we've got to go, Sally. I'm sorry, but we really have to go."

He stood up and, still holding her hand, added, "I'll make you a deal. After this is all over, and you're well again, we'll go out for coffee and doughnuts."

She laughed then. "Do you promise?" she asked, looking up at him.

"Cross my heart and hope to die."

"I don't even know your name."

Chapter 17

Several weeks were required to tie the loose ends of the plot to savage the nation's dairy herd, but even then a few ends were left to fray. Yussef Maidin had died red-handed. The handbag that he had clung to so steadfastly in his failed flight through the upper reaches of the Alliant Energy Center Coliseum contained three vials of livestock serum well laced with the foot-and-mouth virus. The vials were now in the hands of the authorities; the viruses would be preserved as evidence.

Thus ended a conspiracy that began when Yussef Maidin and Dr. Mirza Paracha met in Sneem, Ireland, and became friends. Mr. Maidin eventually confided in his older and better educated friend that his marriage had been a mistake and that he hated America. For his part, Dr. Paracha was soon expounding his views on an Islamic world in crisis, explaining to his young friend how Christians and Jews ruled the world and how their decadent ways had made devastating inroads on the purity of Islam. He introduced his friend to the writings of the Egyptian philosopher Sayyid Qutub who had been executed for supposedly plotting to overthrow the Egyptian president Gamal Nasser. The question was posed how the infidels could be stopped; how a new era of Islamic purification could be achieved. Islamic fundamentalists were denied free expression of their views in the very countries of greatest importance to them: Egypt, Saudi Arabia, Syria, and other Middle Eastern countries. The radicals were killed, jailed, tortured, and expelled from the region.

What is left to us? Dr. Paracha had asked Yussef Maidin.

The plot against America, seen as propping up the heretical regimes of the Middle East, was completed soon after the two conspirators met Basim Hachem at the Finsbury Park mosque in London. Hachem was quickly enlisted in their cause. It had been Dr. Paracha's idea to send Hachem to Afghanistan for training and further religious instruction. He would be the foot soldier. Dr. Paracha would be the brains. Yussef Maidin would be the serious, law-abiding student, clean as a hound's tooth until he struck.

Originally, the plan had been simplicity itself. Yussef Maidin knew that his wife's uncle owned Green Valley Farm and that his mother-in-law would soon die from Alzheimer's. Arranging two accidental deaths was the hard part. With Dennis Mc Quade and Caroline cleared out of the way, and Caroline's mother dead of natural causes, Green Valley Farm would fall into the hands of Yussef Maidin. He would arrange a going-out-of-business sale of the entire herd of the farm's prize-winning livestock. The timing of the sale would be coordinated with Dr. Paracha's theft of the foot-and-mouth virus from the Reeks Animal Disease Research Center and the speedy transfer of the virus by Hachem from Ireland to Plattefield. Infected animals would be shipped all over the country, within the same month if possible. By the time the disease and its source were discovered, it would have been too late to thwart a massive epidemic. It would have been a catastrophe, and Yussef Maidin, Basim Hachem, and Dr. Mirza Paracha would have had ample time to flee to safe harbors.

The first major hurdle of the plot was cleared without a hitch, but then the trouble began. Dennis Mc Quade had been killed by Maidin and Hachem in much the way Detective Patrick Delaney had imagined. Scant evidence of a crime had been left behind. The death of Caroline Maidin would almost certainly have been seen as a hit-and-run accident had it not been for Michael Patriarca's decision one cool April morning to jog down Greenbriar Road. When the attempt to kill his wife failed, Yussef Maidin was forced to improvise. He convinced her they should have a summer home at Green Valley Farm, where, he argued, their children (she was the one eager for children, after all) would learn the virtues of farm living. His real intent was almost certainly to clear the Olsons out of the house at the farm so he and Caroline could move in, thus to facilitate organizing the sale of infected cattle. Working around his wife would be a challenge, he complained in a letter to Dr. Paracha, but he could hardly risk another attempt on her life. A police detective was already suspicious.

Hachem's failure to follow orders, which certainly did *not* call for the amassing of guns and explosives in his house, together with his rotten luck (how could he have known Coach Coneybear had a conduit to a former KGB thug?) had upset the plan, but not in any way that was crucial. The strike against America would be speeded up just in case further police work uncovered Hachem's connection with Maidin and Dr. Paracha. The idea was to strike fast and then run and hide. Hachem's death in a cornfield dealt a serious blow to the scheme. All the animals at Green Valley Farm were tested, quarantined, and closely guarded. Forced into hiding, Yussef Maidin had to find a new way of spreading the viruses in his possession.

Fate had shown no particular partiality to the good guys. True, Michael Patriarca's turn down Greenbriar Road and Mani Malakhov's burglary of Hachem's house were perfectly timed to give the terrorists heartburn, but, on the other hand, the mistaken report of Yussef Maidin's passing through Morocco to parts unknown had been a godsend. The rescheduling of the World Dairy Expo gave Maidin a perfect target, a plum soft and sweetly ripe for the picking. Yussef Maidin never left the country. He didn't have to. With a valise and a pocket full of viruses, he had hurried into a restroom for the handicapped in Kohl Hall as Yussef Maidin and emerged as Lily Siskind.

The real Lily Siskind, it was discovered, lived in Manhattan and worked as a seamstress for New York City Ballet. Her identity had been stolen along with thousands of others from FalEast Healthcare Alliance, as had the identity assumed by Basim

Hachem. Now more than ever the FBI wanted to find out who had stolen the FalEast medical records, but the trail had gone cold.

The case against Professor Suleiman Daoudi was quietly dropped when his chief accuser, Ahmed Hmimssa, forgot some of the lies he had told earlier and began cobbling together new stories that were even less believable than the first. Professor Daoudi and his wife eventually settled in Paris, where his critique of U. S. foreign policy was well received. The students flocked to his lectures, but the professor became an unwitting friend of Uncle Sam by arguing that 9/11 was not an international Jewish conspiracy.

It was established that Mrs. Harriet Hoffnagel had fired two shots from her husband's twelve gauge shotgun to scare away invaders from the United Nations. She insisted that she had not aimed the gun at the men spilling out of the Humvees. The dead chickens that lay on the ground well short of where the Humvees had been parked seemed to support her contention. Ditto the blasted hole in the ceiling of an upstairs bedroom. The District Attorney with jurisdiction over Crayfish County declined to file charges against her. The city of Plattefield agreed to put up the money for a new house.

Chief Smedegard announced his coming retirement at a press conference. In his valedictory, he warned his fellow countrymen that the war on terrorism was best fought by smart police, not smart bombs. The national media were uninterested, but his antiwar stance played well in the local community. This plus the Plattefield Police Department's success in thwarting a bioterrorist threat gave the chief the clout needed to name his successor, which he did: Detective Tom Willison. A senior member of the SWAT team was named its interim leader until the new Chief of Police could find a suitable replacement for Detective Phillip Moran who had begun talking about early retirement.

The identity of the man killed in the explosion at 112 Cowslip Lane remained a mystery along with how he came to die. Dr. Mirza Paracha continued to insist that the bioterrorist plot had been a three-man operation; he could offer no explanation for the strange DNA. Thus, the previous hypothesis remained unchallenged: there had been a fourth conspirator unknown to Dr. Paracha. But why hadn't the fourth conspirator escaped out the backdoor along with Basim Hachem? Had Hachem shot a man deemed untrustworthy in an emergency? Someone best disposed of in a ball of fire and smoke? Among the basket of spent bullets recovered from the ashes was one from a handgun not of police issue, but, of course, there was no way of knowing where it came from short of finding a gun now mired in mud at the bottom of a slough three miles beyond Plattefield's city limits. Hachem had rushed home to keep a burglar from discovering his secret, it was surmised. When he saw the SWAT team, he reverted to a plan developed earlier, which was to open a large tank of propane gas that together with his store of dynamite would assure a massive explosion, one that would destroy all evidence of his Al Qaeda connections. Here, too, fate had smiled on the terrorists, having arranged for Mrs. Schultz's warning Hachem of a burglary in progress.

The loose end of the investigation of greatest annoyance to Detective Patrick Delaney was the identity of the burglar who, by calling 911, had set into motion the entire chain of events that culminated in the thwarting of a terrorist plot. Delaney's colleagues couldn't understand why he kept fretting about it. Most agreed with Officer Wade Johnson who said at a coffee break one morning that Delaney was just being, well, Delaney.

Though soon involved in investigations of domestic disputes, minor break-ins, and teenage hooliganism, the bread and butter of detectives generally, the 911 burglar was never far from Delaney's thoughts. One day he had an inspiration. Once again he listened to the recording of the burglar's 911 call; he asked Detective Willison to do the same. The two detectives agreed: the caller likely had a speech defect. He said "fwicking" instead of "fricking," which was the clue to listen for other r-sounds. But there were no other r-sounds. There were instead odd hesitations and unlikely word choices that seemed based on the desire to avoid words with r's. The detectives began asking around. Did anyone know of a Plattefield lowlife with the suspected speech impediment? A curious reporter for the Plattefield Gazette got wind of this. A small item appeared in the paper centering on the celebrated 911 burglar and speculating whether the man had a speech impediment. The item was then picked up by the local TV station, prompting a few sales clerks to report selling hamburgers, gas, movie tickets, and upscale grooming products to just such a man. The descriptions of both the man and the nature of his speech problem varied widely, however, and were therefore of little help.

Which brings us to Mrs. Laura Osterby. On a wintry afternoon, she and three of her closest friends played bridge at a card table set up in the living room at Mrs. Eileen Parker's house.

North: One diamond.
East: One spade.
South: Oh, my. Let me think. (A pause ensued.)
West: What do you all think about the police going after the burglar with a speech problem. I mean, here's a person who did our country a lot of good, and they're going after him. It's awful.
North: I agree. Laura, honey, it's your turn.
East: Why don't they just leave the poor man alone? What's to be gained from going after him?
West: Yes, well I agree. What's to be gained?
South: Eileen, what do you think. I mean really.
North: Well, I said I agreed didn't I? They should give the guy a medal, not hound him like a common criminal, though I suppose technically he *is* a criminal. I don't approve of burglary.
West: But maybe it wasn't a burglary.
North: Well, when he called 911, he said he was a burglar. Are we going to play bridge or what?
West: Actually, he didn't say he was a burglar. He said something about getting into Hachem's house.

North: I think he said something about breaking in. Isn't that burglary?

South: Maybe he was someone at the university who got to know Hachem and became suspicious. Maybe he was looking for evidence.

East: I never thought of that.

West: Nor had I. I mean, I think they should leave the guy alone.

South: He could be a really nice person.

North: Laura, honey. You look so stressed out. Have you been real busy at the motel?

South: No, it's a slow season for us. It's just . . . I don't know. I'm just upset is all.

North: Maybe we should give up bridge for the afternoon.

South: Oh, could we. I don't know why I've been so upset lately.

The cards, card table, and folding chairs were put away, and Mrs. Parker poured four glasses of Johannisberg Riesling. Fortified by a glass of nice wine and further discussion of how lucky the nation had been in thwarting a bioterrorist attack, Mrs. Laura Osterby headed for home. She drove slowly with her head held high and her shoulders squared. She was filled with resolve. She knew a young man with just the kind of speech impediment that was described in the newspaper. He had stayed in Room 16 for some time while he checked out the campus, trying to decide whether to enroll at the university. He kept his room and bathroom tidy and neat. He was one of the sweetest, nicest young men she had ever met. He was always so cheerful and polite. He once noticed a new scarf she was wearing on her way to church, how it picked up the color of her earrings. She once saw him making like Fred Astaire on the way to his car. And she was aware, too, that once in a while he entertained a male friend. She had heard voices as she passed his door. Well, what of it? she now thought. It's nice that he had a close friend. It's hard enough getting through life even when you have a partner. Every human being is entitled to a partner. Her mind was made up. There was no way in blazes she and her husband would ever go to the police to tell about Mani Malakhov from Los Angeles.

Coach Lawrence Coneybear crawled out of bed with a sore back. He had not had a good night's sleep. In addition to his back, there had been the recurrent soreness in his right leg that often disturbed his sleep. Perhaps he had driven too hard the day before. He showered and shaved and hit the road for LA. He had plenty of time to get there in time for lunch with Mani Malakhov. In the back of his Laredo were two large suitcases and a few boxes holding the only things he would have to start life anew. His trip to California had been leisurely, but lonely. He had used the journey to reflect on his life, where he had gone wrong, and how he might yet salvage what was left of it. Was he too old to find a good woman and rear a family? Be damned if he wouldn't give it a try. There must be a lot of gorgeous divorcees in LA willing to pitch tent with a former coach, he thought; preferably one with a little money. Several plaintive melodies had occurred to him as he crossed the barren expanses of the high plains. He played around with lyrics.

Plattefield now seemed far away. He was astonished at how quickly he had been able to put the place behind him, once he'd made the hard but right decision, which was to resign his position. Now he could breathe again. He was sorry about his marriage, though, but his leaving Jane was merely a coming to grips with reality. He had fallen in love with the wrong woman. She had been tearful at their parting and said she was sorry for the way things worked out. He said he was sorry, too, and that life was a bitch. And that was about it. There was no good-bye kiss, just an awkward hug. Before leaving Plattefield, he said good-bye to all his little friends, too, watching as they swirled round, round, and down in the toilet bowl. And now, nearing the end of his journey (or was it the end of the beginning?) he hadn't yet had a single drink. Out on Interstate 5, winging his way south on a dream and a prayer, a bit wary of California traffic, he risked a quick peek at himself in the car mirror and smiled. For the first time in over fifteen years, he felt good about himself. He'd be OK, once he made it to LA. A little tune came to him just then.

As Coach Coneybear drove south, Mani Malakhov watched the clock, for he was anxious about his meeting with the coach. He had so much to tell. Until he actually saw the coach at Sophia's Soufflés and had given him a bear hug, he would not relax.

He was eager to say that he had become an entrepreneur (it was *so* American), not in the detestable restaurant trade, for godsake. Puke, puke. He had other ventures in mind. He and his family would hang on to Petrouchka's, but its management would be lodged in the hands of the chef his father had hired away from a New York restaurant. And it had been Mani's decision, also, to link the new manager's generous salary to Petrouchka's profitability. Mani had been particularly eager to turn over the advertising to Beta Advertising Inc, for he had long believed that his father's decisions in this particular arena of capitalism had been a disaster. What does an aging gangster-Bolshevik know about advertising? he had complained to sympathetic friends. The new radio ads had already paid off in a surge of business.

Of course Mani was sorry that his papa had suffered a massive stroke and was now confined to a wheelchair and could only gurgle and salivate in an effort to boss his son around. The doctors had assured Mani that his father's stroke wasn't *his* fault: that a massive stroke such as the one his father had suffered could not have been brought on by the sudden appearance of a son sporting a nose stud and a new hair color. Talk about a speech impediment, Mani had muttered bitterly to himself when he first tried to communicate with his father at the hospital. Well, he used to make fun of me, Mani remembered as he looked about the room, at the flowers his mother had ordered and the apparatus supporting his father's bodily functions. But he was not one to hold a grudge, for a loyal son was this Mani Malakhov. He didn't understand that more often than not when his father turned purple with rage trying to speak, he wasn't trying to tell his son how to run Petrouchka's, but rather to say something along the lines of, "Put blanket on top of legs, you moronic poof."

Mani was very eager to talk to Coach Coneybear about his song Bumper Car Baby. He had such *good* news. One of Mani's best friends was a scientist working with others of his ilk in Barcelona on a piece of artificial intelligence called Hit Song Science, a computer program using higher mathematics to predict whether a new song would hit the Top 40. When first told of it, Mani didn't take his friend seriously. He pooh-poohed the whole idea, whereupon his friend went frenetic, gesturing wildly and rattling on and on, occasionally in Spanish, about clustering algorithms, acoustic similarities, and commonalties in popular rhythms, harmonies, and keys. Mani found it all quite incomprehensible. For the fun of it, though, and to indulge a friend, Mani's little rock group taped Bumper Car Baby. When the tape was fed into the computer, Hit Song Science gurgled for a split second and spit out its answer: Bumper Car Baby would hit the charts big time. After hearing the song and getting the computer results, the CEO of Spectacular Compact Discs, Inc., said he was interested and would call Hilly Jones who, he explained, was looking for a knockout number for her next album. Hilly Jones! Mani thought, when he heard the news. Awesome.

But Mani Malakhov had other things to tell Coach Coneybear. When put in charge of the Malakhov family's affairs, he discovered the true extent of his father's wealth, which was staggering. In short order, he hired a realtor to negotiate the purchase of a large but old and rundown supermarket two blocks up the street from Petrouchka's. It would be razed. In its place would rise a fabulous nightclub where people would come to party, dance, and relive the glory of vaudeville. Every Friday and Saturday night, there would be song-and-dance routines, slapstick turns, comedic monologues, and stinging political satires.

Coach Coneybear would be given a title commensurate with his salary, maybe vice president or something. Mani didn't know for sure. The important thing was that he and Coach Coneybear would be joint managers of a fabulous new nightclub. They'd organize a new rock group and invite rock stars to listen to some of the coach's original songs. Mani knew better than anyone that half the waiters and waitresses in LA were waiting for that one big chance. His nightclub would give it to them. In a winner-take-all economy, he and the coach would recruit fresh talent that hadn't yet won the lottery of public recognition. The auditions would be great fun. And what would be wrong if the owner of the establishment did a little soft shoe from time to time, as part of the introduction to a new act, say? It was all so Mickey Rooney and Judy Garlandish. Let's put on a show in a neighbor's barn, only in the case of Mani Malakhov's dream, the barn would cost over $20 million dollars to construct. Perhaps Robin Williams could be hired to kick off opening night, just to get the enterprise started on the right foot. Some day, Mani dared to believe, many of the nation's top comedians, singers, dancers, and musicians would say they got their start, their first big break, at a place called The Malakhov Cocktail.

Winter has loosened its grip on Dairyland. The fragrance of flowering crabs in full bloom wafts over the Willgrubs's backyard on a balmy southern breeze. Detective Patrick Delaney sits in a lawn chair drinking his fourth beer, a little drunk and totally complacent over his three helpings of potato salad and baked beans and his four grilled bratwursts with sauerkraut. It was after all Emily's graduation party. If a guy can't load up on calories and alcohol on such an occasion as this, thought Delaney, when can he?

The party given by the Willgrubs had been small: a few neighbors, a few friends, a few relatives. Delaney hadn't wanted any of his fellow officers invited on the premise that you couldn't invite a few without inviting them all. And what a big boisterous, beer-swilling bash that would have been! And what would Mrs. Willgrubs have said? So instead, the party had been small, pleasant, and, yes, a little boring. In particular, in Delaney's opinion, there had been entirely too much yakking about the bioterrorist plot against the nation's dairy industry. Even so, as he enjoys a solitary moment in the Willgrubs's backyard, with the professor and his wife and Emily inside saying good-bye to the last of the guests, his mind turns to the loose ends of the case he and the professor had done so much to solve. He niggles over a question that came to him during the party. Had Coach Lawrence Coneybear somehow gotten mixed up with the terrorists? It seemed so inconceivable.

Still, why had the coach resigned and given up such a promising career? His letter of resignation had been so unexpected and so unconvincing. He had never before shown an aversion to the pressure of coaching football. On the contrary, he seemed to positively revel in the job. Did his resignation have something to do with the broken desk drawer, a crime that he had neither reported to the police nor discussed with his friends? And why did he lie (at least I think he was lying) when he said he couldn't remember who had called him from the same payphone used by the 911 burglar on the day Basim Hachem's house was blown to kingdom come? The conversation had run on for almost two minutes. He obviously didn't want the police to know who the caller was. Why not? Was the call from a mistress? A gambler? Was the coach into pornography? Mmm. Had his desk drawer contained naughty photos? Basim Hachem had access to the coach's office and could easily have been the one who broke into the coach's desk. Ah, suppose Basim Hachem had broken into the coach's desk and was blackmailing him. Yes, yes: that's possible. And the coach could have hired someone to burgle Hachem's house to retrieve the photos. Yikes, the 911 burglar and the person who called from the payphone could have been the same person. He might have called to tell the coach what he'd found in Hachem's house and to ask what to do about it? Boy, if that's the case the media reports of the 911 burglar's little speech defect must have given the coach the jitters. And after the reports he sure got out of town in a fwicking hurry.

Well, Coach, wherever you are, I hope you've learned your lesson. In the end, you did good.

"How are you doing, honey?" Emily asks. He looks up at her when she musses his hair.

"You look like the cat who swallowed the canary," she says. She bends over to lift his upper lip with a finger, looks at his teeth, and says, "Do I see any yellow feathers?"

He kisses her hand and says, "Oh, Emily, how do I love thee? Let me count the ways. Minus one."

"How would you like it if I pulled your arm hair?

"You wouldn't dare."

"Well, I think that went pretty well," says Mrs. Willgrubs in a good stout voice, coming out onto the patio with a tray to begin clearing away the detritus of her outdoor barbecue.

BVG